"Just so you know." Tatum shifted, stood before him with a breath between them. "While I don't forbid workplace involvement, I don't encourage it, either."

"And just so you know." Cruz dipped his head, just a bit, enough so she could feel his warm breath caress her skin. "It's been my policy not to get involved with someone connected to an investigation. It's frowned upon, in fact."

"Is it?" She arched a brow. "That sounds suspiciously like a challenge." It took every bit of effort she possessed to hold his gaze; a gaze that made her feel as if the world around them had melted into oblivion. "I enjoy challenges. I find them exhilarating." Her hand came up, fingers trailing up his bare arm until it brushed against the short sleeve of his dark shirt. "Do you like challenges, Detective Medina?"

"Almost as much as I like complications."

* * *

Colton 911: Chicago—Love and danger come alive in the Windy City...

* * *

If you're on Twitter, tell us what you think of Harlequin Romantic Suspense! #harlequinromsuspense

Dear Reader,

There are some opportunities that, when they present themselves, you jump at and worry about the what-ifs later. Being asked to write a Colton book (my second!) definitely fits this description and it's already paid off for me in spades. In *Colton 911: Undercover Heat*, Tatum Colton's story, I get to combine two of my loves: romance and cooking. I've been a foodie and Food Network–aholic for most of my life. I grew up with Julia Child reruns on my TV screen and can watch *The Great British Bake Off* 24/7 (please tell me I'm not alone). You can usually tell while reading one of my books which food I was obsessing over because it shows up in the story (this one is no exception). I've been a baking fool these past few months and loved incorporating certain creations into Tatum's journey. A journey that, of course, has her falling hard for Detective Cruz Medina, a man who knows what he wants from the second he walks in the front door of Tatum's restaurant. Or at least he thought he did.

The recipe for this book was straightforward: start with one independent, headstrong female chef; add in a hot, determined undercover narcotics detective named Cruz Medina; toss in a splash of fun with a dedicated, protective kitchen staff; season with drug dealers and traffickers willing to do anything, including kill, to earn their money; and voilà! I did not have to push too hard to get these two together. The sparks are immediate and intense, but beyond the physical, they don't only balance each other out, they enhance the other. And isn't that what the best happily-ever-afters are all about?

I hope you enjoy this latest Colton installment. As for me... I'm off to find something new to bake.

Happy reading!

Anna J

COLTON 911: UNDERCOVER HEAT

Anna J. Stewart

HARLEQUIN
ROMANTIC
SUSPENSE

Special thanks and acknowledgment are given to
Anna J. Stewart for her contribution to
the Colton 911: Chicago miniseries.

Recycling programs
for this product may
not exist in your area.

ISBN-13: 978-1-335-62885-5

Colton 911: Undercover Heat

Copyright © 2021 by Harlequin Books S.A.

For questions and comments about the quality of this book, please contact us at CustomerService@Harlequin.com.

Harlequin Enterprises ULC
22 Adelaide St. West, 40th Floor
Toronto, Ontario M5H 4E3, Canada
www.Harlequin.com

Printed in U.S.A.

Bestselling author **Anna J. Stewart** can barely remember a time she didn't want to write romances. A bookaholic for as long as she can remember, stories of action and adventure have always topped her list, especially if said books also include a spunky, independent heroine and a well-earned happily-ever-after. With Wonder Woman and Princess Leia as her earliest influences, she now writes for Harlequin's Heartwarming and Romantic Suspense lines and, when she's not cooking or baking, attempts to wrangle her two cats, Rosie and Sherlock, into some semblance of proper behavior (yeah, that's not happening).

Books by Anna J. Stewart

Harlequin Romantic Suspense

Colton 911: Chicago

Colton 911: Undercover Heat

Honor Bound

Reunited with the P.I.
More Than a Lawman
Gone in the Night
Guarding His Midnight Witness

Harlequin Heartwarming

Return of the Blackwell Brothers

The Rancher's Homecoming

Butterfly Harbor Stories

Recipe for Redemption
A Dad for Charlie
Always the Hero
Holiday Kisses
Safe in His Arms
The Firefighter's Thanksgiving Wish
A Match Made Perfect

Visit the Author Profile page at Harlequin.com for more titles.

For Patience.
For asking.

Chapter 1

Controlling fire came as easily to Tatum Colton as breathing.

The arc of the flame, the quick flash of pristine blue giving way to brilliant orange as it brushed its heat in time with a quick wrist flick of the sauté pan in her hand. Warmth caressed her arms through the white chef's jacket she wore. The familiar beads of sweat coated her forehead as she moved from the stove to the workstation, where she plated the butter-rich pasta and fresh asparagus. A quick swipe of the towel tucked into the apron string around her waist, and the plate was set on the service table.

"Spring primavera up!" She glanced at the order screen, already mentally sorting out the ingredients as one of her chefs took the prepared bowl to the garnish-

ing station before service. "Simon, how're we doing on
the special orders for table nine?"

"Finishing now, Chef." Simon "Chester" Chester-
ton, one of her newest line chefs, worked magic with
the vegan offerings at True, Tatum's restaurant. True
was a lifelong dream of hers, and just last year, only
their third since opening, she'd earned a James Beard
nomination. The framed certificate hung on the press
wall of the kitchen where they celebrated the accomplishments of all their staff. The nomination hadn't been
her achievement alone. It was theirs. This year she was
determined to take even bigger leaps and make the restaurant a food haven destination in the North Center
neighborhood of Chicago.

The white-noise roar of the gas grills and burners,
along with the scraping of a pizza peel as it slid freshly
kneaded dough topped with imported cheeses and meats
made in-house into the custom-built oven, soothed
whatever nerves she might have had when it came to
feeding her full house. Garlic, roasted spices, and the
ever-present promise of a delicious, perfect European-
inspired meal hung in the air and invigorated her. Her
team moved fluidly and effortlessly through the kitchen
as wait and cleaning staff bustled in and out of Sunday
dinner service.

The employees at True had helped bring her vision
to life. They were the blood that kept the heart of True
beating. This place was her life. She'd put everything—
all her finances, all her energy, all her focus into making it what it was becoming. And it had repaid her in
kind by giving her a place of refuge and solace these
past few weeks.

Grief and anger mingled low in her belly as tears

of frustration and loss burned behind her smoke-filled eyes. If she didn't have this place she'd have been lost in the weeks since her father and uncle had been killed. No, she reminded herself as sternly as her sister Simone would have. They hadn't just been killed; they'd been murdered.

A murder the police still didn't seem to have a decent lead on.

One minute here, the next minute gone.

She grabbed a clean pan, dropped a fresh serving of pasta into the simmering water on the back of the multi-burner stove and got back to work.

"Tatum?" Susan Ford, Tatum's assistant front-of-house manager, dodged two of her line chefs. "There's a customer at the bar requesting to speak with you."

Tatum glanced up at the clock. "I'm not scheduled for my round of greetings for another forty minutes. Who is it?"

Susan shook her head, the unfamiliar expression of befuddlement clear on her face. Normally Susan was unflappable. "He didn't give me his name, just said he needed to speak with the owner as soon as possible."

Meaning Susan didn't know who the man was. And given Susan knew just about everyone in the food industry—from critics to owners to busboys—Tatum continued cooking. "Tell him I'll be out as soon as I can. And give him a drink on the house."

"He's not drinking."

Tatum's eyebrows arched, but she didn't comment. For all she knew, the man could be in recovery. "All right, then, a free appetizer. Provided you're certain he's not a salesman looking to hit us up on a buy."

"Definitely no salesman vibe with this guy." The

grin on Susan's face had Tatum biting back a smile of her own. "He is seriously *h-o-t* hot. Just so you know ahead of time."

"Noted for future reference." Tatum chuckled and reached for the bowl of fresh tomatoes one of her prep chefs had placed nearby. Adding a stop at the bar to her mental list of the usual table rounds, Tatum refocused and worked her way through the continuous run of orders.

Whoever the man was, he was just going to have to wait.

Detective Cruz Medina of the Chicago Police Department nursed his club soda with lime in what had to be a glass made from actual clear-cut crystal. From his seat at the bar, he admired the pristine, oversize cubes mingling about the sparkling liquid. The interplay of clear lines and vibrant colors was reflected in the decor of True, Tatum Colton's upscale, trendy and somewhat pricey restaurant.

Glass and silver fused with displays of lush greenery that brought in a feel of the outside. Clearly a renovated warehouse, he thought, as he surveyed the high ceilings and walls covered in geometric greens and gold that added to the relaxed atmosphere currently on display in the packed house.

Normally he'd have turned down the hostess's offer of a free appetizer while he waited. He was more a pizza and wings kind of guy, but that was because of convenience and a lack of time. After perusing the menu she handed him, he figured he may as well experience what the other half did, and ordered the fried calamari and lemon garlic aioli.

If his normal attire of slacks and loose-fitting T-shirt were out of place, he wasn't made to feel that way. The bartending staff was polite and welcoming, as were the servers who moved as if they had wings on their feet. Their uniforms looked surprisingly comfortable. Dark slacks, white shirts under tasteful floral ones in the same natural tones as the decor. Deep-pocketed aprons held everything from small tablet computers for order taking, and biodegradable straws upon request, to packets of crayons for the few tables where children were handed their own miniature coloring books.

As far as Cruz could tell, True ran smoothly, effortlessly and without drama.

Which made it the perfect cover for illegal activity.

He sipped his soda, shifted around on his stool and scanned the crowd behind him in the mirrored shelves of the bar. He had yet to decide on what tactic he was going to take when it came to talking to owner Tatum Colton. It wasn't going to be an easy conversation, however he approached it. Also, the timing could be better. Given everything the Colton family was going through right now, with the still unsolved killing of Ms. Colton's father and her uncle, this wasn't the best time to present her with his suspicions about her business. But he had a case to solve, and every day he didn't, more addicts stayed on the street and more people became victims of overdose. More families suffered.

The murder of twin brothers Alfred and Ernest Colton had rocked Chicago to its foundation. There were plenty of wealthy residents in the city who wielded their power and finances like weapons, but not the Coltons, and certainly not the brothers. While Cruz had never met either man personally, he was acquainted with plenty of people who had, and their impressions went a long way in telling Cruz what kind of people they really were. The Colton brothers had been good people. Solid people.

And their loss was felt well beyond the borders of their family and friends.

Still… Cruz couldn't turn his cop brain off long enough to avoid considering if Tatum Colton was involved with the drug trade in the city, and whether she was somehow responsible for her loved ones' deaths. The idea sounded as ridiculous as it had the first time it slipped through his mind, but it still left a thread, however thin, of doubt. Until they were cleared, he didn't consider anyone free of suspicion.

Right now the Coltons were a grieving family, and while Cruz didn't want to pile on to an already difficult situation, he had an investigation to finish. An investigation that had already cost people he cared about far too much.

"Ms. Colton should be out in a few minutes." The elegant-looking hostess who had set him up at the bar returned with his appetizer. She was tall, on the curvy side, and wore her copper-highlighted red hair plank straight down her back. "Are you certain it's something I can't help you with?"

"I'm certain, thank you." He offered his most charming and understanding smile to the pretty young woman before glancing at her name tag. "I know she's busy."

"Busy is her eternal state," Susan said with a friendly laugh. "She'll be checking in on her dinner guests first, but she knows you're here. Is there anything else I can get you?"

"No, thanks," Cruz said. "I think I've got enough

to feed a small army." One thing was for certain, he thought, as he focused on the plate brimming with golden, crispy-fried goodness in front of him. True fed to impress. He was not a fan of those "art meals" where the presentation looked as if it took a special design degree to construct. The portions here weren't stylishly scant, but bountiful and appealing and served on heavy, substantial, pristine white plates which made the food the star of the show. The restaurant's dedication to fresh, farm-to-table provisions was more than evident and a testament to why this place had helped revitalize a once forgotten area of the city.

One taste set his taste buds to singing. Any longing he'd had for a cheese-laden cardboard box delivery vanished as he ate. Enjoyed. And watched.

Curiosity, Tatum had to admit, got the better of her by the time she took her front-of-house break. Break was such a misnomer. She wouldn't stop until after she got home well after midnight. Most nights she wasn't in bed until after two. While her happy place was in front of the stove, with a knife in her hand, or creating new recipes, she knew that interacting with her customers was just as important as the food she served them.

"Showtime," she whispered as she let down her hair, changed into a clean jacket and headed out the swinging doors into the main dining room. Faces familiar and new moved in and out of focus as she greeted those who chose to spend time in her creation, feeding both their bodies and their souls with her food. The feedback on the meals was valuable of course, but this was also a way for Tatum to check and make sure everyone was having a good time and to put a face behind the experience. She wanted them all to feel as if they were at home.

When she had worked her way to the tables by the front door, she glanced at Susan, who inclined her head toward the bar. Tatum gave a short nod, and letting her gaze drift to the upper platform, scanned the line of stools and their occupants with practiced ease.

She'd have noticed the man even if he hadn't requested a conversation. Who was she kidding? She resisted the urge to pat her suddenly warm cheeks. She'd have noticed him if he'd been standing in the middle of a crowd.

In Tatum's experience, there were men who commanded attention. There were men who captured a woman's gaze as ferociously as a hunter caught his prey. And then there were men like the one sitting at her bar: the kind of man who turned a woman's normally locked-down, practical mind toward spinning images of very intimate, almost erotic encounters.

She shook her head as if trying to dislodge the thoughts. Not an easy task, considering those dark, fathomless eyes had found her as if she'd been a beacon he'd instantly honed in on.

Tatum let out a long, slow breath, bade good evening to the last group of guests and made her way toward the bar.

Everything around her faded into silence. He lowered his feet to the floor, stood to his full six-foot height and had her inching her chin up to meet his eyes. Shaggy dark hair brushed against his shoulders. His brown skin was accented by a neatly trimmed beard and mustache that outlined full, rounded lips and camouflaged a jawline indicating not only stubbornness, but determination. His body was trim, streamlined and inappropriately tempting beneath his dark slacks and shirt, which showed off biceps that spoke of an attention both to fitness and a woman's intimate desires.

He was, Tatum thought in the moment before he took her hand, a man who could make a woman forget everything about her life before he walked into it.

"Ms. Colton?" His voice was as smooth as the imported cognac she kept in stock for her most discerning customers. "Cruz Medina. I appreciate you taking some time. I know how busy you are."

"Always happy to speak with one of my customers." She motioned for him to take his seat, then slid in between him and the empty stool beside him. Resting her arm on the edge of the bar, she gave him her full attention. "I see you chose the calamari. Did you enjoy it?"

"I haven't had better since I was in San Francisco," he said, his eyes twinkling with something akin to mischief. No doubt he was well aware of the effect he had on women. Or, Tatum thought, her specifically. "I appreciate the service and the experience."

"That's what we are here for." Pride had her steeling her shoulders. "Is there something I can help you with, Mr. Medina?"

"There is." He wiped his mouth, pushed his empty plate away and reached into his back pocket. When he flipped open his wallet, Tatum found herself looking down at a shiny gold badge. Her heart did an odd *kathump* in her chest as the breath left her lungs. "It's Detective Medina, actually. I'm here to ask you about the drugs being run through your restaurant."

Chapter 2

It would forever remain a mystery, Tatum would later think as she closed herself in her kitchen office after closing, how she'd made it through the rest of her shift. Her anger threatened to bubble over, and the ringing in her ears even now grew louder as she paced the upstairs space she used as a refuge.

She tried to lose herself in the faint, cacophonous, almost frenetic noise of the nightly cleanup echoing up the staircase. The dishes being washed, pots and pans being run through the industrial fast-working washer. Tables being pre-set for their next open night's service. The down-to-business but still good-natured ribbing that ricocheted through the kitchen. She looked down through the wall of windows that gave her an eagle-eye view of her pride and joy and, for a moment, felt as if she was about to lose everything.

While she might not sleep at True, it was her home. Her center. The people who worked here were her family. She loved them. More important, she trusted them.

The idea anyone would come into her home slinging accusations, accusing people she cared about of... drug trafficking?

"It's absolutely ridiculous." She grabbed the rubber stress ball her sister Simone had given her and smacked it off the desk, sending it soaring across the room. There was a short rap on the door before Susan poked her head in.

"Everything okay?"

"Yeah, fine," Tatum lied before she centered herself. She couldn't let one completely unfounded allegation throw her. Yet. Her future demeanor would depend on the conversation she planned to have with the good detective now that the doors were closed. "Just needed a couple of minutes of relative quiet."

"Hmm." Susan's eyebrow arched in that lie detector way she had. "I'm thinking something else drove you in here. Is he about six feet, has devastating eyes and looks like he should be sipping tequila on the Riviera?"

Tatum turned her back and removed her chef's jacket, tossed it onto her chair with her purse, then unclipped her hair. "He's definitely made an impression," she managed, barely keeping her temper in check. "You ready to take off?"

"Yeah. I've got the day's printouts and cash bundled up. You want to take them or should I leave them for Richard for tomorrow?" She held out the bank bag she'd filled from the two in-house registers. Normally she'd let Richard Kirkman, her manager, deal with it. He took

Sundays off and did all the "office" work on Mondays, when they were closed to customers.

"I'll take them with me." Something told her she wasn't going to be sleeping much tonight. And not because of anything Susan might be thinking.

"Okay, then, I'll be heading out." Susan gave her a quick if not confused smile.

"Hey, Susan?"

"Yeah?"

Choosing her words carefully, Tatum walked around and leaned back on the edge of her desk, her arms crossed. "I'm a pretty good judge of people, right?"

"Well, you plucked me right out of business school graduation, so I'd say yes." Susan's gentle laugh almost made Tatum smile. Almost. "Sorry. I would say yes. You're an excellent judge. The people you've hired, we all fit. And believe me, that's not an easy thing to do in any business, let alone a restaurant."

Susan's answer should have been a relief. "So there's no one you'd say doesn't work right or seems…out of place."

Susan frowned, stepped back inside and closed the door. "No one I can think of. Why? What's going on?"

"I don't know." Tatum rubbed a hand across the back of her neck. "Maybe nothing. Just…do me a favor and let me know if anything looks, sounds or feels…" She waved her hand in the air, struggling for the right word.

"Hinky?" Susan supplied.

"Yeah, hinky."

"All right. Well, to be honest, my boss is currently sounding like something's bothering her, and it sounds like she both does and doesn't want to talk about it." Susan inclined her head. "That's a bit hinky."

Tatum couldn't help it. She laughed, and the pressure that released in her chest allowed her to breathe for the first time in hours. "That might just be exactly what I needed to hear."

Another knock on the door had Tatum standing up straight once more. "Yes?"

"Sorry to interrupt." Detective Medina leaned in, looked between the two of them, his dark-eyed gaze completely unreadable. "You said to come up once you closed."

"Come on in." She waved him in, moved around him and shooed Susan toward the door.

"You know you're going to have to tell me everything, right?" Susan mock-whispered.

"Go home, Susan." It was all Tatum could do not to roll her eyes. "Enjoy the day off."

"Right." Susan leaned back, craned her neck and grinned over Tatum toward Detective Medina. "It was nice to kind of meet you."

"Nice to meet you, too, Susan."

Tatum glared at him as he took her spot, propped himself against the edge of her desk and stretched out his legs. He looked, she thought, like a cat who had finished off the last bowl of cream.

"He knows my name," Susan whispered with a grin before Tatum shoved her the rest of the way out the door and closed it.

When she was certain privacy was in place, she swung on Detective Medina, hands planted on her hips, the anger burning a hole in her chest. "What the hell do you mean coming into my restaurant and accusing me of being a drug dealer?"

He barely moved. The only indication he gave he'd

even heard her was a twitch of those lips that not so long ago she'd had serious fantasies about. When he spoke, she could tell it was with deliberate care, which only scraped on her frayed nerves. "I didn't accuse *you* of any such thing," he said finally. "I do, however, think True is being used as part of a drug distribution chain in the city."

"That's the most ridiculous thing I've ever heard," she snapped. "What on earth led you to that conclusion?"

"Six months of investigation." He sounded so casual, as if they weren't talking about something that could destroy her life. "I've got players in this from all over the city, including the restaurant business, and funnily enough, a lot of the paths I've followed lead right through your doors."

"Who are these players? I want names. If I've got criminals working for me—"

"You have two ex-cons on the payroll, actually." He inclined his head as if imparting information she didn't already know. "Sam Price and Ty Collins."

"Three," she added with a smirk. "You missed Bobby Quallis. All three were nonviolent offenders, and all three have served their time and fulfilled their probation obligations. They also attended culinary training at community colleges and haven't been in trouble since." She'd wanted to be able to give back to the community in some way, to offer her employees chances other businesses might not. "I'd stand up for any one of them."

"Noted." He shrugged. "You're the trusting sort. Good to know."

"I know people," Tatum said. "More important, I like them. Well, most of them. You certainly aren't on the top of my list right now. What actual evidence do you have that True is involved in whatever case you're investigating?"

For the first time since she'd seen him in the bar, she saw him tense. Not a lot. Just enough to let her know she'd hit some kind of target.

"Actually, it's evidence I'm hoping to find. Right now all I have is a hunch."

Relief surged through her and had her shoulders sagging. "A hunch." The word tasted like cheap vinegar on her tongue. "I've been breathing fire for the past three hours because you have a hunch?"

He held up his hands as if she were going to attack. "*Hunch* is maybe the wrong word. I have very good intuition about these things and my gut is telling me there's something here. Not necessarily with you."

"You mean I'm not a drug dealer?" She pressed a hand against her heart and sighed dramatically. "Oh, that's such a relief." She stalked around the desk and dropped into her chair. He stood, but slowly, so that she got a very up-close-and-personal look at his very fine butt. Irritation sizzled through her veins. She pursed her lips and shoved her mind back on track. "You can take your hunch and your intuition and everything else you brought with you and get lost."

He sat in the one empty chair across from her, the entertained expression fading from his face. "I can't do that, Ms. Colton."

"Why not?" She should have poured herself a glass of wine before she'd come in here. Hell, she should have grabbed a whole bottle.

"Because." He waited until she looked him full in the eyes again. "My hunches are never wrong. True is being used in the distribution of narcotics in and around Chicago. I wouldn't be here if I didn't believe that. I also wouldn't be talking to you about it if I thought you were personally involved. We'd be discussing it down at the station with you under caution."

"Down at the station." Tatum rested her elbows on the desk and lowered her head into her hands. "Suddenly I'm in an episode of *Law and Order*." He didn't laugh. He didn't respond. And when she met his gaze again, she felt her stomach pitch at the sympathy she found on his handsome face. "What do you want from me? Access to my books? Employee files? Phone records?" She could hear their family attorney screaming in protest. "You can question my employees, but I won't hold it against them if they request a lawyer."

"Since you're offering, I'll say yes to all of that. But that isn't why I'm here." He leaned forward, clasped his hands between his knees and offered a smile that had her heart skidding to a halt. "I want you to give me a job."

Cruz had to give Tatum Colton credit. He'd thrown a lot at her in a short amount of time and she'd taken each hit like she was wearing a bulletproof vest. Every bit of information struck home and had no doubt stung and even bruised her, but she'd barely flinched.

And that, Cruz thought as he watched her process his request, told him more about her than the dozens of media and news features he'd read about her. He knew the stats—her birthday, her very single marital status, and where she lived. He also knew after his first glimpse that she was a knockout—from that rich honey-blond hair to those stunning, sparkling blue eyes of hers, down her very fit figure to the tips of her cushioned, black-sneakered feet. The definition in her arms, along with the sweat-kissed tendrils of hair surrounding her face, told him she wasn't just the pretty public face of the restaurant: she was the constantly humming engine behind it. But from the way she absorbed the information he shot at her, the play of tense emotions that first dulled then sharpened that pinpoint gaze of hers, he knew his gut instinct was right.

Tatum Colton wasn't a drug trafficker. She wasn't a criminal.

What she could be was useful.

His request for a job wasn't completely impulsive. It was an option he and his lieutenant had discussed as a possibility. Not the first option of course, but that would have only happened if Tatum had somehow collapsed immediately and confessed.

Cruz watched Tatum blink her way through his words as if spitting out Morse code. He'd been a cop long enough he could have a second career as a lie detector. He'd bet his future pension she had no involvement in the drug activity he was convinced was being conducted through True. No one, not even Academy Award winners, could act so convincingly. He didn't pick up on nerves or guilt. But he definitely felt a surge of anger shimmering through the air.

He also felt a spark of attraction. One big enough to set this whole building on fire. But that wouldn't get him anywhere but in a whole lot of trouble.

"Would you excuse me for a moment? I'll be right back." Tatum pushed out of her chair and headed for the door. He winced as she gave the knob a particularly nasty twist before stepping out. He heard every

single foot-pounding step she took downstairs, then
a few minutes later, every single stomp back up. She
stormed back in and, as her hands were now full with
a bottle and two of those pristine cut-crystal glasses,
kicked the door shut behind her.

She sat again, all but ripped the cap off the bottle and
poured two healthy portions before pushing one toward
him. She tossed back a shot and slammed her empty
glass on her desk, arching a perfect brow at him. "Are
you joining me?"

He felt his lips twitch as he reached for the glass,
followed suit and downed what he now realized was
one of the smoothest aged tequilas he'd ever ingested.
Cruz grabbed the bottle, nearly balking at the label that
would have set him back a good couple of weeks' pay.
"Well, hell." He sat back, enjoying the burn as the alcohol made its way down. She reached for the bottle.
"Are you sure you want to do that?"

"Oh, yeah." She poured again, a bit more generously
this time, but he covered his glass with his hand, shook
his head.

"I have to admit," Cruz said with more amusement
than the situation called for. "This wasn't exactly the
reaction I expected."

"I'm a constant surprise to people." She toasted him,
then tossed the second drink back, poured a third. This
time when she looked back at him, her eyes were swim-
ming with tears, but she blinked them away and let the
anger shine through. "Tell me something." She pressed
the back of her hand to her mouth. "Is this theory of
yours about drugs being run through my restaurant
common knowledge among your fellow cops or is this
something you're sharing with me first as a courtesy?"

"I wouldn't say it's common knowledge," Cruz said. "My lieutenant is aware, as are a few other detectives in my squad. Why?"

"Why?" She blinked again. "Because the second word gets out you're investigating True, everything I've worked for will disappear. Even just the hint of illegalities will shut the doors to this place faster than I can toss a pizza. I might never get them open again."

Cruz knew he should have felt like squirming under that heated, penetrating gaze of hers, but he didn't. He couldn't. He had a job to do. An important one. Stopping the flow of drugs into the city had been his sole focus from the time he joined the department seven years ago. He wasn't going to back off now because his investigation might inconvenience a few business owners here and there. He'd promised his partner. His brother-in-arms. A brother whose life would never be the same again. And Cruz never, ever gave up on a promise. "Hurting your business is not my intention."

"Intention or not..." She capped the bottle and sat back in her chair, filled glass clasped between her hands, and looking, Cruz had to admit, a bit more relaxed and even sexier than before. "That's what's going to happen."

"Look." Cruz, not known for his diplomacy, found himself choosing his words carefully. "Contrary to how this looks, I've approached you quietly. Off the radar. Because my gut is telling me this is where I'm supposed to be. I'm good at my job, Ms. Colton. Very good at it. Part of the reason I am is that I don't let anything stand in my way. We could have done this officially, called you into the station house for questioning, asked to see your books, your records, your employee files..." He held up his hands when she opened her mouth to speak. "All of which you just offered me free and clear. But I didn't do all that. I'd like to do this clean, where it would cause you and your business the least amount of damage and publicity." It wasn't a lie.

But it also wasn't the truth.

She considered him with a narrowed gaze. "What if I say no?"

"No to what?"

"No to giving you a job." She rested her cheek in her palm and looked at him, not with the resentment and anger he'd seen before, but with a barely shrouded gaze of desperation. "No to cooperating with you. What if I tell you to conduct your investigation as you have been? From outside. And before you answer, remember you haven't shown me anything to prove anyone here is involved with the drug trade. All you've done is tell me who you are and that my business is a front for drugs. Why should I believe you?"

"I don't think it's a front," Cruz said. "I have no doubt your business is exactly what you mean for it to be. A successful, neighborhood-rejuvenating restaurant that serves some pretty incredible food." Once again, he found himself pulling back from his normal bulldozing ways. He needed an in. He needed more evidence to convince his lieutenant he was on the right track. He didn't have nearly enough for warrants, court orders or even surveillance. Which meant he needed to find another tactic.

And from what he could tell, the best way in was through Tatum Colton.

"Someone is using your business, Ms. Colton. Someone is using what you built to bolster their own criminal enterprise. I'm sorry to have to tell you this, but those are the facts."

"The facts as you see them," Tatum challenged as she downed the last shot. "The facts as I know them tell me you're wrong."

"Then let me prove it one way or the other." He inclined his head. "If I'm wrong, I'll back off and you'll never see me again. But if I'm right…" He shrugged.

"If you're right, your investigation could destroy everything I've worked for in my life." She eyed the bottle of tequila, seemed to shake off the idea, as if she realized that wasn't going to solve anything. "I need to think about this."

"I thought you might." Feeling as if some progress was being made, he stood, reached for his wallet and pulled out one of his cards, set it on her desk. "When you've decided, give me a call. Day or night. My cell is always on."

She let out a short laugh. "I bet you say that to all the girls."

"Tonight I'm saying it to you." He found himself smiling. He liked her. He hadn't expected that. He liked her a lot. "I don't always mean it, though."

"Yeah, well, I bet not all your ladies can help you investigate drug running in Chicago." Instead of putting his card away, she pocketed it. "I'll let you know."

"I do have one other question before I leave." He faced her at the door. He was close, not too close, but close enough to catch the faint hint of olive oil and smoke wafting off her skin. "This one's a bit more personal."

"Can I plead the Fifth if I choose not to answer?"

She really did have a way of making him smile. "Why tequila?" he asked.

"Because it gives me the most bang for my buck and never disappoints." When her face relaxed and she leaned against the doorframe, he found himself suddenly reluctant to leave. And not just because when she crossed her arms over her chest he caught a significant glimpse of cleavage beneath her tank top. She caught his eye when he lifted his gaze back to her face, and her grin widened. "But I also chose it because I figured you could match me shot for shot. It was nice to meet you, Detective Medina." She held out her hand. "One way or the other, I'll be in touch."

"I look forward to hearing from you." He shook her hand, gave it an extra squeeze just to test the waters. When she squeezed back, he felt that bolt of attraction hit him dead square in the chest.

As he left her office and headed downstairs to the kitchen and then the front door, he found himself wondering when he'd last been on anything resembling a date. He couldn't remember. When he reached his car, he tried to recall the name of any woman who had captured his interest over the past... It didn't matter how far back he went, the list didn't exist.

But he had one now.

And it began with Tatum Colton.

After letting the rest of her staff know she'd be sticking around to close, Tatum locked herself back in her office and stashed the bottle of tequila in the bottom drawer of her desk for what she assumed would be a need later on. She pulled open her laptop and began skimming through the last six months of her business accounts.

Assessing the numbers had, until recently, been a nightly ritual. These days, she left most of the office work and number crunching to her manager, Richard. He'd been a godsend from the start, popping up right after the unexpected resignation of her last manager, who had sadly been killed in a car accident a few days later. And then since her father's death, he'd stepped up and in, eagerly accepting the challenge of expanding True's catering options even as he took over food and supplies ordering, employee schedules, and payroll. All of which freed Tatum to do what she did best: cook.

Looking at the network-shared spreadsheets, accounts and banking statements, she didn't see anything amiss. It was a cursory check, but she knew her business well enough to spot red flags. Revenue was up considerably, but they'd had a full list of reservations for nearly two months now. An uptick in cash made sense. She clicked open the catering spreadsheet, noticed that currently the expenses were definitely outweighing profit, but that wasn't wholly unexpected. As of now they only had a few bookings and only two recurring clients. Time to start pushing for more. She jotted down a note to discuss the catering with Richard ASAP.

Not for the first time tonight, she picked up her cell, her fingers itching to reach out to the one man who had always been her shoulder to cry on, her confidant. Her protector. She tapped open the number pad before she remembered her father wouldn't answer. He was gone.

She bit her lip, pressed the phone against her forehead and squeezed her eyes shut until she saw stars.

Alfie Colton had been so proud of what she'd made here, the changes she'd helped to bring to this community. Both her parents had always instilled the importance of giving back, of making a difference, and of building something lasting in her life. Not only for Tatum, but for her sisters, as well. January and Simone had taken different tracks to get there—January as a social worker and Simone as a psychologist—but they'd accomplished the one thing all the Colton sisters had as a goal in common: making their parents proud while living completely independent lives.

The air in her lungs seemed to vanish. For the first time since her father's murder, as much as she missed him, as much as she could have used Alfie Colton's advice, she was grateful he wouldn't witness whatever fallout there was from what had started tonight.

Anger and bitterness cut through her like a honed porcelain knife. How could she think such a thing? Shoving her laptop away, she sank back in her chair, drew her knees up and stared at the too-bright screen.

Tears trailed down her cheeks as she wondered for what felt like the millionth time what, if any, progress the police were making in finding whoever was responsible for her father's and uncle's deaths. It had felt as if their family had been swarmed with detectives and officers early on, but in the last few weeks since the funerals? She'd been questioned not once but twice, and she resented the notion of having to give them her irrefutable alibi. She'd been here, at True, when her father had been killed, just as she was every night. That she—or any of her sisters or close-as-sibling cousins—was considered a suspect had bile rising in the back of her throat.

It seemed to have taken forever to convince those detectives that they were a family that loved each other without reservation or hesitation. Not that there weren't issues. Of course there were. But for those issues to lead to murder?

It had been the most preposterous accusation she'd ever heard. Until tonight.

Now the detectives were going longer and longer between phone calls and new information. Her mother and aunt, both beyond heartbroken at having lost their husbands in the same violent way, were standing strong. They were, after all, Coltons, even if only by marriage. A Colton was a Colton, and if there was one thing her family was, it was strong. They might bend, but they never, ever broke.

Tatum as well as her sisters and her three cousins were all adrift with grief and anger, but also more cognizant than ever of how important family truly was.

She was not, Tatum decided as she swept her fingers under her eyes and stopped the flow of tears by sheer will, going to let one hint of scandal hit True or the Colton family. She couldn't. Not only because the restaurant was her livelihood and her life, but because she would not taint the Colton name.

"Let him investigate on his own," she said to the empty room. "He won't find anything."

Chapter 3

Cruz stopped at his parents' house on his way home. Because he saw the kitchen light on, he told himself. Not because he was feeling slightly uneasy about having lied to Tatum Colton about taking the damage potentially done to her restaurant into consideration. He couldn't afford concerns.

"Stop worrying about that," he muttered as he pulled into the driveway and climbed out. "You're doing your job." He couldn't take collateral damage into consideration. Not if he was going to make a dent in the drugs streaming into his city. Streaming? Ha. In recent months the trickle had turned into a flood and people were dying. Long-time addicts and the newly curious. And kids. So many, too many kids.

The crisp March air had him shivering despite his lifelong acclimation to the Windy City. Growing up in a working-class neighborhood had been a paradise of bike riding, baseball games and trick-or-treating for him and his younger siblings. Lawn mowers rumbled on the weekends and cars moved in and out of garages and driveways with consistency. Being raised in an area where his neighbors were friends, where he had been exposed to multiple cultures and family types had been the best preparation for becoming a cop. He liked people. He understood people. And he loved his neighborhood.

He would do whatever he had to in order to protect it.

When he ran up onto the porch, he found himself wishing he'd worn his jacket, but that thought vanished the instant he stepped inside. The two-story brick structure had been his parents' home for the past thirty-two years, and he found himself encased in the instant, familiar warmth.

He didn't, as he had all those years growing up, call out to them. Instead he closed the door, wiped his feet and ducked into the kitchen, where he found his mother precisely where he expected to find her on a Sunday night—sitting with his father at the polished round table, going over the family budget.

"Cruz." Patricia Medina's all-seeing, all-knowing brown eyes narrowed in suspicion as she pulled off her reading glasses. "It's after midnight. What are you doing here?"

"Just thought I'd stop on my way home."

"You working a case?" Saul Medina picked up his coffee mug and headed to the ancient, sputtering pot as Cruz pulled open the fridge. "Or just raiding our fridge?"

"Yes and yes." Cruz grinned at his parents. "Unless

Frankie and Inez polished off tonight's leftovers already?" The twins, his college-age brother and sister, ten years his junior, were notorious for their all-night study sessions that usually left the refrigerator and cupboards bare and the kitchen sink overflowing.

"Midterms are over. Our food supply is safe for a while." His mother moved in behind him, waving him away even as she brushed a gentle hand over his hair. "I'll fix you a plate."

"Let the man-child feed himself," Saul told his wife as he reclaimed his seat. "He's capable."

"Feeding him lets me pretend he still lives here."

"He hasn't lived here in over a decade, Patty." Saul rolled his eyes as Cruz took a seat beside his father. "Sometimes I think she's living in a time warp."

"School going okay?" Cruz asked his college professor dad.

"I admit the older I get, the more I look forward to the summers," Saul said. "But I have a good group of students this semester. Most of whom even seem to want to be there."

"Always a good sign," Cruz agreed. "Ma?"

"Your mother and I were just discussing her job, actually," Saul said and barely grimaced when Patty shushed him. "What? He's going to find out eventually. Your mother's school is implementing cutbacks. They've offered her early retirement, but if she goes, so does the library."

"What?" Cruz almost choked on his coffee. "But they can't do that. How can you have a high school without a library?"

"Spoken like my favorite child," Patty said with

what to Cruz looked like a soul-sad smile. "Funds are stretched thin in this district. They are in every district."

"But you've been there twenty-seven years."

"They see numbers, Cruz," his father said. "Not people. There's talk of a fundraiser, both to save the library and your mother's job."

"Along with the assistants," Patty said, setting a reheated plate of her unique albeit delicious, spicy spin on shepherd's pie, along with a fork, in front of Cruz. "I'm not staying without them."

"And so the conversation continues," Saul said. "We'll be fine," he told Cruz, who was already trying to figure out how much his parents owed on their mortgage. "Are you still working that narcotics case you can't talk about? The one you and Johnny were on?"

"I am." Guilt swam through his stomach, trying to stifle his appetite, at the mention of his partner. Cruz spooned in the comforting tastes and textures of his childhood and felt instantly better. "Have a new lead I'm following and it'll probably mean I won't be coming around very much for a few weeks."

"You're not going undercover, are you?" Patty's voice took on that edge of fear Cruz hated to hear.

"Not really. Not dangerous undercover," he added at his mother's narrowed gaze. "I promised you and Dad I wouldn't do that again." Especially after what had happened to Johnny. During his two years in deep cover, Cruz had earned enough scars, not all of them visible, to last him a lifetime. He wasn't looking to add to them. "I'll be working at a restaurant, actually. Which no doubt means free food." If Tatum Colton agreed to his request. As of now, he was guessing that was a big if.

"Well, that'll save us money on groceries at least,"

Saul teased, then sobered. "I saw Jackie and Carlo Ruiz this afternoon. They're still having a hard time adjusting."

"Do any parents ever adjust to losing a child?" Patty asked and added a slice of homemade cheesecake to the table.

Cruz winced and kept eating. Benji Ruiz had been only the latest in a list of overdose victims they knew from the neighborhood. This one had struck closer and harder than most, as Cruz's sister, Inez, had babysat Benji for most of his elementary school years. Kids like Benji—the ones they'd lost and the ones he could still save—were what kept him going. He worked every single day to ensure his parents, his siblings and friends would never have to attend another drug-induced, before-their-time funeral.

"So this new avenue of investigation," Patty said as she slid back into her chair. "Will it leave you much time for a social life?"

"Dad, I thought you were going to get her to back off." Cruz sent his father a warning look, but Saul just shrugged. "No, Mom, I don't think it will." Even as he said it, he could hear Tatum Colton's rich, sultry voice ringing through his head. He wondered what her laugh sounded like.

"Once, just once I'd like to meet someone you care about, Cruz." Patty shook her head in that disapproving way she had that made Cruz feel like a misbehaving teenager again. "Such a shame. You should be going home for a hot meal and not stopping off here. You need someone in your home, Cruz. You need someone in your bed."

"Jeez, Mom!" Inez Medina came skidding to a halt in

the kitchen doorway, her anime-inspired pajama pants and matching pink tank glowing like a beacon. "Lala-lalala." She covered her ears and ducked around them to grab a bottle of water. "Can we please not discuss Cruz's sex life? Ick."

"Ick is right," Cruz agreed and gave his sister a grateful wink. "Find a way to conquer our ever-expanding environmental issues yet, kid?"

Inez, who took after their mother with her short stature and thick, dark hair, came over to stand between her parents. "I'm working on it. Speaking of which, we're organizing a protest march for next week. A new pharmaceutical company is opening up offices downtown. They've been fined multiple times for illegal disposal of their waste and inhuman animal testing. I'm in charge of the permits for the protest."

Food had never held so much interest for him before. He didn't need to look up to know both his parents had pinned their eyes on him. "Contact Sheryl Cunningham at the city offices. Tell her who you are and what's been planned and where. She'll get you set up."

"Oooh, I get to name-drop? Cool! Thanks, Cruz." She kissed both her parents on the cheek and hurried back upstairs.

"Cruz." His mother's warning was loud and clear, but this was one instance where Cruz felt secure.

"She's asking about permits, Ma. She's thinking ahead because she's smart and she's planning for every contingency." Of course she was. She was prelaw and already clerking at a local ACLU office. "It's not like you and Dad didn't do the same at her age. Isn't that about when I was conceived? At a pro-immigration rights rally?" He heard his father guffaw and took it as a win.

"It was after the rally," his mother said without missing a beat. "And if Inez protesting endangers her scholarship? What will we do then?"

"Knowing Inez, she'd vlog about it on YouTube and end up with a GoFundMe campaign that would get her through graduate school." This from Saul before Cruz could put the words together. "We've raised activists, dear. Nothing we can do about it now."

"At least Frankie keeps his nose in his books and off social media," Patty said. "I bet he'll be the first one to give me grandchildren."

Cruz snorted but quickly covered by finishing off his late-night dinner. Science-minded Frankie hadn't taken his nose out of a book long enough to even recognize that girls flocked after him like he was a one-man K-pop band. He would, eventually, though. Then they'd all be in trouble.

"Only you have the power to make her stop talking about grandbabies," Saul told Cruz in the same tone he remembered when he'd been warned about preventing forest fires. "Maybe give that some thought, would you?"

Cruz rolled his eyes. He wasn't about to admit that seeing his parents this way, coming home the way he had—the way he did most weeks—was something he longed to create for himself. But this kind of life—quiet nights worrying over household budgets, raising children and eating leftover shepherd's pie and cheesecake, that wasn't possible for him. And it wasn't fair to expect someone to be able to live it with him.

It was an argument he'd had with himself and his

parents so many times he'd lost track. But as he trudged back to his car, filled with the warmth and love only his parents could provide, instead of lamenting the impossibility of a family of his own, he found himself thinking of a honey-blonde, spitfire chef with bright blue eyes and a taste for tequila.

And wondered if maybe there was hope after all.

Whatever dreams Tatum had of losing herself to oblivion and sleep vanished when she pried her eyes open after only five hours. She groaned, squeezed her eyes shut and tried to ignore the digital evidence that 8:00 a.m. was creeping close. "So much for sleeping in on my day off," she grumbled into her pillow and burrowed deeper.

Instead of the blissful unconsciousness she'd hoped to drop into, dreams of an intensely erotic and squirm-inducing nature had descended, with one central, irritating law enforcement character on center stage. It wasn't fair. Mondays were normally her catch-up-and-rejuvenate day. Her reset day. Her create-new-recipes-and-be-inspired day. Instead she was going to spend some of it telling an estrogen-spiking detective he could get bent.

She groaned, felt the faint hitch in her stomach and pounding in her head. The tequila was not going to leave her system without a very painful goodbye, it seemed. Rolling over, she stared up at the ceiling and tried to shove all thoughts, images and feelings about Detective Cruz Medina out of her cluttered, sleep-and-man-deprived mind.

She smashed a pillow over her face and wished time to rewind. Just a day or two or… Tears burned behind her shut eyes. Five weeks ago. What she wouldn't give to take everyone back five weeks and stop her dad and uncle from leaving the office when they had.

Voices echoed in her ears. Muffled, insistent and all too familiar. She yanked the pillow clear just as her bedroom door swung open. "Mom!" Tatum sat up in bed, clutching her sheet and duvet against her pajama-clad chest. "What are you doing here?"

"Tatum." Farrah Colton stood in the doorway, a book of fabric samples dangling from one hand. "What are *you* doing here?"

"I live here," Tatum reminded her, and for a moment, the last month faded away. "Or so it says on the lease."

"But it's Monday. You stay at the ranch house Sunday night." Farrah glanced over her shoulder, her stylish, shoulder-length curly brown hair brushing against the yellow fabric of her shirt. "Oh, um." She cringed and looked more than a bit guilty. "Darn it, this was going to be a surprise."

"Trust me, it is," Tatum muttered as she slung back the covers. As her feet hit the floor, an identical albeit thinner face popped up behind her mother. "Aunt Fallon, not you, too."

"Always me, too." Fallon Colton offered a somewhat dimmer smile than her twin sister. "Why aren't you at the ranch house?"

"I didn't feel like driving out there last night after we closed." Mainly because she knew she shouldn't be driving. She dragged herself out of bed and stood there, feeling oddly like a teenager caught after curfew. "Do one of you want to tell me what's going on? What are you doing here?"

"Oh, well, it's meant to be a—"

"Surprise, yeah, got that. I need coffee." And about ten aspirin. Then she might be able to function with the flood of information streaming into her head.

"Put on a pot, would you, sweetheart?" her mother called. "We'll be quick in here so you can take a shower."

Tatum stopped halfway down the hall, mouth open, question poised, but she shook her head, left them to whatever they were going to do in her bedroom, and headed into the kitchen.

It was the kitchen that had sold her on the space, even before she'd fully decided she needed a place in town while she worked. The loft-like setting, the hardwood floors, the beautiful picture windows overlooking the neighborhood, that was all nice.

But it was the six-burner gas range, the smooth gold-and-black marble countertops, the bay window filled with pots of fresh herbs, and the dual wall ovens with warming and proving drawers that made the place irresistible.

Contrary to how most women thought, the way to her heart was definitely through an electrical appliance. She loved her ranch house out in Livingston, had from the moment she'd first seen the house on sprawling land that acted as a retreat as well as a home. But it was too easy to bring the pressures of work there. This one-bedroom condo, only a ten-minute drive from True, was the perfect solution. Although at the moment she was seriously regretting handing out keys to her family.

As her mother suggested, she set an entire pot to brew rather than her cup-at-a-time pod and began rummaging through the refrigerator for the makings of an omelet.

"I've never understood how you do that," her mother said a few minutes later when she joined her in the kitchen.

"What? Cook?"

"Ha ha."

Tatum couldn't help teasing her mom. Farrah Colton was many things: a warm, caring and sometimes over-attentive mother, a brilliant woman with a successful and expanding interior design business. And she'd been a happy, devoted, if not challenging wife. But Farrah had never mastered the kitchen. Or what came out of it.

Tatum set aside chopped onion, peppers and mushroom, and popped open the carton of eggs. "Are you two hungry?"

Her mother shrugged, and then, after glancing over her shoulder, nodded. "If you cook for her she'll eat. And I meant I never understand how you can cook all night, every night, and still want to do it on your day off."

"Because it makes me happy." And that, Tatum thought when she glanced up at her mother, was all the answer Farrah needed. She set a pan on the stove, dropped in a mother-gasping amount of butter and set the burner to low. "So when are you going to spring it on me? This surprise you two have cooked up," she added when Farrah looked purposely confused.

"We are redecorating your condo." It was her aunt who answered as she joined them, setting down her own pile of fabric swatches and wallpaper books. "We need a project to get us back into a creative space, and this was on the top of our list."

"Oh." Tatum frowned. "Is it really that bad?" To be honest, she hadn't paid much attention. It had what she needed: a bed, a bathroom and a kitchen. The beige walls and brown curtains had been in place when she moved in a little over two years ago. Sure, the muted colors were a bit boring, but… "Never mind," she said when her aunt gaped at her. "I see it now. It is."

"You don't mind, then?" her mother asked.

Even if she did, she wasn't going to turn them away. For the past few weeks she'd watched her mother and aunt struggle daily with getting through the endless hours of grief as they were thrust into widowhood. Tatum's grandmother had been instrumental in helping her daughters put one foot in front of the other. Even after her stroke last year, Abigail Jones was a commanding enough presence the family looked to in times of turmoil.

Losing both her sons-in-law had taken its toll on her as well, but she led by example, and it seemed, considering her mother and aunt were currently standing in Tatum's condo looking as clear-eyed and determined as she'd seen in weeks, that example was to persevere. Just as every Colton would.

"As long as you leave my kitchen alone, the rest of the place is yours," Tatum told them. "Have at it. But you know the rules."

"Don't worry, we learned our lesson when you were sixteen," Aunt Fallon said. "No orange—"

"No flowery froufrou—" Tatum's mother chimed in.

"And no frogs," Aunt Fallon finished for her twin. "Although I still don't get the no-frogs thing."

"Blame your son for that one." Tatum shuddered, remembering when Fallon's youngest boy, Jones, had left a rather slimy toad in Tatum's sleeping bag during one notorious backyard campout. "Not that any of you particularly cared," she chided good-naturedly. "The fact that Daddy fell into the pool because he was laughing…" She stopped, a wave of grief so large, so suffocating, overwhelming her she felt sick. "I'm sorry." She shook her head and turned away, having to press a hand against her chest to remind herself to breathe.

"Tatum." Her mother's hand came to rest on her shoulder, turned her around so she could cup her face in her palms. "I know it's hard. I know you miss him. Miss them. I do, too." The grief was there, reflected in her mother's deep green eyes. And it broke Tatum's heart. "Some days it's almost impossible. But we have to go on, don't we? It's what he would have wanted."

"I miss him so much." Tatum's voice broke as she stared down at the sizzling butter. "He should be here. Teasing me about what color you're going to paint my walls."

"Or leaving a stuffed frog on your bed," Farrah said with a laugh.

Tatum choked on her own chuckle, wiped the tears from her cheek. "What a housewarming present that was. Oh, Mom." She glanced to Aunt Fallon, who was dealing with tears of her own.

"There's to be no more of this, Tatum Colton." Her mother's hold on her tightened. "We remember with joy and gratitude and leave the sorrow and grief for the night. And in the morning, we start again. You know what he always said. We do what's right, and we do what's good. Even when it feels impossible."

An image of Cruz Medina floated into her mind: an image of a determined, sure-footed detective who had asked for her cooperation. Cooperation she now realized she would have to give him. On one condition.

She'd do what was right.

But she would also protect what was hers.

It was, after all, the Colton way.

Chapter 4

There were few places that brought Cruz Medina any sense of peace, especially on a Monday. And by peace he meant someplace that provided enough noise and distraction he could stick his earphones in, kick back and attempt to sort through the mess that was his investigation into the Nacio drug cartel.

Feet up on his desk, the mind-numbing tones of classic rock blasting in his ears, he leaned back and closed his eyes, mentally programming his respite to end in ten, nine, eight...

His chair tipped back and Cruz kicked out, flailing as he struggled to right himself. When he pitched forward and braced himself on his desk, he spun his chair and glared up at the interloper. "What the what, Cunningham?" He ignored the ego-checking chuckles coming from his fellow detectives.

Sheryl Cunningham, all five feet eight inches of her, stood, arms crossed over her chest, obsidian eyes glinting. She was not only stunning in her designer fuchsia suit that complemented her black skin, she was also glowing for two as she neared her delivery date. "You sicced your little sister on me, Medina."

"Ah." Cruz choked back a laugh. Mostly because he didn't feel like dying today. Sheryl arched a brow, clearly waiting for a response. "Problem with Inez?"

"The only problem is now I know there's two of you." Sheryl grabbed an empty office chair and wheeled it over, sat down and let out what Cruz could only imagine was a sigh of relief. "Someone should have warned me you had a Mini-Me. Why send her to me? What did I ever do to you?"

"Well, I didn't do that." He pointed at her very pregnant belly and earned a hearty snort. "I wanted to make sure she had what she needed for the protest. You don't let anything slip through the cracks. I trusted you with her."

"Well, hell." Sheryl sagged a bit. "That's all right then, I guess. And I have to admit, the idea of a protest march against that creepy drug company will make my day brighter. I'm on her list now, aren't I?"

"I want her to know who she can trust," Cruz told his former flame. A flame that had flared quick and bright and left them as friends. "She's prelaw and looking to save the world."

"It's the Medina family motto, isn't it?" Sheryl's face softened. "How's your mom?"

"Lamenting the fact I'm not settled down and giving her grandchildren."

"We're all lamenting that," Sheryl teased.

"What brings you down here?" Cruz popped out his earphones and tossed them onto his desk. "You could have reamed me over the phone about Inez."

"I needed an excuse to take a walk. Kid's coming up on overdue and I want her out. Doctor said physical activity would help, and seeing as I'm not feeling particularly sexy these days—"

"Understood." He held up his hands in the universal male TMI surrender gesture.

"Yeah, well, I also have that information you requested." She handed him the manila envelope she had in her hand. "Permit checks on that restaurant, True. Ran you off copies of everything on file. Most recent one was from a little over a month ago."

"Oh? What for?" He slipped the papers out, skimmed them.

"Restaurant's expansion into catering. Wouldn't be surprised if a food truck's next. That place sounds mighty tasty. You been?"

"I was there last night, actually," Cruz admitted. The name on the permits, building, liquor license, catering, everything had Tatum's signature. "Good calamari."

"Huh." Sheryl looked impressed. "Guess you got some taste after all."

"Thanks. Sorry if Inez gave you a bad time."

"Nah." Sheryl waved off his concern. "Gave me something to rag you about, though. Seems like a good kid. Definitely a cross-her-t's-and-dot-her-i's kinda girl. You find yourself needing someone to have dinner with at True, you let me know. It's on my and Luce's list of must tries."

"Before or after the baby?"

"I wouldn't say no to before." A wistful expression crossed her face. "Do they take waddlers?"

"Save it for after." Cruz tried to sound nonchalant. He didn't want people he cared about anywhere near that place until he knew it was safe. "It'll be worth it, I promise."

"Uh-huh." Sheryl's brow went back up. "Don't worry. I won't tell anyone it's under investigation."

"I'd appreciate that."

"Sheryl, you're early." Lieutenant Lucille Graves came out of her office, joined them, gave her wife a quick kiss and Sheryl's belly a quick rub. "I thought we said noon."

Cruz looked at his watch, then back at his boss. "It is noon, LT."

"Smart answer for everything," Graves said with a smirk. His commanding officer had a constant if not bewildering sense of humor. She also had ten years, a good twenty pounds and about fifty IQ points on him. "You get what you wanted from Tatum Colton?"

"Waiting to hear." Cruz had been avoiding his LT most of the morning. He liked to think he'd been persuasive, but he wouldn't put it past Tatum to tell him to get lost just to see where it got her. He wasn't sure himself, considering he didn't have many other ideas at the moment. His cell phone rang, and after a glance at the screen, Cruz had to wonder if his luck had just changed. "Hang on, LT." He held up a finger, took the call. "Ms. Colton."

"I think—" Tatum's voice floated over the phone and had him sitting up straighter in his chair "—given the fact we'll be working together, you'd best call me Tatum."

"All right, Tatum." He grinned, glancing back at his boss and her wife. Luce and Sheryl both rolled their eyes, as if lamenting the fact another female had fallen under his spell. "I take that to mean we should get together and discuss some things?"

"You take it correctly. Since the restaurant's closed today, why don't you come by my place and we can work out the details here." She rattled off an address. "Anytime after... Mom! Get off that chair! It's not... Darn it."

"You live with your mother?"

"Heaven forbid," Tatum said in a tone Cruz completely understood. "She and my aunt are doing some redecorating for me. It's keeping them busy."

Cruz winced. He'd almost forgotten about her father and uncle.

"Anyway, how about you come by after three. They should be gone by then. I hope. Please let them be gone..."

"Three it is."

"Oh, and you'll need to do some shopping beforehand. You have a pen handy?"

By the time he hung up, he found Sheryl and his LT peering over his shoulder at the most unusual shopping list he'd ever written.

"Wonder what you two will do with all that olive oil," Sheryl teased.

"Let's go. Where do you want to go for lunch?" Luce Graves asked Sheryl as they left the squad room. "I'm thinking pizza."

"Really?" Sheryl winked back at Cruz before they turned the corner. "I have a craving for squid."

* * *

It took twenty minutes, a care package of fresh-baked sourdough bread for both her mother and her aunt, along with a promise to be out of the condo as of ten tomorrow morning, to get them out the door.

She was cutting it close. It was quarter to three, and she did not want to become family gossip by allowing her mother to see her with a man in her condo. That was one distraction Tatum most definitely did not want to use on her mom.

If her instinct was right—and it usually was, thank goodness—her sister January was on the verge of being engaged. The second her mother and aunt had a wedding to plan, the pressure to entertain, distract and worry would ease, and Tatum might, *might* start to feel her life slip back on track.

"I bet you're getting a real laugh out of this, aren't you, Daddy?" Tatum brushed a finger over her father's photographed face. The picture had been taken at Tatum's culinary academy graduation. Where her sisters had caps and gowns, Tatum had donned a chef's jacket and worn it and her honor ribbons as proudly as a princess wore a tiara. Her father had worn his pride and love not only on his sleeve, but on his face.

The downstairs buzzer blared into the condo, making her jump. She hurried to the front door, clicked on the intercom. "Yes?"

"Medina delivery service," came the sardonic response. He was irritated. Tatum grinned. Perfect. "Second floor. Two-oh-four." She buzzed him in.

Something tingled inside her. Unease? Nerves? Anticipation, maybe? "Get a grip, girl," she told herself as she tightened her ponytail and tugged down her blue

T-shirt. "He's investigating you for a crime, not taking you out on a date." She heard the footsteps outside and opened the door before he could knock. "Hi. Come on in."

"Thanks." He carried two fabric totes, one in each hand. "Can I put these over there?"

"Yeah, sure. On the counter's fine." She twisted her hands together. She'd thought maybe her attraction to him last night had been the result of the tequila, yet here she was, stone-cold sober, and admiring every single fit inch of him. Dark slacks and T-shirt again, and the blazer he wore today looked slightly more worn than last night's attire. She couldn't help wondering how he looked out of those clothes. "Did you get everything on the list?"

"Enough to make my credit card whine," he confirmed. "I'll unload and you store."

"Yeah, sure. That works." She hurried forward. "I kind of took advantage. There were some things I needed to restock, so—"

"I figured. Let me guess? My penance for last night?"

"Maybe a little." She couldn't stop her lips twitching. "You are familiar with the concept of penance, then?"

"With twelve years of Catholic school, I ought to be."

"Catholic school?" She wasn't sure why she was surprised. "Did you go to Sacred Heart?"

"Saint Ignatius," he corrected. "All-boys. My sister went to SH, though. You?"

"Saint Mary's. Me, my sisters and my cousins. There were a lot of Coltons on the roster for a while." She was babbling. And talking about silly, meaningless stuff. She hadn't been nervous around a man since...who was she kidding? Men didn't make her nervous.

But she'd never met Cruz Medina before.

She stashed the gallon of olive oil in the cabinet near the sink, dumped all the produce into the basin where she'd wash it later for storage. The eggs, butter and various proteins she'd had him grab went into the fridge.

"So I've been thinking about my job," Cruz said.

"As a cop?"

"No. My job at the restaurant." He looked at her as if he was surprised she didn't understand.

"Right. That job." She considered pouring herself a glass of wine, then realized what trouble that might get her into. "I've already taken care of it. You want a beer?"

"Yeah, sure. Thanks. You have?" Surprise filled his eyes. Along with something else she couldn't quite define. He accepted the imported beer with ease, knocked off the cap.

"Yeah, well, it isn't like we've got a lot of openings at True right now. I have low turnover. People like working for me." She meant for it to sound like a warning of sorts. For him to remember that his investigation would affect more than his case; it would affect her business and her employees. "The only job we have right now is for a sous-chef."

"That sounds…complicated. I was thinking more of bartending."

"Like I said, we're pretty full with employees and we don't need another bartender." She didn't really need another sous-chef, but it was the one position Richard had recommended adding another of. "How are you with a knife?" She grabbed a bottle of water for herself, then led him into the loosely serviceable living room. "Ignore the paint swatches on the wall. My mom and aunt were testing colors."

"I like the blue," he said, gesturing to the dark peacock-inspired color. "Cozy."

"I will definitely consider telling them I like it, then."

Cruz smiled and settled into the corner of her sofa. "Before we talk more about the job, I wanted to say, and I should have said before, how sorry I am about your father and uncle."

She ducked her head, longing for the day when the mention of her father wouldn't feel like a gut punch. "Thank you. It's been…" she shrugged "…difficult. I'm sure you know. You deal with cases like this enough, I suppose."

"I deal with a lot of death," he said. "But I don't think anything can ever prepare you for losing someone, or in your case, two someones the way you did. Do you know who's running the case?"

"Ah, yeah." She rubbed her fingers across her forehead. "A Detective Joe Parker. He seems very competent."

"He is. He's good people. He'll take care of them."

"I suppose family members are always the first suspects in a case like this." It was impossible to keep the disgust out of her voice. She'd witnessed firsthand how the accusation against her cousin Heath, president of Colton Connections, had been handled, the effect it had on him.

"I did a little investigating of my own," Cruz said. "Just asked around a bit to get a feel for the case and how the investigation's going. They've cleared the entire family as suspects."

"I'd say that's a relief, but it's not." Tatum faced him,

stretching out her arm along the back of the sofa. "They still aren't anywhere close to finding out who did kill them. Or why. They never hurt anyone. It doesn't make any sense."

"It rarely does," Cruz told her. "Even when we find a motive or explanation, it still won't make sense. I'm sorry you're all going through this."

"Not sorry enough to stop you from investigating my restaurant."

"No." He didn't seem ashamed by it, or even contrite. "I won't apologize for doing my job."

It was admirable, she supposed, despite his determination putting her smack-dab in the middle of one of his cases. "I won't apologize for doing mine, either. Which brings us back to you being a sous-chef."

"Yeah, about that. I really think—"

"It's a done deal." Tatum had been waiting for the right moment to reveal her morning and early-afternoon activities. "I called my manager a while ago and told him I'd hired you. I said you came highly recommended by a fellow chef friend in New York. While you'll be a sous in title, you'll do various jobs…prep chef, line chef. We'll get your résumé together, get you acclimated as to how a restaurant kitchen works. How are you in the kitchen, by the way?"

"Passable." His grin was slow, almost flirtatious, as if he was conjuring images he shouldn't be. Then he shook his head. "I don't like to cook but I'll do it. I used to help my mom when I was growing up. Doing all the chopping and stuff for her."

"Perfect." Covering her surprise with a long drink of water, she continued. "Then you're already on your way. Being a sous is mostly about prepping. For you, anyway. For others it's a rung on the ladder to head chef. You're backup to me, but you also move in and out of the kitchen doing whatever needs doing, especially when people take their breaks. I did think this through," she said when he looked mildly impressed. "Being a sous gives you access to almost every area of the kitchen and also the restaurant at large. You want access, you'll have it. You can get to know your fellow employees, wheedle out which one of them might be running drugs out of our freezer."

"You still don't believe I'm right, do you?"

"No." Tatum didn't leave any room for doubt. "I don't. I can't. These people are my family, Cruz. Believing you're right, that one or more of them are working against me, committing crimes using my restaurant? I honestly don't think my heart can take that right now."

"Fair enough." He took a long pull of his beer. "So when do we start my sous lessons?"

"You hungry?"

"Always."

"Perfect. Then we'll start now."

Chapter 5

"Don't take this the wrong way," Tatum said as Cruz effortlessly used the back of his chef's knife to scrape chopped peppers into a waiting bowl. "But I assumed your definition of passable meant you knew which side of the knife was sharp. You're actually pretty good at this."

"Not sure there's any other way to take it." His smile, even as he kept his eyes on his prep work, made her insides do that inconvenient albeit insistent dance. "When I was ten my mom and dad had a surprise pregnancy."

Tatum frowned, set her bowl of hand-crushed tomatoes aside. What did that have to do with—

"I like to say the surprise was that it was twins," he continued. "But in truth, it was *Surprise! You're old enough to help more around the house!* My parents gave me the choice between cleaning and cooking. As the vacuum cleaner and I had multiple disagreements over the years, I went with the kitchen." He shrugged, as if that said it all. "They timed things perfectly with the advent of all those cooking shows, even though my mom loved watching old Julia Child reruns."

"I love Julia Child." Tatum couldn't help but be entranced. Not just by his voice and the obvious affection he had for his mother, but with the elegant way he moved around her kitchen, as if he'd been working in it all her life. How did a big-city detective fit so effortlessly into whatever setting he stepped into? "So you have twin siblings?"

"Frankie, well, Francisco, and Inez. They're nineteen. Just started college last fall. But when they were ten they got the same lecture I did, and both ended up in the kitchen. The Medina family will never starve, that's for sure."

"Well, I have to say you're easing my mind about how well you'll fit in at True. You follow instructions well, at least for the prep work."

"Speaking of prep, you're using me again, aren't you? Getting your *mise en place* done for the week?"

"Listen to you with the jargon. Yes, and no. Not for the whole week. Just the next few days." She chuckled at his *uh-huh*. "One thing you'll need to know how to do is pasta."

"I take it you mean I won't just be opening a box."

"No." She shook her head, retrieved the eggs she'd left out earlier. "All our pasta is made fresh. Not to order, but fresh every day. And we make a lot of it." She pulled over the organic flour, salt and imported olive oil. "When you're done with those." Tatum gestured to the last of the vegetables she'd set out for him, then returned to her laptop to finish typing up a list of things he'd need to know coming in. "What first put True on your radar?"

"GPS mapping." he answered, unfazed, then took his knife and cutting board over to the sink. "In part. The cartel I'm investigating has a number of connections and dealers in and around this neighborhood. True is right in the middle of it all."

"You're ready to blow up my entire life over the GPS readings of drug dealers?" How did the crazy continue to spiral into surreal?

He dried his hands, leaned back against the sink and looked at her. "You're acting as if this is somehow personal, and it isn't, Tatum. It just is what it is. I go where the evidence—"

"You said you didn't have any evidence yet."

"I go where the trail leads me," he finished as if she hadn't interrupted. "None of this makes me happy, Tatum. I don't want to tarnish your business or your reputation. But I'm not going to give up seeing something through because it inconveniences you."

Inconveniences her? "You really don't get it, do you? All you see is your case. Black-and-white. Right or wrong."

"Actually, no, I don't. I'm more than familiar with all the varieties of gray. But I have a job to do."

"Right. And your job is more important than my livelihood. Just because True pops up on your GPS analysis it doesn't mean it's involved!"

"It doesn't mean it's not, either." If he understood she was spoiling for a fight, he didn't rise to the bait. If anything, her arguing with him seemed to steel his argument. "We can go around and around with this forever,

Tatum. We aren't going to change the other's mind. The investigation is moving forward with or without your help. Isn't it easier, wouldn't it be better if we agreed to disagree while working toward a common goal?"

"Forget police work. You should run for office." She'd rarely heard such a rational, almost practiced argument that both irritated her and made complete sense.

"Something tells me that'll be what my sister does at some point. Look." He tossed the towel down and walked over to her, the warmth of his closeness tempting her to lean closer, to lose herself in it. To surround herself with it. "I understand what's at stake for you, Tatum. But I need to stop this group of traffickers before more innocent people get hurt or killed. If we're lucky, by the time we're on the other side of this, True will be free and clear and so will you and your employees. It'll be a blip on your professional history that no one will even remember a few months from now."

"It'll only be a blip if no one hears about it," she tried again.

"How about this." He covered her hand with his, moved closer yet again and lowered his voice. "How about I promise to do my best to protect your business? Within the confines of my job, of course. I can't promise anything beyond that."

She looked down to where he touched her, the feel, the heat of his touch racing up her arm and sliding through her entire body like she was sinking into a warm, sensuous bath. "I suppose it's something."

Tatum could almost feel his smile even before she glanced up. That mouth of his, those lips that widened to expose a perfect, white-toothed smile that very nearly reached all the way to his somewhat jaded dark eyes.

"How magnanimous of you." He lifted his free hand, brushed a solitary finger down the side of her face.

She shivered and resisted the urge to turn into his touch. "Just so you know." She shifted, stood before him with a breath between them. "While I don't forbid workplace involvement, I don't encourage it, either."

"And just so you know." He dipped his head, just a bit, enough she could feel his warm breath caress her skin. "It's been my policy not to get involved with someone connected to an investigation. It's frowned upon, in fact."

"Is it?" She arched a brow. "That sounds suspiciously like a challenge." It took every bit of effort she possessed to hold his gaze, a gaze that made her feel as if the world around them had melted into oblivion. "I enjoy challenges. I find them exhilarating." Her hand came up, fingers trailing up his bare arm until it brushed against the short sleeve of his dark shirt. "Do you like challenges, Detective Medina?"

"Almost as much as I like complications." His mouth brushed across hers, featherlight, as if testing the waters of a particularly tempestuous river.

"I strike you as complicated?" She breathed out the question, surprised she could find the voice to speak. His beard scraped against the softness of her skin, making her shiver. The energy surging through her system, the absolute desire she felt at this moment, as if she would literally burst into flames if he didn't shut up and kiss her, had her struggling against reason. This was a bad idea.

A really bad, horrible, messy...

"You strike me as a lot of things." He pulled his hand free of hers, and for a moment she thought he was moving away. Instead, he took that last, final, cavern-sized step closer and took her face in his hands. "Something tells me this is going to open up a whole new area of complicated," he murmured an inch from her mouth. "That okay with you?"

"Uh-huh." She wet her lips, the anticipation suffocating whatever rational thought she might still have. "It would just be a kiss," she reasoned and saw the humor flash in his eyes. "It doesn't have to change anything. Or mean anything. We'd still be partners."

"No," he said with a sharpness in his eyes. "We aren't partners. But on the other thing? Let's test that theory." But he didn't kiss her. Not right away. For what felt like an eternity, he did nothing more than stand there, holding her face gently between his hands, his thumbs caressing her cheeks as if they were made of precious spun gold.

Tatum was not a patient woman. Not when it came to what she wanted, and right now all she wanted was Cruz Medina's mouth on hers. Hot. Hungry. Commanding. And when he made no move to give her what she wanted, she slid her hands around to his chest, fisted her fingers in his shirt and dragged him in.

It was as if his kiss ignited a lifelong dormant pilot light inside of her. Instant heat. Instant combustion. Instant desire. All three mingled into a dance that had her moaning against his mouth. He wasn't coy about it. Didn't take his time to investigate or coddle. He simply dived in and took, demanded, and pulled her solidly into arms that folded around her.

She met him moment for moment, touch for touch. She'd kissed her fair share of men over her twenty-nine years. She liked men. She liked sex and had no trouble finding it when she needed or just wanted it. But this encounter, this experience, this *man* was different. Everything she thought of doing to him he was a step, a stroke, a thrust ahead of her as he kissed her deeply. Completely.

When he lifted his mouth, she could see her own surprise, her own desire, reflected in his uncertain if not shocked gaze. "Well." He stroked his thumb over her lips before he stepped back. "I guess that answers that question."

"And raises a few others," she managed and held up a hand when he appeared to want to step forward again. "I think it would be safe to say we have a healthy attraction toward one another."

"I don't think we can call any of what we just started safe."

"No," she agreed. "I don't think we could. Intense sexual attraction can't override the need for rational behavior. As you said, getting involved would be ill-advised on your part."

"And on yours?"

Oh, how she wanted to leap at him and kiss that cocky grin off his face. "On my part it would be self-destructive. For a number of reasons, but mainly because I know you don't have my best professional interests at heart." Hearing her own words echo in her ear doused the still raging flames of desire she felt for him. "Despite your promise, I have the feeling that given the choice, you're going to do what you have to in order to solve your case. Even if it means hurting me."

"It's your business that's in trouble, Tatum. Not you."

"That's what you don't seem to understand, Cruz." She planted a hand on his chest and pushed him away.

"They're one and the same. So." She pulled herself together, shoved what might have been down to where she couldn't access it, and refocused on the only thing that mattered. "Let's call that a completed experiment, accept the results and get back to the job at hand as partners." The sooner he was out of her business, out of her life, the better. She reached for the canister of flour and a measuring cup, handed the latter over to him with a barely trembling hand. "Measure out two cups."

Cruz kicked the door to his two-bedroom bungalow closed behind him and carried an oversize tote into his own meager, completely uninspired kitchen. For a man who prided himself on following plans, he'd sure taken a serious detour today.

He returned to the living room, turned on a few lights and tapped a finger against the glass of the oversize aquarium that housed Norbert, his pet tortoise. The creature lifted his wrinkly head, blinked his teeny eyes, then seemed to let out a silent sigh of irritation that his nap had been interrupted before he tucked back into his shell. "Serves me right for not getting a dog."

He clicked on the TV, grateful for the background noise, then returned to the kitchen to unpack.

Not only had Tatum sent him home with enough pasta to feed him for a few nights, she'd also given him homework in the guise of an advanced, illustrated techniques cookbook and a number of books on the restaurant business.

"I want you to walk in the door to True on Wednesday as if you can jump into the job immediately," she'd told him as she'd pulled books from her dedicated case against the wall between her kitchen and living room. "I'll have your résumé tweaked and done by tomorrow morning and will email it to you. I suggest you memorize it to be safe."

The detached professionalism didn't sit well with him. Clearly, they could now divide their history as BK and AK. Before kiss and after kiss. He much preferred the BK Tatum Colton.

Before he realized exactly how much heat there was between them.

He should have known touching the flame would get him burned, and Tatum Colton had most definitely scorched him. Cruz set the leftover containers in the fridge, grabbed a beer and lugged the books into the living room, where he flipped around until he landed on an exhibition game between the Cubs and Cardinals. Before he'd been summoned to Tatum's condo, he'd had plans to watch the game down at Santino's, the sports pub two blocks away, but as he was fond of reminding Tatum, he had a job to do. And work had to come first.

"Even before kissing beautiful chefs," he told himself. He wished he knew what he'd been thinking, giving in to that impulse. An impulse that clearly she'd shared. It was, after all, she who'd hauled him closer to get the deed done. And in that one instant he understood just how powerful attraction could be.

The revelation could not have come at a more inconvenient time.

He took a pull of his beer, set the bottle down, then settled in on his sofa to read. He was a skimmer by nature, a fast skimmer who could absorb information like a sponge. Speed-reading was a natural ability for him and had served him well in the various undercover operations he'd been a part of since becoming a cop. He also had a memory like a steel trap. Not eidetic exactly, but pretty close. One of the reasons all his partners had been thrilled to work with him. No one did paperwork as efficiently or with as much detail as Cruz Medina.

Johnny had been pretty darn good at it, too. He'd even enjoyed doing it. For once Cruz had been happy to turn that part of the job over to his partner.

Cruz winced, tried to focus for a few moments on the game. It had been two months. Two months since he'd last sat with his partner, his friend, and laughed as they tried to navigate this crazy profession they'd both chosen. Two months since Cruz had been able to tease his fresh-off-the-farm partner about his tooth-achingly sweet plans to propose to his long-time girlfriend. Two months since Johnny had dragged Cruz with him to pick out the ring he planned to surprise his Jade with.

Johnny wasn't laughing anymore. He wasn't spouting proposal plans or even planning a wedding. And chances were pretty damn good he never would.

Cruz finished his beer, resisted the urge to get another. One thing he'd learned early on in this job was to limit his chosen coping mechanisms. Whether it was women, alcohol or hours at the firing range, they were all to be enjoyed in steady, limited amounts.

But he hadn't gotten close to his limit of Tatum Colton. He knew it as soon as his mouth had brushed hers. There was something different about her, about them. Something he had never expected to find for himself. Something he didn't want to find.

"Focus on the books, Medina." He returned to reading, to skimming, pushing all other thoughts firmly out of reach.

The sooner he got this case solved and behind him, the better. More important, the sooner he could distance himself from Tatum, the better off both of them would be.

Chapter 6

"Tatum, you got a minute?"

"Sure." Tatum glanced up from her menu notes when Richard knocked on her door midmorning on Wednesday. Her manager was tall, a little on the bulky side, and possessed a mind born for the business world. He waited for her to wave him in, and then entered. "What's up?"

"About this sous-chef you hired." Richard reminded her of a Ken doll, very well put together, perfectly presentable, and happy to reside in the shadows of a successful woman. They only rarely butted heads, which usually told her she needed to consider things from another perspective. Most important, he knew when to pick his battles.

She let out a long breath. Clearly, this was going to be one of those times.

"Cruz Mendoza?" Her stomach clenched as the moment she'd been dreading arrived. Richard had been in and out of the restaurant most of the day overseeing the catering deliveries. He looked slightly haggard and stressed beneath the pressed dark suit and blue tie he wore. She motioned for him to sit and reminded herself yet again she was doing what had to be done. For now at least. "What about him?"

"I was just wondering how or where you found him." He waved a printout of the résumé she'd fabricated for Cruz. "I had a list of potentials lined up."

"Yeah, sorry about that." She kept her voice even, scribbled meaningless notes to appear somewhat normal. "Kelly Spangler recommended him." Her colleague was currently on maternity leave and had gone incommunicado. "They worked together a couple of years ago when he was just out of culinary school." She'd committed Cruz's false history to memory while she and the detective had worked out the details. "He moved here to be near family, so I reached out. Why?" She glanced up and frowned. "Is there a problem?"

"No. Not really." But she could tell by the strained expression on his face there was. "I guess I've gotten used to taking care of the employment aspects of the job. Plus, I got the feeling I hadn't quite convinced you we needed someone else."

"It felt right." She added a shrug. "Right time. Right person. He's coming in this morning. You good to show him around?"

"Ah, what time?" Richard glanced at his watch. "I have a meeting at eleven thirty with a potential new catering customer."

"Don't worry about it." She waved him off. "I went ahead and set him up in the payroll system. I got back early from the farmers and fish market so jumped at it. Deliveries should be here in a little over an hour." They opened for dinner at five, but there was always prep work and planning that needed doing. And of course staff dinner, which all the employees ate together a few hours before they opened. First thing she'd done when she'd come in today was put on a huge pot of her employees-only minestrone. It would simmer the next few hours and soon the aroma of fresh-baked bread would begin wafting through True. "Since I'm ahead of things I can take care of getting him acquainted with the restaurant."

"I can call Susan," Richard offered. "Have her come in early?"

"It's fine." She didn't want to hand Cruz off to anyone else. "I'll introduce you when you get back. Anything else?" Her cheeks strained with the effort it took to smile.

"We've locked down the Wilmington wedding in July and the Eppes' Bar Mitzvah next month for catering jobs. I'd like to set up some tastings for them in the next week or so."

"Shouldn't be an issue." She scribbled a note to herself to do a little research on both families. She liked, if possible, to add special, personal touches to events like this, incorporating familiar or comforting menu items that would be that added attention to detail. "How's Jeremy working out as driver? I bet he's glad to get out of washing dishes once in a while."

"Pike?" Richard glanced down at his notepad. "Yeah, doing okay. We get along okay and he likes the change." He shrugged. "Can't ask for more than that, can you?"

Of course she could; she always asked a lot of her

employees and she expected the best. Given the catering program had been in Richard's hands, navigating her interest could be...tricky. She didn't want to come across as taking over when it was a job he was more than qualified and eager to do. But if Cruz's appearance in her life didn't teach her anything else, it taught her that she needed to keep a closer eye on what was going on in all aspects of her business. Although the kitchen would always be her main priority, and Tatum would never relinquish control over the food she and her staff produced.

"Over the next few weeks I'd like to work on getting some consistent summer events booked," she said. "I know a lot of people think of us as high-end, but we need to appeal to smaller businesses and activities as well, to ensure long-term success." If all went well, she could look into expanding next door with a dedicated and separate catering operation. She already had some ideas as to who she'd like running it, once they were solidly in the black.

"I can go through the list of city festivals and events, see if anything pops there." Richard tapped away on his phone. "There's always Eataly, and it is one of Chicago's premier food festivals, but that's this month and they're probably booked out for booths. Maybe someone's canceled."

"Can't hurt to check. What about those business lunches we've been catering for the past few weeks?"

"Belma Trade? They want to sign a long-term agreement. Gourmet lunches for their employees and board of directors. About a hundred and fifty meals every Thursday. Nothing fancy so far, but enough to keep things moving and word of mouth rolling. Sam's doing good overseeing the preparation. He and Colby seem to have it running well."

What would she do without Sam? "What's that costing us?"

Richard glanced up. "We're not quite in the black yet. Why? You want to see numbers?"

"I've looked at the sheets, but I'd like specifics and an accounting report. Is that a problem?"

"No." But Richard's brow furrowed. "Of course not. I'll put one together for you this week."

"Great, thanks." Her gaze shifted over Richard's shoulder when a familiar and distracting face strode into view. "Cruz. You're early." She got to her feet, ignoring the surge of excitement that shot through her at seeing him again, which didn't make sense because she did not want him here.

He'd taken her advice and come dressed to work, from his loose-fitting slacks to the cushioned shoes on his feet. His shirt was a shade of blue that reminded her of lazy sails on the ocean and long, languid dives into the deep. Heaven help her, this was going to be more difficult than she thought.

He carried a backpack like most of her employees, and his hair was tied back in a short ponytail at the base of his neck. She didn't see any hint of the intense, intractable detective she'd been dealing with. "Cruz Mendoza, this is Richard Kirkman, my manager and all-around right hand."

"Pleasure." Cruz stepped in and held out his hand. "Thank you again for this opportunity, Ms. Colton. I can't tell you how relieved I am to have a job again."

"We're looking forward to working with you," Richard responded for her. "So how's Kelly Spangler doing these days? I had lunch with her a few months ago. She'd just been promoted to executive chef at Ladle and Spoon."

Tatum's eyes went wide for an instant before her gaze flew to Cruz. Darn it! She'd thought she'd chosen someone completely off Richard's radar.

"Sounds like you're spending too much time in a Tardis," Cruz said easily and with a chuckle. "Kelly left Spoon just before she had her first baby. She's at Bread and Butter now. Or she will be once she's back from her second maternity leave."

Richard snapped his fingers. "That's right. I forgot. She's running their bakery, isn't she?"

"Once they open it, yes. This sounds like some kind of test." Cruz played the concerned applicant with deference, but the ease with which he lied had Tatum's stomach looping into uneasy knots. "Have you changed your mind about hiring me?"

"No, we haven't." Tatum found her voice again, came around her desk and put an end to the inquisition. "I don't think Richard appreciated me going around him to hire you. But seeing as it is my restaurant, it is my prerogative." It was perfectly okay for Richard to do his job and make recommendations, but when push came to shove, decisions like this were hers. It must have been a while since she'd reminded her manager of that. "Isn't that right, Richard?"

"Of course. No offense meant." Richard nodded, stuffed his hands in his pockets. "Normally I'd be the one to get you all set here, but I'm afraid I have an appointment. I believe Tatum will be taking care of you from here on. I'll let you know how things turn out with the new client, Tatum," he said on his way out.

Tatum stood where she was until she was certain he was out of earshot, then turned her still wide eyes on Cruz.

"Would it be out of line for me to just call him Dick?" Cruz muttered under his breath as he closed the door.

"He means well." Tatum bit back a grin. "And you are early. Why? Is there something wrong?" Had he realized he'd made a mistake? Did they not have to go through with this charade after all?

"No. Just anxious to get started." He glanced around her office, gave what she took as a nod of approval. "I didn't have anything else to do, so I figured I'd best jump in. What's first, boss lady?"

He spoke so casually, as if what he was doing here wasn't spying on her business. How was this so easy for him? And how had he brushed aside what had happened between them yesterday? Okay, so she'd been the one to insist they keep things professional. Still, it would be nice to know she wasn't the only person who'd had her circuits fried.

"That's Chef while we're working. Tatum is fine the rest of the time. How'd you know all that about Kelly?"

"It's my job to know my legend inside and out." Cruz shifted his pack higher on his shoulder. "The internet is a detective's best friend. I did a search on everyone you mentioned in my résumé. He was testing me, wasn't he?"

"Probably." She pulled open the door again. "He's been very meticulous about who we've hired. It's a point of pride with him."

"Meaning I wouldn't have passed muster if you'd left it up to him?"

"Meaning there was no guarantee, and as you said,

we don't have a lot of time to play with. Drug trafficking being what it is and all."

Given his arched brow and his pursed lips, she must have sounded snarkier than intended. "How about I show you around," she said. "We'll get you a locker, and you can meet some of your fellow employees."

Whatever Cruz had been expecting as an employee of True, his downtime, whatever there was of it, would definitely be a plus. The employee locker room, as it was loosely called, was, well, something he would have expected to see in an upscale gym or private club. The walls were painted the same green as the restaurant ceiling and accentuated with swirls of gold. The requisite bank of polished wooden lockers sat against one long wall, and on either end were doors leading to both men's and women's rooms.

Behind those doors were areas that included changing rooms as well as well-stocked showers. That he didn't find a monogrammed robe behind his narrow, numbered locker door came as something of a surprise.

The break area consisted of a couple of tables with multiple cushioned chairs as well as a flat-screen TV, something he couldn't quite wrap his brain around. And was that an...an old-fashioned movie-style popcorn machine?

"We've got a staff of baseball fans," Tatum told him at his befuddled expression. "They watch games on their breaks."

"And throw popcorn at the screen when we lose," someone chimed in.

"We also get the best leftovers in town. I'm Sam Price." One of Tatum's staff members introduced himself as he slipped on his white chef's jacket. He was Black, slightly shorter than Cruz, and had what Cruz could only describe as a mischievous twinkle in his eyes. "Still time to get in on this year's pool, Chef."

"You know I can't tell a shortstop from a midfielder," Tatum said.

"Yeah." Sam grinned. "That was kinda the point."

"How about you, new guy?" The woman who sidled over was compact, reached almost to Cruz's bicep, and wore her stark pink hair in a face-tightening bun on the top of her head. Tiny, tattooed stars dotted the side of her neck. "You a baseball fan, Mendoza?"

"Since I could hold a bat," Cruz confirmed. "Cubs fan to the marrow."

"Cool." As if he'd passed another test, she offered her hand. "I'm Colby Quinn."

"Nice to meet you, Colby."

"My man." Bobby Quallis, all of six feet four inches, towered over Cruz and gave him a hearty slap on the back. "You being a Cubs fan earns you bonus points. You see that exhibition game last night? Vicious."

"I might have caught an inning or two." Cruz did his best not to wince in pain. He could already feel a bruise forming between his shoulder blades even as his mind circled through the larger man's history.

Quallis had played football once upon a time, before serving two years for auto theft. The fact he was caught because he'd pulled over to help an elderly woman cross through a nasty intersection of traffic had earned the two-time offender a sentencing break along with the hearty reputation as a behemoth with a heart of tarnished gold.

Tatum introduced him to the others, the bartenders and wait staff, the dish room crew and busboys, most of whom were young women working their way through college or culinary school. He quickly put faces to names but couldn't get much more without looking at their employee files. Cruz was waiting for the right moment to ask for those.

"Cruz is going to be working with you tonight, Sam," Tatum said. "I want him acclimated to how we work before we throw him in the deep end as my sous. That work for you?"

"Pizza duty's the best in the kitchen." Sam raised his fist in a mock bump. "You good with your hands?"

"I do okay." Cruz swore he could feel Tatum's face heating up from here. "Do you throw or stretch?"

"Combo, my friend," Sam said with a wide smile. "I'll teach you what you don't know."

"I'm up for anything."

Tatum cleared her throat and, as Cruz suspected, when he glanced at her he found her cheeks had turned an amusing shade of pink. "On that note, I will leave you in their capable hands. Thanks, guys. See you in a few."

Cruz turned to stash his bag in his locker once she'd left, not surprised to find the locker room had gone oddly quiet. "Something I can help you all with?" He glanced behind him in the mirror on the interior of his locker door.

"So, you, um, known Tatum for long?" Colby asked, then yelped when a tall, thin, almost anemic-looking young redheaded man elbowed her in the ribs. "Ow! Geez, Chester. I was just asking."

"Snooping for gossip, you mean. Ty Collins." The third of Tatum's former parolees stepped forward. The almost-fifty-year-old looked as if he'd seen a lot more life than most, with his haunted gray eyes and sad smile. A look at his file had told Cruz the man hadn't caught many breaks over the years. "I work mainly pastries and desserts. And I think what Colby meant to say was however you got this job, welcome aboard. Looking forward to working with you."

However he got the... Cruz covered before he blinked in shock. They seemed to be under the impression he and Tatum were...involved. "Ah, thanks. I guess." He cleared his throat and earned a knowing laugh from his new coworkers. It took him a few seconds to realize he'd made the exact same sound Tatum had before she'd left the room. "Look, it's nothing like—I mean, Tatum and me—"

"Don't sweat it." Quallis loomed over him, slapped a hand on Cruz's shoulder and nearly made his knees buckle. "Just know if you hurt her we know how to get rid of your body." His smile was quick, surprisingly friendly, and came with a warning glare that, as a protective big brother himself, Cruz completely understood. "But keep it out of the kitchen," Quallis added with a wink. "In there, it's all about the food. No drama. No personal crap. It stays outside."

"Truer words were never spoken." Sam stood and straightened his jacket, finished the last of his coffee. "The kitchen gets hot enough. Leave whatever it is you've got simmering with her outside."

"But there's nothing..." Cruz trailed off, gaping at the knowing, amused expressions on the faces that trailed out and headed to work. It wasn't until he was alone that he realized that by hiring him the way she had, by being as bad a liar as she was, Tatum had inadvertently given him an added layer of protection. If her employees were focused on his supposed relationship with Tatum, they'd never even consider he was anything more than that.

He shrugged out of his zip-front hoodie, hung it in the locker and pulled out the white chef's jacket Tatum had instructed him to pick up at a local uniform store. He'd also grabbed a few pairs of the relaxed pants and a good pair of solid work shoes. His backup cell and wallet—filled with new IDs that matched his current working identity at True—were in his pack, along with a few innocuous items a man might keep with him on a long workday that included a loaded-to-the-gills e-reader and a fresh pair of clothes.

His detective badge and real ID were locked away in the safe back home in his bedroom, but he had his gun secured in the bottom of his bag. From the time he stepped foot outside his house, for the foreseeable future, he was Cruz Mendoza, sous-chef and devoted son of two elderly, ill parents.

The back of his neck prickled. Now that the break room was empty except for him, he had the strangest feeling he was being watched. He glanced around the ceiling edge. He didn't see any cameras, nor had Tatum mentioned any, and she would have, wouldn't she? Until he was sure, he'd postpone his search of his fellow employee's lockers. Maybe convince Tatum to let him come in after hours so he could take a more thorough look around.

The warrant he'd got was already burning a hole in his pocket. It covered the restaurant and everything inside it for the next seven days. That was the judge's call, having severely narrowed Cruz's requested three-

month window. He had a short time to find the evidence
he needed to expand the warrant and that time was already running out.

Buttoning up and tugging his jacket into place, he
rotated his shoulders, trying to get used to the added
fabric. He'd be sweating in no time, and he could only
imagine how restricted his movements were going to
be. How did she—how did any of them—wear this day
in and day out, night after night? He slid a finger under
the collar, rotated his neck. One thing was for sure.

He had the distinct feeling this was going to be a
very, very long day.

Tatum took an extra half hour over the night's special menu, going over it more times than usual. She told
herself she was being cautious. That she just wanted the
perfect choices possible from her trip to the farmers and
fish market earlier that day.

But that wasn't it.

Being down in that locker room with her staff, she'd
felt almost sick at the idea of what was really going on.
Cruz was here because he believed someone was running drugs out of her restaurant. And there she'd stood,
talking about baseball and blushing to high heaven because of a throwaway comment by someone she considered a friend.

For the first time since she'd opened her restaurant,
True didn't feel like a haven or an escape. It felt like a
trap where every single one of them had been caught.

The only way, the absolute only way to get through
this with her business still intact, was to make sure
the case was never brought to anyone's attention. She'd
prove Cruz wrong. Easy as that.

And if he's right? That irritating little subconscious of hers would not stop pestering her with that question. "If he's right, I'll find a way through it." But he wasn't right. There were no drugs in True.

She'd bet her life on it.

Who was she kidding? She *was* betting her life on it.

Forget butterflies, she had a swarm of murder hornets buzzing around in her stomach. And that buzzing grew more intense as she headed down to the kitchen to begin preservice prep.

She stopped outside the swinging door, pressed a hand to her stomach. She hadn't been this nervous in the kitchen since she'd landed her first *sous* job. Nerves. Jitters. Uncertainty. And it was all because of Detective Cruz Medina.

"Mendoza," she muttered. "Mendoza, not Medina."

"You all right there, Chef?" Quallis came up behind her.

"Fine, thanks." She turned around and pushed her butt into the door to open it. Clipboard in hand, she called her team of chefs and servers together to run through the night's menu. She watched them gather, felt a swelling of pride lift her confidence even as she caught Cruz's gaze. She could do this. Tatum took a deep breath. She could do it.

"Okay, so tonight we're going Mediterranean. Italian and Greek. We're doing branzino with early spring vegetables and a lemon rice pilaf as our main special. Colby, that'll be you on fish with Chester on backup. We've been slow on vegan lately, so I don't want you getting overwhelmed, Colby, and you two work well together," she added when she saw the young woman's brows pinch together. "Sam, you and Cruz are handling the pizza. I added the pear and gorgonzola back to the menu for tonight as an appetizer. Let's see how it does now that we've got the reduced balsamic glaze."

"We've got it," Sam called.

"Great." She recited the rest of the menu items, made note of the few changes she'd made to some of their mainstays. "We're going with chocolate lava cakes with a caramel ice cream as our recommended dessert. Ty, you've already gotten started on the baklava, right?"

"On it," Ty confirmed. "I was also going to recommend a honey gelato as an option for the future. We got a bottle of lavender honey with our market delivery today."

"Oh, that sounds good." She made a note. "Yeah, we'll work that in this week. As usual, I'm open to menu suggestions. I want to keep things fresh. For tonight, let's just focus on being fast and being good. I want every plate that leaves this kitchen to be pristine." She glanced at her watch. "We open in three hours. Soup's on for us in ninety minutes. Any questions?"

The nerves had mostly vanished by the time everyone went back to their stations. Soon the familiar, comforting sounds of True began ringing through her ears. It was going to be okay, she told herself even as she shifted her gaze through the kitchen and found Cruz in the back corner by the imported stone pizza oven. She watched as Sam showed him how to load the wood, shoving it through the flames into the back to maintain the constant fifteen-hundred-degree heat. It made for quick pizzas, especially given how thin their crusts were.

She took a step back, her lips curving as Cruz and Sam worked as a team; it was a good match. One she'd purposely made. Sam knew everything that went on at True whether people wanted him to or not. It was a good connection for Cruz to make. A good friend. She needed the detective to see that the people who worked for her were more than employees, more than names in a file or people with records. They were real people with real lives and she didn't doubt for one minute that they were loyal to her.

Still. She cringed. She really hoped this wouldn't blow back in her face.

Cruz took a step back, planted his hands on his narrow hips and turned his head. His gaze found hers, and for a moment, just like the other night in the bar, the world seemed to move into silence. His smile, when he offered it, scraped against her heart. As beautiful as he was, as effortlessly as he seemed to fit, he didn't belong here. Her own smile faded.

He didn't love this place like she did. To him, it was just another element to his case. Another circumstance he could brush off and move beyond, while to her it was the air she needed to breathe.

"Chef?" Colby waved at her. "I think we might have a problem with the branzino."

Just like that her trance was broken. "Coming," she called, and got to work.

Chapter 7

It took less than the full shift for Cruz to gain a new respect not only for chefs, but for restaurant staff in general. Sure, he'd seen his share of TV docuseries spotlighting the "real world" behind the swinging doors, but that was nothing compared to being in on the action. The nonstop, hot, sweaty, ear-splittingly frenetic activity. The rolling with the punches that could be anything from a food allergy to a food critic.

Despite his crash course at Tatum's condo, there had been no way to properly prepare for this new job. Words and videos, warnings and advice might have helped, but this was being in the trenches, and he felt like a gangly cadet pushing through his first radio car shift.

If he'd expected to have a "getting to know you" conversation with Sam, that idea flew out the pizza door oven from almost the moment service started. There wasn't time to talk. And if he thought he'd slip into this without any difficulty, the overcooked pizzas that had piled up before he finally got the timing right was a definite ego check. They'd made good snacks for one of his breaks, though. On his other break he'd taken what he hoped was a new guy exploratory walk around the storage area, loading bay and alley behind the restaurant. He'd spotted the cameras he expected, but not in the most convenient of places, and not all of them seemed to be working. Interesting.

"Good job, everyone!" Susan Ford, True's hostess, gave them a quick round of applause as they ended the evening at just after eleven. "We had a full house that sent many kudos back to all of you."

Cruz watched Susan walk over to Tatum and speak to her for a while before they both headed out. Before Sam could comment on Cruz's distraction, Cruz refocused his attention and followed the cleanup routine Sam had down to military precision. Once the pizza station was sparkling, they shifted their way down the line, helping the various sous-chefs with their own cleanup, loading the dishes, pots, pans and everything else that had touched a morsel of food into the far back.

"You guys are the definition of a well-oiled machine," Cruz said and earned appreciative smiles from the two dedicated dishwashers currently elbow-deep in suds. "We didn't get introduced earlier. I'm Cruz Mendoza."

"Bernadette Chavez." Dark, frizzy curls sprang up around her sweat-dotted, freckled face. "It's nice to meet you."

"Jeremy Pike." The other dishwasher jerked his chin up in greeting. "Welcome to True." He continued loading one of the three industrial-strength rapid dishwashers while the dirty plates piled up.

"Thanks, Jeremy."

"Just Pike is fine. Only my mother calls me Jeremy." He was tall, only an inch shorter than Cruz, and leaned toward the lanky side. Beneath the collar of his T-shirt Cruz could see the edges of tattoo work, including a distinct symbol from the armed forces.

"You serve?" Cruz asked.

"Nah." Pike shrugged. "My dad. Marines. He was KIA when I was a kid."

"Sorry to hear it."

"Yeah. That's how life goes." Pike turned his attention back to the dishes while others filed in and out, resupplying the kitchen with the just washed and warm plates.

"It usually takes us about an hour after closing to get everything ready for the next night." Ty took a stack of plates from Cruz and set them in their open metal cabinet. "You did real well for your first night here. You ready to do it all again tomorrow?"

"I am, actually." Although he winced as he said it and earned a laugh of sympathy not only from Sam but from some of his other coworkers. Given that he was supposed to be used to working in a restaurant, he couldn't exactly complain, but man. The gym had nothing on this place when it came to physical exertion.

"Most of us are heading over to O'Shannahan's across the street for an afterwork beer," Sam told him as they returned to the washing room for another load. "You're welcome to join us."

"Unless you're ready to go home and collapse," Quallis teased.

He was, but that would be admitting defeat. Besides, a beer with the crew was the perfect way to open up new avenues of information for him. "I'm more than ready for a beer." He was also hungry. How was that even possible after he'd scarfed down that amazing minestrone, fresh-baked bread and more than a fair share of scorched pizza?

"Great. We'll see you there." Sam, Quallis, Chester and Colby all grinned far too widely before they filed out, leaving Cruz surrounded by the remaining mountain of dishes. He groaned. He'd be lucky to be out of here by dawn.

"Let me guess," he said to Ty Collins, who appeared to have taken pity on him and was grabbing an armful of serving utensils. "Dishes are True's version of hazing?"

"You survived trial by fire," Ty told him, looking far more energetic than Cruz despite his added twenty years. "Better than Sam did his first night. He set off the fire alarm twice and ruined so many pies Tatum had to make a fresh batch of dough. Come on. I'll help you finish up."

By the time the kitchen was clean and the last of the kitchen staff was on their way home, Cruz completely understood why the locker room included shower facilities. And also why Tatum had suggested bringing a change of clothes with him. He gave brief thought to drowning himself under the hot water as it melted some of the soreness away, and felt some regret that the night was not over. One job was done. Now his real work began.

"You coming for a beer?" Cruz asked Ty back in the

locker room as the older man tugged on a jacket over a fresh T-shirt and jeans.

"Not tonight." Ty offered an apologetic smile. "Not that I don't want to celebrate your inauguration into the trenches, but I have somewhere I need to be."

Cruz moved his cell onto the top shelf of his locker before he closed the door and spun the combination lock. "No worries. Have a good night."

"Yeah," Ty said with a nod. "You, too."

After-closing was Tatum's favorite part of the day. Not because it boosted her pride to see the receipts for the night, although that did give her a shot of satisfaction. And not because she could retire to her office after delegating the busy work she'd spent years doing in other people's restaurants. Tatum loved this part of her day because there was something special about retreating to her office and looking down at the empty, silent, dimly lit creation she'd brought to life.

True slept now, exhaling in relief as the last of her staff trickled out the front door. She watched them leave every night, enjoying the banter and camaraderie that had built up over the past few years. They'd spend an hour or so at O'Shannahan's, venting whatever they needed to get out of their systems in a safe place she didn't dare intrude into. As much as she would have enjoyed joining them for a beer, having the boss show up like some kind of after-hours overseer just felt… well, it felt rude.

Cruz wasn't in the first flood out. She chuckled to herself as she wandered over to her desk, unbuttoned and shrugged out of her chef's jacket. She stretched her arms over her head, untied her hair and shook her hands through it.

He'd have been given the brunt of the grunt work tonight. Sam would have seen to that. The ritual breaking-in of the new guy—and by guy she meant man or woman—had become a right of passage for her crew, one she fully embraced while staying completely, well, mostly, hands off. And it gave Cruz one more way to see who these people really were.

So it might be a bit passive-aggressive on her part. It wasn't as if he was unfamiliar with the practice. Tatum sorted through the various paperwork and receipts Susan had given her from the registers, the computer printouts. While it was part of Richard's job to maintain the books and accounts, this was one aspect of her business she hadn't quite been able to let go of completely. She liked seeing the numbers add up, and could still remember the thrill of seeing her profit margin move out of the red and solidly into black.

If Cruz was right and True was being used in some way, it had to show up somewhere in the books, didn't it? Her second skimming of the records didn't provide any new answers or suspicions. His investigation was, she decided, going to be quick, cursory, and a complete waste of time. She heard the faint echo of voices as the final group of employees, Cruz included this time no doubt, headed out for the night.

Casually, she knocked her hand against her laptop to wake it up, sorted through the papers and notes, and jotted down totals to keep track of the meals that had been preferred for the evening. When she was ready to put the information into her personal spreadsheet, she pulled her computer closer.

A loud bang followed by a door slamming had Tatum jumping in her chair. She took a deep breath, silently cursed Cruz for making her so darned jumpy, and tried to refocus. She'd had to pull the branzino off the menu special due to its suspicious quality, something she planned to discuss with her supplier first thing in the morning. It wasn't the first time this particular business had tried to slip something past her, but it would definitely be the last.

There it was again. Not a bang this time, but a crash, as if someone had run into something in the kitchen.

Tatum got up, pulled open the door and stood on the top of the landing, leaned over and yelled, "Richard? Are you still here?" She could have sworn she'd seen him leave with the others, but he wasn't exactly a joiner. He also wasn't the workaholic she was and had a tendency to take care of most of the business early in the morning.

Their styles might not be exact, and he did have the tendency to walk around with his nose in the air, something that came in handy with her snootier clientele. He was, above all else, an excellent schmoozer and marketer, and in just the last few months he'd helped her and True make their mark in Chicago's food world. One place he did not excel, however, was in the kitchen. Which was exactly how she wanted it. "Richard?"

Restaurants weren't the safest place in the world for non-chefs, and it was that thought that had her moving quietly down the stairs through the silent confines of True.

After successful nights like this she could almost hear the restaurant's heartbeat; her business was alive, had been from the moment she'd swiped her first paint sample on the wall. The bar and main dining room were bathed in dim light. The kitchen was dark, but she could move through True blindfolded. She wound her way around the counters and appliances toward the back office near the back alley and loading bay, past the walk-in refrigerator. "Richard?" she called again. "Are you all right?"

Something scampered behind her. An odd shuffling of feet and fabric. Tatum spun around, wishing she'd clicked on the light. "Darn it," she told herself in a harsh whisper. "Stop letting him spook you." Cruz. Her eyes narrowed. Was he behind this? Snooping around? Or was he deliberately trying to scare her into believing she had drug dealers in her midst? "You're being ridiculous." Then again, after having seen that cool determination in his eyes earlier this evening, would she put it past him? "Ha, ha, very funny, Cruz." She backtracked, stopped at the edge of the stainless steel work counter, and clicked on the lights. Electricity buzzed overhead as they flickered on. Rather than ease her nerves, the hair on the back of her neck prickled as she caught sight of the walk-in refrigerator's door standing open.

"What on earth?" She stalked toward it, ignoring the warning bells going off in her head. She poked her head inside the walk-in, reached for the light switch. She heard a shuffling behind her, more than a scamper this time, but before she could turn around, she was shoved forward into the icy room. She flailed, struggled to catch her balance, and smashed headfirst into one of the metal shelving units.

Before she could catch her breath, the door slammed shut.

Cruz had situated himself by the front window of O'Shannahan's to nurse his one-beer limit. The True crowd apparently had attained their own dedicated table in the seventy-five-year-old establishment. The throwback-style pub had a history as rich and diverse as Chicago itself, from the scarred yet polished bar that had been salvaged and shipped from a now defunct hotel in Dublin, to the framed news clippings featuring Irish-influenced accomplishments and successes lining the faux brick walls.

According to the stories he'd heard over the last forty minutes, O'Shannahan's had nearly gone under a few years ago. Then True had opened. The rejuvenation of the neighborhood gave the beleaguered owners new hope. Rather than closing up and giving up, they'd taken the chance on a bit of rebranding and marketing, and now enjoyed a new lease—literally and figuratively— along with a steady clientele. A clientele that included True employees who, as a continuous thank-you from the pub, were all given half-off drinks their first hour each night.

"It's not like Ty not to join us after work," Colby said with something akin to motherly concern shining in her eyes. "Is everything okay with him?"

"Who knows." Sam shrugged and took a pull of his beer. "He's not exactly the chattiest in our bunch." He grinned at Colby, who rolled her eyes. "If he wants us to know, he'll tell us." When Cruz continued to watch the restaurant, Sam gave him a friendly nudge on the arm. "Can't leave it alone, can you?"

Cruz shifted his attention to the table, but only for a moment. The lights in True were low; he couldn't see a thing other than the steady glow in the back right corner, precisely where Tatum's second-floor office was located. Given the frenzied activity that took place most of the day, after-closing was the ideal time for anything illegal to go down. "Can't leave what alone?"

"Work," Sam said. "Feels good to find where you fit. Where you belong."

Hearing the sentimentality in the younger man's voice, Cruz stepped through the verbal door that just opened. "Is that what happened to you? To all of you?" he added so as not to single Sam out. "You found where you fit?"

"You know it." Sam toasted him with his bottle. "That woman over there? Tatum? She gave me the chance I needed in this business."

"She's saved a lot of our lives," Quallis chimed in. "Not many folks with her stellar reputation would hire ex-cons like us."

"Ex-cons? You've served time?" Cruz leaned forward. He feigned his surprise, but not his interest. There was always a lot more to people than what their criminal records said. "Both of you?"

"Three of us," Sam corrected. "Ty, too."

"You mind me asking what you were sentenced for?" Cruz knew of course, but reading a file and hearing about it firsthand were two entirely different things.

"Accessory after the fact. Armed robbery," Sam said with a familiar flinch of remorse.

"You didn't accessorize anything," Quallis told him, then looked to Cruz, who forced a smile at the intentional joke.

"Quall, drop it," Sam said with more than a hint of irritation. "I got seven years."

"Kid didn't know what his buddies had just pulled off. He just gave them a ride," Quallis qualified. "Turns out they'd knocked over a convenience store earlier that night, then hoofed it over to where Sam was working and begged a ride."

Sam glared at Quallis. "You going to let me tell it my way or not?"

"They gave you seven years for that?" Why was he surprised? The sentencing of Black defendants typically skewed into the unjust realm. Cruz wasn't immune to the societal inequities; he had a close-up view every single day. As a Hispanic cop, he'd dealt with more than his share of racism and prejudice on both sides of the system. He liked to think he was making a small difference at least. He sure hoped so.

"They gave him seven years because he wouldn't rat out his friends," Quallis continued on his rant as if Sam hadn't spoken.

"I was out in three." Sam's voice quieted, as if he'd changed his mind and wanted to be discussing anything else.

"That sucks," Cruz said. Things had gotten better in the last…he took another drink of beer and longed for another. Who was he kidding? It was going to take a long time for things to get significantly better where the judicial system was concerned. It was a shame Sam had lost even that much of his life for a first-time offence. That said, there was something noble, if not misguided, about the young man not having ratted out his friends. "I'm sorry."

"I found a way through it," Sam said and shrugged. "Kept my head down. Didn't make trouble. Got a job in the prison kitchen. Took classes online and then finished my degree at a community college when I got out. I worked my butt off in a pizza place near my mom's house to pay for it. Now look at me." He toasted to True.

"I'm a top sous-chef for Tatum-freaking-Colton. One day I'm gonna have my own place, serve my own food my way. But for now? I'm where I'm meant to be and learning everything I can."

"We're all where we're meant to be. Speaking of—" Quallis glanced over his shoulder "—Tatum's running late." He checked his watch, frowned. "She's usually heading out about now."

Cruz looked back at the light, saw shadows moving in and out. "You know what time Tatum leaves?"

"Why do you think we chose a table by the window?" Colby chimed in. "None of us go home until she does."

It took a lot to surprise Cruz. They'd managed to do so multiple times in just one night. "She doesn't know, does she?"

"Nope. We've worked hard to keep it that way." Quallis's crystal blue eyes narrowed. "So if she suddenly finds out we'll know who squealed." That grin of his spread slowly and reminded Cruz of a certain maniacal comic book villain.

Cruz chuckled, recognizing a challenge when he heard it. He leaned forward, reached into his back pocket for his phone. He swore, checked his other pocket, patted the front of his jeans. He swore again. "I must have left my phone in my locker."

"Uh-huh." Sam finished his beer. "That's believable."

"Agreed," Quallis teased. "A likely story."

"Work on your creativity, Cruz," Colby suggested. "You'd best get over there before she locks you out for the night."

"Right." He got to his feet, grabbed his bag, pulled a ten out of his wallet and tossed it on the table. "I'll see you all tomorrow."

Tatum had only been truly terrified three times in her life.

Once when she was seven and had gotten separated from her parents and sisters at a Halloween fair, and found herself lost in a haunted corn maze. The second time had been shortly after she'd gotten her driver's license and had white-knuckled it through a thirty-minute downpour on the highway. Number three hit just a few weeks ago when the police had notified the family of her father and uncle's murder. The feeling of her heart lurching inside her body, as if it had forgotten how to beat, was something she'd never wanted to feel again. Something she'd never forget.

But she felt it again now. Surrounded by pulsating silence trapped in the one place she had always been, always felt safe. Tatum dived toward the beam of light streaming in through the small, square window. She grabbed the metal lever handle, but pushing or pulling proved futile. The handle wouldn't budge.

The door remained closed.

In those other instances, tears had broken through the fear, released her from the paralytic inability to think clearly. Even if she had the inclination to cry now, any attempt would have evaporated beneath the steam of anger building inside of her.

Tatum turned her back on the door, slammed her fist against it as her head throbbed. She touched cold fingers to her scalp, fingers that came away bloodied. She swallowed the panic climbing into her throat. Control and calm would get her through. She had to blink constantly to stop her eyes from burning against the cold. She found the light switch, flicked it on and breathed a sigh of relief when the bare bulb overhead fizzled to life.

"Cell phone." She found it in her back pocket, the one place she tried not to keep it because of her tendency to sit on and crack screens. Thank goodness for bad habits. Tatum almost kissed it as she tapped the screen. Until she saw she had no bars. No signal. No way out. Cursing, and as the cold began seeping into her bones, she started to pace. This wasn't supposed to be able to happen. She'd purposely chosen a walk-in refrigeration model that prevented someone being trapped. Which meant one thing.

Someone had locked her inside.

Chapter 8

The cold air snapped through Cruz like a whip as he jogged across the street. True's dimmed interior displayed its elegant facade in the darkness of the night. Streetlights hummed and buzzed, and his footfalls echoed into the darkness. He tried the front door first, not surprised to find it locked. He rapped on the glass, but seconds ticked by without any response.

Cruz took a step back, then walked around to the front of the building where he could get a better vantage into the second-floor office, but as he found the right line of sight he spotted Tatum descending the stairs and circling into the kitchen.

He almost knocked again, then decided to wait until she came back out. He didn't like the idea of her being alone like this. Not at this hour. The neighborhood might have become safer in recent years, but as he well knew, no place was 100 percent safe.

Cruz stood there, staring at the outline of the swinging kitchen doors, mentally willing her to come back out so he could get her attention. When the seconds continued to tick by, he'd had enough. He raised a hand to knock on the glass.

Just as a figure in black streaked out of the kitchen and up the stairs to her office.

Cruz immediately dropped into cop mode. Whoever that was, was too big. Too frantic.

Too male.

Cruz swore, and as he ran around the corner of the building to the back alley, he dragged his backpack in front of him, rummaging inside for his gun. He tossed the bag aside and, pistol in hand, came to a skidding halt when he spotted the taillights of a dark SUV parked directly in front of the metal door of the loading bay. Cruz ducked behind a dumpster, staying out of sight of the idling car as he considered his options. He could call for backup, but that would risk blowing his cover. Once the cops set foot in True, he'd be out, and he had too much at stake to give up so fast. Besides, by the time anyone got here, they'd be long gone. The streetlamps were still blazing, but the nearby ones weren't close or bright enough to give him a good look at the license plate.

He needed to get inside. Tatum was in there. For a moment, impulse overruled reason and he nearly revealed himself. Tatum. His heart jackhammered in his chest. Exciting, entrancing, trusting Tatum who had been so certain no one on her staff could be involved in criminal activity. Anger and frustration boiled their way through his blood. She could be hurt or…worse. Cruz gritted his teeth, gripped his free hand around the edge of the dumpster, poked his head up as someone inside the car pushed open the passenger door.

Voices exploded in the night. Muffled, indistinct, unrecognizable. The shadowy figure he'd seen moments before ducked out the half-raised loading accordion door and into the vehicle. Cruz began moving when the car did, sticking close to the wall, focusing his attention on the grime-covered plate. He caught two numbers and a letter, but the popular make and model of the car would make it nearly impossible to trace.

He ducked into the loading bay, tucked his gun into the back waistband of his pants and hurried through the darkness as quickly as he could. Passing by the bright white catering van with True's logo painted on the outside, he collided with crates along with some boxes in his rush to get to the kitchen, but the gossamer quality of the plastic tarp draped between the main kitchen door and the loading bay acted as a beacon.

He stepped inside the creepy silence of True. "Tatum?" His voice echoed back at him as he made his way through the dish room, into the kitchen and around to the other side. "Tatum?"

He forced himself to stay in one spot, to listen and look. He turned in a slow, deliberate circle. There! A bang. Dull. Heavy. Weak. He inclined his head, and when it came again, he shifted his attention to the walk-in refrigerator.

Son of a...

The metal lever handle of the walk-in had been wedged closed with an oversize metal ladle. She was inside.

The bang sounded again, and this time the light inside flickered. "Tatum!" he yelled as he grabbed a towel and grabbed hold of the utensil to pull it free. He dropped it to the ground with a clang, but before he could open the door, it sprung open and Tatum, hands and arms filled with something he couldn't identify, flew out.

He caught her around the waist before she slammed face-first into the stainless steel counter. Her scream when he lifted her right off the ground had his ears ringing. She kicked and twisted, trying to hit him with whatever reddish brown rock-solid block she carried. He turned his head to the side to avoid being knocked out. "Tatum, stop! It's me. It's Cruz!" He set her down before he dropped her.

"Cruz." She went limp in his arms. Her knees folded and he kept hold of her, kept her on her feet as she caught her breath. "Okay. It's okay." She inhaled deeply, still clutching her battering ram of choice in her arms. "I'm okay."

"What on earth is that?" Cruz asked.

"This?" She hefted it up and nearly hit him in the chin with it. "It's an imported ham. It's the heaviest thing I could find in there," she added at his look of disbelief.

"Let's put the pig down, shall we?" He plucked the ham out of her hands and set it on the counter. When he faced her again, his gaze fell to the trickle of blood trailing down the side of her face. "You're hurt." He reached out, but she flinched before he even touched her. Cruz swore, grabbed a stool and pushed her onto it. "Stay here. I'll get the first aid kit."

"I'm fine." But the fact she sank onto the stool told him otherwise.

"It's either me or the ER. Take your pick." He didn't

stop moving until he'd retrieved the red plastic box from the unisex bathroom off the dish room. When he returned to her side by the refrigerator, he found her staring into its chilly depths, her eyes slightly unfocused. She was shivering. Whether from the cold or the aftereffects, he couldn't be sure. "Maybe the ER is the right move."

"No." She shook her head, flinched a bit, but when she looked at him he saw her eyes were clear again. "No emergency room." She brushed her fingers against her scalp. "Head wounds always bleed like crazy." She pulled the medical box over and rummaged around, set out what he himself would have. "No one else is with you, are they?"

"No." He uncapped the antibacterial spray and got to work dabbing and trying not to make the cut on her head hurt worse. Cruz moved her hair behind her shoulders, took an extra moment to tuck it behind her ear. He looked down at her pale face, at what he could only assume was anger and hurt spinning in those endless eyes of hers. He cupped the back of her head, tilted her head back. "Are you sure he didn't hurt you?"

"Are you sure it was a he? Never mind." She sighed. "Of course it was a man. He just gave me a shove and then slammed the door. Momentum's a bi—" She pinched her lips together. "Took me a second too long to catch my balance. I hit one of the metal racks face-first." She lifted her hand, but he stopped her, caught it in his and curled his fingers around hers. "You know what really makes me mad?"

He couldn't resist, not when she looked so uncertain, so unsure of what to do or think next. He lifted her hand and pressed his lips to the back of her knuckles. "Tell me."

He wasn't sure whether to be impressed or insulted that his attempt at comfort and affection didn't distract her.

"He did this to me in my home, Cruz. He made me feel scared and afraid in my home." Her jaw tensed. "Did you see him? Do you know who it was?"

"No." He released her hand, refocused his attention on her head. "I was standing outside when you came down from your office. I knocked earlier but you didn't hear. Whoever it was moved too fast for me to get a good look"

"I heard someone down here." She was reciting it as if dazed. "I guess I thought maybe it was Richard or one of the employees. Or you."

"Me?"

Her smirk seemed almost normal. "I thought maybe it was you trying to teach me a lesson about being too trusting. You know, freak me out so I'd be more agreeable to your *investigation*."

As insulting as the prospect was, it wasn't a bad lesson for her to have learned. "I wouldn't have done that, Tatum."

"I know. But that's what I was telling myself when I came down here." She scrubbed a hand over the uninjured side of her face. "And before you say anything, I know it was stupid. Just like those idiotic dimwits in horror movies who go up to the attic in the middle of the night because they heard a noise."

"Or the basement," Cruz attempted some levity. He grinned at her irritated glare. "They make for good entertainment."

"The girls or the movies?"

He chuckled and stretched a small butterfly bandage over the cut in her hairline. "Both."

"Typical," she snorted. "Yeah, well, this wasn't scripted and I should have stayed in my…" She stopped. "What else did you see?"

Now it was his turn to wince. "Whoever was here went up to your office." She slid off the stool and shoved past him so fast it was as if he'd flipped a switch. "Wait, Tatum. Hold on." Darn it! He left the medical box open on the counter and hurried after her. She was already halfway up the steps before he caught up. "Let me go in first, okay?"

"It's my office, Cruz." She jerked her arm free of his grasp.

"And someone just broke in here to find something. Just…" He moved around her, backed up the last few steps to the landing. "Let me go first."

"Whatever, Mr. I-Have-a-Penis-and-You-Don't."

Hand braced on the door, he inclined his head. "That's not what this is about."

"Sure it is." She pointed to his back. "Gun, penis. Same diff as far as I'm concerned. There's no one in there, Cruz. They're gone, remember? You saw them leave yourself."

He pushed open the door and stepped into the dimly lit room. He stepped just inside, a bit stunned by what he saw.

"Well?" Tatum moved in behind him.

"Well nothing." He planted his hands on his hips. "The place is immaculate." Just as he remembered it. He'd expected it to be tossed. Whoever had been here had been in a rush. It shouldn't be this neat. Unless they knew exactly what they were looking for and where to find it.

"Well, then." She moved around him this time and headed to her desk.

"Do you see anything that's been disturbed? That's out of place?"

She sat in her chair and did a slow rotation to check the room. "Not really, no." She tapped on the keyboard of her laptop. "This is what I was working on when I heard the noise, and nothing new has been opened." Her gaze hesitated on the tall wooden filing cabinet. "Hang on." She got up and pulled the top drawer open.

"What?"

"This is supposed to be locked," she said and began sifting through the files. "I keep the key in the frame of that picture." She pointed to one of her and her sisters. "Everything seems in place, though. They're a bit more messy than I like, but that could have been me. Huh." She pulled out one file from the middle of the drawer. "This is in the wrong order. I'll give you one guess whose employment file this is."

"Given the look on your face, I only need one." He plucked it out of her hands and flipped open the now empty file. "It's mine."

Tatum stayed in Cruz's SUV while he ran the towel-wrapped ladle that had nearly sealed her doom into the precinct lab. She hadn't been up for another argument, which was why she agreed to let him drive her home. Although why he hadn't done that first before coming here was beyond her.

It was closing in on 1:00 a.m. and her body was

screaming for relief in the form of a shower, a handful of aspirin and sleep. Not necessarily in that order.

Resting her arm on the door, she pressed gentle fingers to the sore spot, which would no doubt transform into a lovely shade of eggplant by morning. She supposed that years from now, when she'd rediscovered her sense of humor, she'd find this entire situation borderline hysterical, but for now? For now she was definitely going to have to take things one minute at a time.

She closed her eyes, felt her head loll forward, but before her eyes drifted shut, she saw a shadow heading her way. Tatum jumped, suddenly wide-awake, and instantly realized it was Cruz. She glanced at her watch. It had been almost an hour since he'd parked.

Tatum shifted in her seat as he opened the door and dropped in behind the wheel. "Sorry. Paperwork's always a pain. You all right?"

"I'm fine." Given it was the tenth time he'd asked her that question since they'd left True, she managed this one through gritted teeth. "Will you take me home now?"

He grinned, starting the engine. "Sure."

She rolled her eyes, which added to the pain in her head. "Just drop me off at my front door, Valentino. I'll walk in tomorrow."

"Valentino, huh?" he echoed with that side-eyed smile of his. "Charming, romantic, the epitome of male virility—"

"In the *silent* movie age," she cut him off.

"Not to mention the fact Rudolph Valentino was Italian and I am—"

"Not." She smirked, ducked her chin before he saw

the conversation was actually entertaining and thus distracting her. "Do you like silent movies?"

"I do, actually. Buster Keaton is one of my favorite silent stars. Who's your favorite?"

"Clara Bow." She'd always thought the women of that era had gotten the shaft when it came to the history of film. "They're having a silent movie retrospective in Edgerton Park next week. Before tonight I was thinking about taking Thursday off and going."

"How does tonight change that?" He made a U-turn at the light and headed toward her condo.

"Call me overly cautious, but I'm not feeling particularly secure in leaving my restaurant in someone else's hands right now." She knew once the fog lifted from her brain she was going to have to deal with the fact that someone—someone she trusted and considered family—was probably responsible for her getting shoved into the Deepfreeze.

"When was the last time you took a day off?"

"Monday, remember?" She could feel her eyes beginning to droop again and stifled a yawn.

"I mean a day that wasn't already designated. You're the boss. You should take a day every once in a while."

She rolled her head against the back of the seat to look at him. "When's the last time you took a day off?"

"February 17," he said without hesitation. "My brother, Frankie, was participating in a debate competition."

Tatum's mouth twisted. Sometimes Cruz Medina seemed entirely too good to be true. "I think my staff would fall over in shock if I took a day off."

"All the more reason to do it." Cruz shrugged. "Put

them off guard. Maybe see what happens as a result." He glanced at her. "You might be surprised."

"Speaking of putting them off guard," she said slowly. "Thank you for letting it look like we were leaving separately tonight."

His lips twitched. "Not a problem."

"They watch out for me," she explained. "They're protective. They actually wait at O'Shannahan's until I leave True for the night." One of the reasons she didn't like to leave too late. "Isn't that sweet? What?" Tatum asked when Cruz glanced out his window.

"They think you don't know." That grin of his needed a dimmer. "Don't let on you know. I'm under strict orders not to tell you."

"I'll keep your secret if you keep mine. I'm just glad they didn't see us leaving together." She sank back farther in the seat as she felt her body begin to loosen. The adrenaline and nerves were fading. "The last thing either of us need is for them—"

"To think we're involved?" He took a left and slowed down as they came up on her street. "Hate to tell you, but I think that ship hasn't only sailed, it's beyond the horizon."

"What's that mean?" All thoughts of sleep and relaxation faded.

"They think we're sleeping together."

"What?" She shot forward in her seat only to have the seat belt snap her back. "Why would they think that?"

"You said yourself the way you're hiring me was a little out of the norm. Plus, you aren't great at deception. You can't lie worth a da—"

"Some people would consider that an admirable quality," she grumbled.

"It didn't help that you blushed to high heaven when you introduced me today."

"I…did not." Her hands flew to her cheeks that were warming even now. "Did I?"

"We could have roasted marshmallows on your face. Don't worry. It actually works to my benefit if they think we've got something going on."

"Well, it doesn't work to mine," she snapped, and then, curious, shifted to face him. "Sleeping with one of my employees. How…cliché. How exactly does it work to your benefit?"

"Us being involved is a good distraction. Not to mention it is a stellar explanation as to why I'm suddenly around. Getting the prime jobs. Having private meetings with the boss." As his humor increased, her irritation grew. "If they're thinking I was hired because we're involved, they won't even consider the real reason I'm there."

"But…" She shook her head. "Us sleeping together would be unprofessional." Not to mention completely out of character for her. Doesn't mean she hadn't thought about it. More than she should have. "And it's a lie."

"Yet not wholly untrue." He pulled into the driveway of her underground parking lot, hit the universal emergency code into her security gate and waited for the metal gate to rise. "We did share a pretty steamy moment in your kitchen the other day. That could qualify as involved."

It qualified as Tatum trying to get Cruz Medina out of her system, she thought sourly. Unfortunately, it hadn't worked, and had, instead, only increased her curiosity, not to mention her desire for the man who could literally destroy her life. "The deal was," Tatum said with exaggerated patience, "I let you work for me so you can prove your theory about drugs being run through my restaurant." As he pulled into her parking spot, left vacant since her car was still at True, she felt compelled to remind him, "It didn't include deceiving my employees into thinking I'm hot for one of my chefs."

"Yeah, well, deals change. Speaking of changing things." He got out and came around to open her door. The next thing she knew he went into his trunk and pulled out not only the pack he'd carried into the restaurant, but also a small duffel bag.

"What's that?" she demanded, but she already knew, by that sly expression on his face. "No. Absolutely not." Her insides sprung into this odd, unfamiliar dance that had her palms sweating. "You are not moving in with me."

"Just for tonight." He took her arm and steered her toward the elevator.

"I said no." She pulled her arm free and took a step back. "You've already invaded my restaurant, turned me into a nervous wreck around my employees and worried someone enough to shove me into a freezer. You are not staying here tonight."

"Let me break this down for you." He took a long breath, let it out. But this time when he smiled, there was no humor behind it. No friendliness. It wasn't Cruz Mendoza, sous-chef and employee of True, looking back at her. This was Cruz Medina, the determined, almost detached cop. "Even if you didn't believe me about the drugs, someone broke into your restaurant tonight. They knew you were there and they came in anyway. They had a plan, Tatum. And it's only blind luck you don't have anything worse than a bump on the head and a case of the chills."

"It was your information they took, not mine," she argued.

"We don't know that for sure. For all we know, taking my file may have been a cover for what they were really after." He pressed the elevator button and stepped back when the doors slid open. "What we do know is they were confident enough in your routine that you'd be alone." He held open the door and waited for her to step inside. "And while the case is my top priority, I'm certainly not going to take a chance with your safety. Not tonight." He hit the button for the second floor. "So whether you like it or not, for tonight at least, I'm your roomie."

There was something immensely satisfying about Tatum Colton in a simmering temper. For years Cruz remembered hearing what a turn-on an angry woman could be, but he'd never gotten the appeal. Clearly, it all depended on the woman.

He wandered around the semi-chaotic living room, where the sparse furniture she did have was out of place and covered in paint tarps left behind by her interior decorator mother and aunt. Cruz had already whipped the coverings off the sofa and coffee table, onto which he set the gun and badge he'd retrieved from his place, along with his phone so all would remain in reach.

It was funny. She'd made it abundantly clear she didn't appreciate his intrusion, and when it came to stubbornness he could think of few rivals. He'd always said he could never be with anyone who wouldn't stand up to him and push back, at least not without irritating him. It had acted as a kind of emotional safety barrier no woman had been able to cross. Enter Tatum Colton.

The more time he spent with her, the more he admired her. Not just admired, but liked. For once, he might be willing to put up with the complications that came with getting involved. Except this would be taking one whopping chance given everything that hung in the balance. The case, the job always would have to come first, always did. Getting distracted by one seriously hot chef was only going to blow up both their lives. And not in any way that was good.

From his spot on the couch—a couch significantly more comfortable than his own bed—he listened to the sound of the shower running. She'd given him the tour beyond the kitchen, the only room he'd inhabited on his previous visit. The kitchen turned out to be the largest, most organized and well-stocked room. It made sense, he supposed. Her love of cooking didn't stop at the doors of True, as evidenced by the spills of herbs lining the small garden window over the sink and the meticulously arranged appliances, utensils and collection of antique rolling pins that made up an odd kind of wall sculpture.

He changed into sweats and a T-shirt, and gave the space outside her bedroom a thorough once-over by checking the windows and the sliding patio door. He double-checked the front door and added suggesting she put a second dead bolt on for added security to his mental list. A single woman couldn't be too careful. Especially if said single woman had drug dealers hovering around her business. But that could wait for when she'd burned off her mad.

He stashed his bags in the small half bath off the kitchen and had made up the couch with the sheets and blanket she'd delivered with her special brand of resentment. Those eyes of hers could scorch glass, and time after time he found himself smiling in the heat of them. It was no doubt obnoxious of him, to take personal delight in what he knew was a difficult situation, but he had a job to do. Tatum's wounded pride and feelings couldn't enter into it.

Lights dimmed, he sat on the couch and checked his voice mail and email. Nothing new to report except... his heart clenched at the text message he'd missed from Jade. He glanced at the time. Too late to message her back now, except...

He typed quickly, his pulse racing as he promised to stop by the Stanhope Rehabilitation Facility tomorrow morning. Hitting Send, he wanted his former partner's almost fiancée to know he'd responded when he could. It wasn't a minute before his notification banner glowed with a simple TY.

Cruz clicked off the light, lay down on the couch and squeezed his eyes shut, trying to block out the rush of memories, the torrent of guilt that flooded through him. He could replay that night in his mind a million times and he'd never see any other way out. But he should have done better, should have done more to protect Johnny. Johnny, who had so much more of a life to live for than he did. Johnny, who had put his life in Cruz's hands only to have things go horribly, horribly wrong.

He needed noise, he needed a distraction. He needed

this condo not to smell like jasmine and fresh-baked bread, scents that only evoked endless images of Tatum Colton and her wild, sexy, untamed mane of golden hair. The only image, it seemed, capable of pushing the guilt and anger into the back corners of his mind.

Even now, as he tried to block everything but the thought of sleep, he could feel her, smell her. Hear her bare feet padding across the hardwood floors…

"Cruz?"

He opened his eyes, tried not to inhale too deeply, but he caught the scent of flower-rich soap on her freshly scrubbed skin. Her damp hair was tied up in a knot. She wore a tank top that clung to every curve of her tight, tempting body, along with boxer shorts that confirmed those legs of hers really did go up as far as he'd imagined. He'd dreamed what those legs would feel like wrapped around him, drawing him near her, closer into her. "Yeah?" He didn't move for fear he might shatter.

"This is a one-off."

He turned his head, arched a brow. Seeing her there, standing in the barely-there light of her kitchen, suspecting what temptations lay beneath the fabric concealing her form from him, had him clearing his throat. "Oh, yeah?"

He couldn't help it. He loved watching her eyes narrow like slit arrows of anger.

"I don't need you here," she said. "More to the point, I don't want you here."

"I know." He sighed as if the argument had become tiresome. "Deal with it." When she didn't move away, he continued. "How's your head?"

"Fine."

But he could see it wasn't. She was scared. Despite

trying not to be. It was in the sudden shift of her eyes, the way she hugged her arms around her waist. It was all he could do not to wrap his own around her and draw her down beside him.

"I won't change my schedule for you. I won't change my life any more than I already have."

"Change it for yourself, then," he said. "And get some sleep."

"We need to be out of here by eight," she said. "I mean it. Eight a.m."

"Right. Eight. Got it." He looked away, snuggled deeper into the sofa and threw his arm over his eyes. "Go to bed, Tatum."

Still, she didn't move. He could hear, could feel her breathing.

"I mean it, Tatum." He'd never growled a statement before in his life. But he did so now. It was the only way to push the words free. "Go to bed before we both do something you'll regret."

It took longer than he expected, and she didn't scamper. She moved away without another word, but the hesitation in her steps, the slight sound of her increased breathing, had him realizing it was only a matter of time before he was in her bed.

Bap! Bap bap bap!

Cruz shot awake, reaching for his gun, and was on his feet in the blink of a sleepy eye. When he looked to the source of the sleep-shattering noise, he lowered his sidearm and glared across the room and into the kitchen.

The sun was peeking in through the kitchen window, announcing the start to a new day. And instead of an in-house rooster, Tatum Colton's alarm consisted, it seemed, of her bashing a significant round of dough against her floured counter. Plumes of white puffed up and around her, coated her skin and set his pulse to jackhammering.

"Sorry." She sounded anything but as she grabbed the dough, whipped it up and over and slapped it back down. "It's almost five."

He pressed his thumb and forefinger into his eyes. "You say that as if it means something."

"I didn't want us to be late. We need to be out of here by—"

"Eight a.m. Yeah, I got the memo." She'd all but carved it into his brain last night. "What are you doing?"

"Making bread." And she seemed scarily focused on it. "Baking is one of my coping mechanisms." She winced, shifted the dough around and began to knead it with a ferocity that had Cruz wincing. "I couldn't sleep."

With sleep a forgotten desire, he made his way to the kitchen, poured himself a cup of coffee from the pot she'd already brewed, and took a seat at the bar. When he set his gun on the countertop, her eyes shifted briefly before she refocused on her task. "What's wrong?"

She snorted, a sound that had him torn between laughing and offering sympathy. Rather than provoking her, he simply sipped appreciatively and waited.

"True has been open for three years. Three." Slap. Bang. Slap bang. "Years. Never once in that time have I felt remotely unsafe in its walls. Among my people." Slap bang bang bang. "And now…" She folded the dough over, shoved at it with the heel of her hand and began kneading again. "And now…"

"And now you aren't sure who you can trust." He

heard the tears in her voice. Not the feel-sorry-for-me tears of a woman whose business might be in serious jeopardy, but the hot, angry, frustrated tears of not being able to do anything about it. "I'm sorry, Tatum."

"Are you?" She slapped the dough hard enough to make him jump, grabbed it to whip it around again only to have it fly out of her hand. He caught it one-handed as it arced over his head, as if he'd caught a home run at Wrigley Field.

The horror in her eyes kept the humor off his face. He reshaped the ball of dough before handing it back to her as a peace offering. "Yes. None of this is your fault. Someone's taking advantage of you." And the generous nature that was bound to get her into trouble.

"Don't say that," she snapped, and after poking the dough, seemed to decide it and she had had enough. She retrieved a prepared and parchment-lined loaf pan from behind her. "That makes me sound like some dimwitted dolt who can't see what's happening in front of her face."

"No," he argued, wishing he was feeling a bit more coherent for this conversation. "It means whoever is doing this knows what buttons to push. I'll figure this out, Tatum. I promise."

"*We'll* figure it out, you mean." She pressed the bread dough into a rectangle, folded over the ends and pinched it together. Within seconds she had it settled in a loaf pan and set to the side for a rise beneath a towel. "We're partners, remember?"

"No," he said and purposely looked into the dark liquid of his cup. "We are not. I'm the cop. You're a chef. You keep your nose in your area and I'll do my job. That's the deal."

"See, I don't like that deal. You have nothing to lose if this all goes heels up. Whereas I lose—"

"Everything. Yes, again, I know." His cell phone vibrated, the sound reaching him from the coffee table. As it gave him the perfect excuse, he walked away from the counter to get it. The text message was another reminder from Jade. Just three words: Please don't forget.

I'll be there by nine, he replied, and before Jade could respond, he set the phone back down.

"Bad news?" Tatum had come around the counter, had her own mug of coffee in her hand and looked over the rim at him as she sipped.

"Just an appointment I have to keep this morning."

"Oh. It looked like it was bad news."

She wasn't wrong. But the bad wasn't new. It was old enough to have sunk into his bones so deep that it made him ache. "A friend of mine's in the hospital. A recovery facility." He shrugged as if it wasn't a big deal.

"I'm sorry. Look, Cruz—"

He held up his hands, not in surrender, but in emphasis for her to listen to him. "I need you to hear me on this, Tatum. And I need you to understand. We are not now, nor will we ever be partners. You watch out for your business. I'll watch out for the bad guys. You've gotten me in to where I need to be and I will take it from here, all right? All you need to do is just keep cooking, keep acting as if everything is as it should be, and if perchance you come across anything that's amiss or doesn't sit right with you, you tell me. Got it?"

"I don't know." Her frown disappeared behind her mug. "Could you maybe tell me all that again in a less condescending tone? I don't want to miss any of my agreed-upon obligations."

He swore, vehemently enough that his mother would have smacked him on the back of the head, but instead of looking surprised or even offended, Tatum rolled her eyes and returned to the other side of the counter. "You're going to have to do better than that to offend me. I got in trouble more times than I can count in school for swearing. And far more creatively than that."

"You did not," he accused.

"Oh, I sure did. Sister Damien sent me to the principal's office so often you could have called me ricochet. I ended up in detention for a month the first time. After that I just planned it into my schedule. I even got points for creativity. Off the record, of course."

"Sister…Damien?"

"Ironic, right?" Tatum's lips twitched. "Look, I get it. You have a job to do. But the sooner you realize you aren't in this alone, the better off we'll both be."

"You think so?" He strode toward her, partly because he knew she wasn't paying attention as she turned on her oven.

"I do think…oh!" She almost bashed into him when she stood up. "Well. Good morning." She pressed a hand against his chest, just over his heart. He could feel the warmth of her skin through his shirt, as if she was slowly branding him with her touch. "What's this, then?"

"I'm just wondering if there's any way to get you to stop talking." He said it while purposely looking at her mouth, a mistake, he realized too late, as he could only imagine what those lips of hers were capable of.

"And I'm wondering if maybe I should ban you from my kitchen." Instead of backing away, like he thought she would, like he hoped she would, she straightened her spine and inched up her chin. "We got in trouble like this before, Cruz. Are you sure you want to give it another try?"

"I shouldn't." It was like being tempted by a decadent dessert and knowing he was allergic to the ingredients. It didn't dim the want, the desire, even as he knew the aftereffects could be dangerous. "You've got an escape route," he told her even as her smile widened. He knew that look by now, that challenge only she could offer. There was something about this woman, something he couldn't define if he tried to, that pushed all thoughts of rationality and reason away and left him only with want.

"I'm not the kind of woman who runs," she told him as she traced her index finger down the center of his lips. "You're a big part of the reason I couldn't sleep, you know."

"Oh?" He leaned in, brushed his mouth, ever so lightly, across hers.

"Uh-huh." She returned the favor, upping the ante by nipping at his bottom lip, catching it between her teeth with the barest hint of pressure. "Maybe we just need to get this out of the way. You know. Scratch the itch."

He caught her hand as it slipped up his chest, almost curved around his shoulder before he threaded his fingers through hers. "You really think one time would do it?"

She kissed him, with only her mouth and hands touching him, and set him on fire from head to toe. When Tatum pulled away, she left only a breath between them as she bit her own lip, lifted her gaze to his. "I'd be willing to find out. Let's see." When her lips opened in silent invitation, he slipped his free hand around her waist and, pressing his palm flat against the base of her spine, pulled her against him. He wanted, he thought as he claimed her mouth, for her to feel what she did to him. From the fire raging through his blood to how ready he was to take her right now, right here, in her personal fortress.

He was used to being in control, in every aspect of his life. But as he felt her grab hold and hook her bare foot around the back of his calf, when she opened her mouth wider so that he could slip deeper into her, he relinquished it eagerly. She matched him move for move, touch for touch, breath for breath until he could feel her heart beating to the same erratic rhythm as his own.

Her hands released him and he felt himself slipping away, until those nimble, strong fingers of hers trailed down his sides and beneath the hem of his shirt. The second he felt her hands on his bare flesh he grabbed hold of her hips and turned her against the counter, pressing his hardened arousal against her.

Her gasp was like a bullet to his system, sharp, intrusive and strangely exhilarating. As her hands roamed over his back and her mouth and tongue continued to enrapture him in blind capitulation, he knew there was only one place for this to end. There was only one place he wanted to be. In Tatum Colton's bed, with her wrapped around him.

"Tatum." He murmured her name against her lips, felt the ever so faint acknowledgment of understanding as her mouth pulled away. "Just how important is eight a.m. to you?"

"What?" The dazed, foggy look in her eyes nearly had him throwing reason and caution out the window and hauling her back into his arms. "Eight oh...oh!" Reality seemed to hit her like a bucket of ice water.

"Jeez. Okay, you're right. Stop." She planted her hands on his shoulders, but instead of pushing him away, she simply looked at him.

Was that regret he saw? Or did he just imagine that because he felt it, too?

"If you don't believe anything else I say to you, Cruz, believe this." Tatum seemed to have a hard time catching her breath. He couldn't wait to make that happen again. "If we aren't out of here by eight, both of us are going to regret it in ways you cannot even imagine."

"So…" He nipped at the side of her neck, felt her shudder, and suspected it wouldn't take much to put that warning out of her mind. "Is it okay to use your shower?"

"Yes." She drew in a shaky breath. "Yes, good idea. Go." She shoved him playfully, and hard enough for him to understand it was just as difficult for her as it was for him to stop. "I'll have breakfast waiting for you when you're done."

She'd make waffles, Tatum decided. Fluffy, buttermilk waffles stuffed with bacon, cheese, and topped with thick, sugary maple syrup that would send even the most recovered carb addict into a blissful coma.

"Yeah, that should make me stop thinking about whatever that kiss was." She had her virtual media player turn on the music, not so loud as to disturb the neighbors at this hour, but definitely so she could lose herself in the frenetic beat. All the better to drown out the sound of the shower running in her bathroom.

She would not think about Cruz Medina being naked in her shower. Or how his firm, toned torso had felt beneath her far too curious fingers. Nor would she entertain the all too easy notion of joining him to finish what both of them had clearly been far too eager to start.

"Think food," she sang in time to the melody. "Food is your safe place."

Pulling out the waffle maker had always been a signal to her family she was stressed or uncertain about something. Come finals time the freezer would be set to overflowing with the varying recipes she tried, bulking up the basic recipe she'd memorized before she'd gotten through grammar school. One of the largest cabinets in the kitchen was filled with the selection of waffle irons she'd gotten for Christmas from someone she'd grown up with. It had become something of a Colton holiday tradition, and while it was something they laughed about every year, it was also one of her favorite collections. There was always one to suit whatever mood she was in.

"Don't think anyone's gotten me one for sexual frustration yet," Tatum mumbled to herself as she dug through the cabinet. She bypassed the small, heart-shaped novelty waffle maker and went for the traditional, oversize, chunky square machine that couldn't be interpreted—or misinterpreted—in any way.

Batter made and resting, she slid a cookie sheet of thick-slab bacon painted with maple syrup and topped with a sprinkling of brown sugar into the oven. Within minutes the air was filled with what she considered the most wonderful aroma in the known universe.

Out of habit, she started toward her bedroom to get dressed, only to stop short when she heard the water turn off.

"Bad idea, bad bad bad idea." She pivoted so fast she almost tripped, then let out a panicked gasp as she heard a key snap open the lock on her front door. Tatum whimpered, cast a frantic look at her closed bedroom door and dived forward as her front door swung open. Her mother and aunt, deep in conversation, weren't even looking as they walked in. "Mom!" She tried, but there was no stopping them. "You're supposed to come after I've left for the day."

"Pfffth." Farrah Colton waved her off as if she was a pesky fly at a picnic. "We needed your input on the drapery fabric."

"No," Tatum said. "You really don't. I don't care what fabric—"

Farrah sniffed the air, elbowed her twin sister and earned a smile in return. "I told you if we were early enough we'd get breakfast. Oh, honey, you've made waffles. What's wrong?" She dumped her armload of fabric samples onto one of the tarp-covered chairs and strode into the kitchen. "Did something happen at work?"

If they only knew. "I just wanted waffles," Tatum protested to no one who would believe her. "Can't a girl just have waffles for breakfast when she wants them?" She couldn't stop herself from glancing back at the bedroom door. Her heart hadn't beat this fast since… her cheeks warmed. Well, since just a few minutes ago when Cruz had his hands on her. "I'm sorry. I had a difficult night."

"I can see that." Aunt Fallon walked over and touched a gentle hand to Tatum's scalp. "That looks like a nasty cut. What happened?"

"Tatum?" Farrah's concern shifted. "You hurt yourself?"

"It's nothing," Tatum said in such a rush her tongue nearly knotted itself. "I bashed into one of the racks in the freezer. I got distracted. Really, Mom, it's nothing." She held up her hands and backed up as her mother approached. "Can we do this another time? I've got—"

"Oh."

Tatum froze and closed her eyes. Never before had one male-uttered syllable threatened her sanity more.

"Sorry." Cruz's amused voice floated through the room. "I, uh, forgot my bag in the other bathroom."

When Tatum opened her eyes, she found both her mother and aunt exchanging unreadable looks before they turned their mutual attention first on Cruz, then on her. "I can explain," Tatum managed in a whisper.

Then she turned around and found Cruz standing just outside her bedroom door, skin and hair still dripping, one hand gripping the edges of the towel draped low across his hips. She swallowed hard, unable to stop herself from taking pulse-pounding inventory. Her imagination hadn't come close to the reality of him. Nor, it seemed, had her subconscious.

Detective Cruz Medina had been beautifully made by nature, and clearly enhanced by meticulous attention paid at the gym. There wasn't a part of him that wasn't sculpted, from his distinct abs right down to those hip muscles that drove women like her over the edge of reason. The way his dark hair lay damp against his shoulders and tiny beads of water dotted his neatly trimmed beard had her internal thermometer spiking into the danger zone.

"Then again." Tatum covered her mouth. "Maybe I can't. Ah, Cruz, this is my mother, Farrah Colton, and her twin sister Fallon. My aunt. Mom, Aunt Fallon, this is Cruz—" she hesitated at the flash of warning in his gold-flecked brown eyes "—Mendoza."

Tatum caught his gaze when it flew to hers, and prayed he could somehow read her mind. *Don't make this worse*, she silently pleaded. *Please don't make this...*

"Ladies. Pleasure to meet you." As if he was wearing an imported suit and welcoming them to a night at the opera, he strode forward and offered his free hand to each of them. "Apologies for my current appearance."

"No apology necessary," Tatum's mother said. "Except from us, of course. We had no idea we'd be interrupting anything by coming over early. Tatum, why didn't you say you had company?"

"Ah, I...um." Despite rarely being at a loss for words, she couldn't seem to find any at the moment. "Cruz, don't you think you should go get dressed?"

"Right," Cruz said and darted into the guest bathroom for his things. "I'll just..." He backed his way toward her bedroom. "Carry on, ladies."

"Uh-huh." Fallon nodded. "He didn't have to leave on our account," she said and earned a snicker from her sister.

"Or get dressed," Tatum's mother added.

"I guess I should be glad you didn't have your work crew with you." Desperate for escape, she hurried into her personal safety zone of the kitchen.

"He seems nice." Farrah took a seat on one of the stools, leaned her chin in her hands. "Known him long?"

The fact her aunt joined her mother at the counter was a sure sign this conversation was happening whether she wanted it to or not. "A while," she lied. "He's, ah, working at the restaurant."

"Really?" It was her Aunt Fallon who spoke. "I didn't think you approved of workplace romances."

Tatum set a stack of plates on the counter with a

bang. "That's not what this is. Exactly," she added at their skeptical looks. "It's complicated, okay?" No way was she going to tell them the truth, that her restaurant was being used as a possible front to distribute drugs. Or that an undercover detective was investigating the claim. "Trust me, it isn't going to last."

"Just getting him out of your system?" her mother asked far too innocently.

"Really, Mom?" If Tatum's face was any hotter she could cook breakfast on it.

"There's nothing wrong with a healthy physical and sexual relationship," Farrah continued in a way that had Tatum wanting to cover her ears. "Although he looks more than capable of dealing with you on a more permanent basis."

"Definite son-in-law material, for sure," Fallon agreed.

"Son-in...okay, stop right there." Tatum pushed out the words over her reaccelerated pulse rate. "You run a design business, not a wedding planning one. And don't you dare start shifting attention away from the job you've started here. Keep on track, you hear me?" Tatum glanced over their heads as her bedroom door opened again and Cruz emerged. "No interrogations. And no teasing. He's a nice guy, Mom," Tatum said when her mother got that gleam in her eye. "He really is."

Farrah's amusement faded, replaced by understanding that still contained more than a hint of interest. "All right. We'll behave."

"Speak for yourself," Fallon teased, then sobered at Tatum's huff. "Oh, let us have some fun, Tatum. You haven't been this smitten about anyone since—"

"Smitten?" Tatum gaped. "I'm sorry, did we just join the road cast of *Oklahoma!*?"

Apparently a glutton for punishment, Cruz emerged from her bedroom, fully dressed and completely appealing.

Her mother began humming an all too familiar show tune as she spun around on her stool. "So, Cruz. How about while Tatum finishes breakfast, we get to know each other?"

FREE BOOKS GIVEAWAY

2 FREE SUSPENSE BOOKS!

2 FREE SUSPENSEFUL ROMANCE BOOKS!

GET UP TO FOUR FREE BOOKS & TWO FREE GIFTS WORTH OVER $20!

We pay for everything!

YOU pick your books – WE pay for everything.

You get up to FOUR New Books and TWO Mystery Gifts...absolutely FRE[E]

Dear Reader,

I am writing to announce the launch of a huge **FREE BOOK[S] GIVEAWAY**... and to let you know that YOU are entitled to choose up to FOUR fantastic books that WE pay for.

Try **Harlequin® Romantic Suspense** books featuring heart-racing page-turners with unexpected plot twists and irresistible chemistry that will keep you guessing to the very end.

Try **Harlequin Intrigue® Larger-Print** books featuring action-packed stories that will keep you on the edge of your seat. Solve the crime and deliver justice at all costs.

Or TRY BOTH!

In return, we ask just one favor: Would you please participate in our brief Reader Survey? We'd love to hear from you.

This FREE BOOKS GIVEAWAY means that we pay for *everything!* We'll even cover the shipping, and no purchas[e] is necessary, now or later. So please return your survey today. You'll get **Two Free Books** and **Two Mystery Gifts** from each series to try, altogether worth over **$20!**

Sincerely

Pam Powers

Pam Powers
For Harlequin Reader Service

Complete the survey below and return it today to receive up to 4 FREE BOOKS and FREE GIFTS guaranteed!

FREE BOOKS GIVEAWAY
Reader Survey

1	2	3
Do you prefer stories with suspensful storylines?	Do you share your favorite books with friends?	Do you often choose to read instead of watching TV?
◯ YES ◯ NO	◯ YES ◯ NO	◯ YES ◯ NO

YES! Please send me my Free Rewards, consisting of **2 Free Books from each series I select** and **Free Mystery Gifts**. I understand that I am under no obligation to buy anything, as explained on the back of this card.

❏ Harlequin® Romantic Suspense (240/340 HDL GQ3J)
❏ Harlequin Intrigue® Larger-Print (199/399 HDL GQ3J)
❏ Try Both (240/340 & 199/399 HDL GQ3U)

FIRST NAME

LAST NAME

ADDRESS

APT.#

CITY

STATE/PROV.

ZIP/POSTAL CODE

EMAIL ❏ Please check this box if you would like to receive newsletters and promotional emails from Harlequin Enterprises ULC and its affiliates. You can unsubscribe anytime.

Chapter 9

"I am so sorry."

"Don't be." Cruz wasn't sure what entertained him more. Her mother and aunt's completely unsubtle interrogation over the best waffles he'd ever eaten, or the fact that Tatum continued to provide him with more layers of cover. Both lost out to Tatum's mortified reaction. He hadn't had this much fun in a long time. "I thought it was funny."

They took the stairs down to the parking garage in her building, leaving well after the previously designated eight o'clock escape hour. He now completely understood why she was determined to get out before Fallon and Farrah arrived. That said, he wouldn't have changed anything—and he meant *anything*—that had happened this morning for the world.

"Of course it was funny for you. It wasn't your

mother who walked in and found us…well." She made a motion with her hand that went up and down his body.

"True enough. If it had been, we'd have been looking for a justice of the peace by lunch."

Tatum snorted and laughed until she saw his face. "Oh, my…you're serious, aren't you?"

Cruz shrugged. "Not really. But she hasn't met any of the women I've dated since I moved out of the house. Something she's mentioned on more than one occasion. Along with her growing desire for grandchildren." They reached the bottom floor, and he pulled open the door for her. "Until I hand one over to her I'm pretty much considered a disappointment."

"Do you want kids?" Her own question seemed to catch her off guard. "Sorry. That's none of my business."

"That's all right." He dug out his keys, clicked the alarm off his car. The beep echoed around them. "When I was about six months out of the academy I was first on scene to a domestic call. It was Christmas Eve, the first one I wasn't spending at home. I walked into this house behind two other senior patrol officers." He opened the passenger door, let her in, then stood there with his hand braced on the door as she looked up at him. "They'd been there before. To this house. Abusive situation, the husband with the wife, the wife with the kids. It just…" He shook his head, flinched against the all too familiar imagery that still haunted him. "As bad as you can imagine, it was worse. I remember thinking, why would anyone bring children into the world if you aren't going to love them. Three beautiful, traumatized kids whose last moments on earth were filled with nothing but violence and rage."

For an instant he was transported back, to another day that haunted him, another that had defined him.

"Cruz." Tatum reached up and covered his hand with hers. In that moment, her touch felt like a balm on his heart. "I'm so sorry."

"Yeah, me, too." He tried to cover, but there were times he was reminded of how truly hopeless his job seemed sometimes. "In answer to your question, it was a while before I could even let myself think about maybe having a family. Kids deserve the world, you know? They deserve attention and love and the promise of everything good. Like my parents gave to us. Like your parents did for you."

Her smile was sad, and he knew she was thinking of the father she'd lost only a short time ago. "So, do you now? Want kids?"

If anyone had asked him a year ago, a month ago, heck, even a week ago, his answer might have been different. Now he found himself saying, "With the right woman, yeah." He squeezed her hand. "I think I do."

Before the conversation went too far off the deep end, he motioned for her to pull her hand inside and closed the door. By the time he got behind the wheel and backed out, the topic was closed. "I'm scheduled to start work around one. I'll do my best to be on time," he told her in a way that reminded both of them that he still had a job to do. "Lab results came back on the ladle. No prints."

"No prints at all?" Tatum frowned. "That means whoever it was wiped them off, right?"

"That's what I'm guessing. I actually came back to the restaurant last night to try to get a look at people's lockers. Since I didn't get to, I need to do that today."

"Right." She was back to being tense, to folding in on herself and tucking into the corner of her seat. "Back to business. Are you going to tell me if you find anything?"

"I'll tell you what you need to know," he said and hoped that was a good enough answer. "The further you stay out of this—"

"I'm already in it, remember? If they're breaking into the restaurant after hours—"

"They didn't break in, Tatum."

"What?"

"They knew how to get in, through the loading bay door. It was partially open. That's how I got in so quick." He waited a beat. "Who all has access to that door?"

"Well, I do obviously." She tucked a strand of hair behind her ear, looked out her window. "Richard and Susan. Sam and Ty, too. And the cleaning crew who comes in on Sunday morning."

"All right." He made a mental note. "I'll see about tracking down their alibis for last night." At this point the only one he knew wasn't involved was Sam, since the young man had been sitting next to him at the bar the entire time since closing. The idea that Ty could be involved didn't sit well; Cruz didn't usually misjudge someone so completely. "Can you give me a list of all your vendors along with copies of your employee files? Anyone who's had anything to do with True since you first opened?"

"Of course." The cool detachment wasn't wholly unexpected. Being with her in her condo had felt almost like a fantasy world where they could leave reality behind. But they were back in the real world now. One that wasn't particularly welcoming for them at the moment.

"Let me out here, will you?" She pointed to the bus stop a few blocks from True. "I need to clear my head."

He hesitated. Cruz didn't like the idea of her being out of his sight right now, but he couldn't be sure if that had to do with the case or his growing attraction for her. He needed to keep things separate, even while giving the appearance of the complete opposite. Besides, he had somewhere to be.

Cruz steered the car into the empty space. "I know this is difficult for you," he said when she pushed open the door. "I do see that, Tatum."

"Even if you do." She didn't smile at him. She only stared straight ahead as if she couldn't bear to look at him. "You've made it pretty clear it doesn't matter. I'll see you this afternoon." She got out and closed the door, hitched her bag over her shoulder, and went around the back of the car to cross the street and vanish around the corner.

"Colby said you're hurt." Tatum's assistant manager hurried into the kitchen just before noon. Susan, undeterred by Tatum's stern expression, scooted around Sam and Quallis, who were both wrist-deep in the endless pile of shrimp delivered fresh that morning. "Tatum, what happened?"

"I should have pinned an announcement on the bulletin board," Tatum said, turning down the heat on the béchamel sauce she was making for the employees' early dinner. "I was taking a look around the restaurant last night and tripped going into the refrigerator. I just banged my head is all." Even now the bruise throbbed as if protesting her story. "It's nothing, you guys, okay?"

"That's horrible! We should check the threshold,"

Susan announced. "You could have been seriously injured."

"Or next time I could turn on a light." She hated having to explain something she'd thought for sure she'd managed to conceal with makeup. But of course all the makeup she possessed sweated off in the kitchen in a matter of seconds. "Just let it go, okay?"

Sam didn't look convinced. The high-intensity expression on his face had Tatum glancing away quickly. It had only been a day since Cruz had been working at True and already she could feel a change. At this rate, by the time he was done with his investigation, her tight ship was going to unravel at the sails.

Her tone must have been enough to get her message across, because Susan withdrew back to the front of the house and the rest of the kitchen fell into an uneasy silence. While Tatum focused on making a revamped recipe of lasagna primavera, something she was testing as a possible late spring menu item, the rest of her crew and staff trickled in. Chester arrived with oversize coffee drinks in his hands while Ty quietly snuck in with a quick nod of acknowledgment before disappearing into the break room. She was sprinkling the final layer of fresh grated parmesan cheese on the top of the pasta when Cruz strolled in.

"Afternoon." His friendly greeting, Tatum noticed when she glanced up, didn't quite reach his eyes. "Cutting it close, I know." He gestured to the clock. Only ten minutes to spare before his shift started.

"Not a problem," Tatum said in what she could tell was an overly happy tone. She saw Sam elbow Quallis, who gave a reluctant nod. Sam washed his hands then, and followed Cruz down the hall. Tatum frowned, her stomach knotting.

"What's that about?" she asked Quallis, who dead-panned his face and just shrugged. "If there's a problem you need to tell me."

Quallis, who she knew came across as a cross between a grizzly bear and a linebacker, merely shrugged. "That goes both ways, Chef."

"Right." Tatum blew out a breath. "I guess I'll just wait and find out, won't I?"

At the sound of raised voices and a distinct crash, Tatum jumped, her eyes widening in alarm as Quallis actually offered an approving nod. "That's probably your cue."

Tatum didn't have to be told twice. Gesturing for Quallis to stay where he was—not that he looked remotely interested in whatever was happening—Tatum hurried into the break room.

It had, Cruz thought as he stashed his backpack and sweatshirt in his locker, been one seriously crap morning. His only saving grace had been the idea he could come here and lose himself in the physical work, and get the last few hours out of his head.

He sank onto the narrow bench in front of the bank of lockers, dropped his head into his hands and squeezed his eyes shut.

The bubble of pressure that had lodged itself in his chest two months ago was expanding, threatening to block the air from his lungs. He'd kept his promise and met Jade at the rehabilitation facility, along with two of Johnny's doctors. As bad as he thought the news was going to be about his former partner, it was worse. Horrifically, heartbreakingly, predictably worse.

"Mendoza." Sam's voice shot into the locker room like a bullet.

Cruz's head snapped up, recognizing the tone and the angry energy catapulting at him. He rose to his feet. "Sam?"

The friendly, easygoing, teasing Sam Price he'd met yesterday was nowhere to be seen. Cruz had to bank his instinct to block the young man from grabbing the front of his shirt and slamming him back into the lockers with a lock-rattling bang.

The nearby water station table shook, sending half a dozen glasses shattering on the floor.

"What the—" Cruz managed to land a solid self-defense punch into Sam's jaw and break loose, but Sam recovered quickly, grabbing for his throat.

"You put hands on her."

"What?" Cruz couldn't for the life of him make sense of the accusation. Not until he saw Tatum running into the room. He saw the bruise on her forehead, looked back to Sam and the rage in his eyes. Obviously the lie they'd come up with to explain her injury hadn't gone over well. "No, Sam, I didn't. I swear—" He raised his foot and brought it down hard on the side of Sam's knee, sending the younger man collapsing down and back.

"That's enough!" Tatum yelled. She hurried over not to help him, but to check on Sam. "Sam, are you all right?" She grabbed the younger man's arm, helped him to stand.

"Is *he* all right?" Cruz heard the cop in his own tone and pulled himself back. He swore, took a few steps away, then placed his hands on his hips and watched

Tatum guide Sam back to the bench. "I barely touched him, Tatum."

"I won't tolerate violence here. Not in any way." She stepped back and glared at both of them. "Not for any reason. Do you hear me?"

"Hard not to," Cruz tried to joke. Sam lifted his chin and glared at him. "Sam." He took a deep breath, forced himself to calm down and not think like a cop. "I didn't hurt her."

"You didn't…what?" Tatum's eyes went wide as she absorbed the information. "Oh, no. Oh, Sam, no." She touched fingers to her face. "This wasn't Cruz." In an instant she transformed from boss to friend. Tatum crouched in front of him, caught his face in her hands. "You lovely, stupid man. While I appreciate the sentiment, I promise you, Cruz didn't hurt me."

"How do I know you aren't saying that because he's standing right there?" Sam demanded.

"Oh, for cripes' sake." Tatum pushed to her feet. "You know me, Sam. Do you honestly believe that if Cruz had lifted a hand against me I'd have let him walk back into True the next day?"

Sam blinked. "I guess maybe not."

"You guess?"

Cruz could feel her temper snap from across the room. Out of the corner of his eye, he spotted Colby, Ty and Chester standing in the doorway. "Is that what all of you thought?" Tatum demanded. "That Cruz hit me?"

"You said it happened last night after we all left," Sam defended himself. "And we all knew he was coming back here."

"Yeah, for his—" Colby air-quoted "—*phone*."

"Next thing you show up with a bruise on your face," Sam finished. "It didn't take much to put it all together."

"Well, your math is wrong," Tatum snapped. "One more time, and for the record, I was stupid last night and tripped and locked myself in the refrigerator. It was Cruz who found me and fixed me up, so forgive me for not telling you the entire humiliating truth."

Realization drifted across Sam's face. "I guess maybe I may have misconstrued the situation." His black eyes shone with regret. "I'm sorry, man. I just saw that bruise and…"

"You were protecting one of your own," Cruz said, admiring Sam's ability to admit he was wrong. "I get it. It hurt, but I get it."

Sam let out a light chuckle and just like that, they were back on even ground.

"Men," Tatum muttered and gave Sam a gentle shove on the shoulder. "I can take care of myself, Sam Price. But I thank you for the assist. Something tells me your knee's going to be killing you later, so take some aspirin now. As for the rest of you—" she snapped her fingers when they began to back out of the room "—one of you clean up this glass, then let's get back to work. We've got a book full of reservations and food to cook."

Cruz headed toward the changing room, only to come up short when Tatum stepped in front of him and put a hand on his chest. She kept her voice low, so only he could hear. The intensity in her voice, the ferocity in her eyes had nothing to do with any attraction between them but everything to do with her anger. "Whatever you have to do to close your investigation and get out of my restaurant, you do it, you hear me, Cruz?" The

flour-coated woman he'd kissed this morning was nowhere to be found. "You do it and get out."

By the time True closed, it was a miracle Tatum
hadn't downed the entire bottle of tequila in her office.
As tempting as it was, Tatum opted instead for two
painkillers and an ice water chaser, following it immediately by locking her office door and retreating to
her desk. She abandoned her nightly ritual of watching
her crew file out and across the street to the bar, wanting, needing the absolute solitude the space provided.

It had, she admitted sadly as she lowered herself into
her chair and leaned back to close her eyes, been one of
the worst days she'd ever had in the kitchen.

Her normally streamlined, fluid employees had spent
the entire night being overly cautious and solicitous or
frantic and uncertain. Sam and Cruz were both out of
sync, and their negative energy trickled down to the rest
of her people. She'd eventually sent Cruz to work with
Ty in food prep, but that just shifted things. It didn't
help she was just as off her game, worrying about her
business and her friends and her future. All of it—all
of it—came out in the food. The result had been multiple returned dishes, displeased customers and a very,
very irritated Tatum.

It was her fault. She couldn't put the blame on anyone else. Leadership began at the top. She'd always led
by example, always stayed focused on what was important: giving their patrons the best experience possible.
Instead, tonight she'd let her annoyance with Cruz and
his "investigation" get the better of her. She needed to
come in with a more positive attitude tomorrow, give
them all a pep talk, or sit them all down and let them

vent whatever they needed in order to get themselves back on track.

The knock on her door didn't surprise her. She'd expected it, especially after last night's break-in. But she remained where she was, staring at the door as if she could laser-beam the man on the other side out of her existence.

"Tatum." Cruz knocked again. "I know you're in there. Open the door, please."

She pressed her lips together until they went numb. Childish, she knew, to leave him out there like that, especially when she had agreed to be at least partially cooperative.

"I'm not leaving." The silence stretched. Just as she was about to get up and let him in, he added, "I still need that list of employees and vendors I asked you for."

Tatum's self-pity party ended in an instant. She grabbed the file folder containing her list of vendors along with copies of her employee files, stalked to the door, flung it open and shoved it into his chest. "Here. Take it and go."

"Tatum." He caught the door with his hand before she could slam it in his face. "I'm sorry about what happened today. I had no idea Sam was going to think I'd hurt you."

He should have, she seethed. If he'd truly done his homework on Sam Price he should have known exactly what the young man's reaction would be to seeing her with a bruised face. He'd grown up in a violent home, one he and his mother had finally escaped from. But it wasn't only Cruz who should have anticipated such a reaction. She should have, as well.

It seemed she should have known a lot of things.

She released her hold on the door, headed back to her desk to collect her things. "I just want to go home, go to sleep and forget today ever happened."

"Right there with you."

It was the way he said it that had Tatum freezing. She stood there, her back to him, half steaming, half curious. When she turned she found him at her window, looking down at the heart of True. His shoulders were slumped, his posture giving every indication of him being dejected, lost even.

"You've learned something, haven't you? About the case," she added when he glanced over and his brow furrowed. "Something you've been wrong about?"

He shook his head, turned and leaned against the sill. "More like I'm reevaluating my approach. I should have handled things with Sam differently. You were right. The way this place operates, my presence is disrupting everything."

"Maybe not everything." Tatum hesitated. It was such a small thing, but that voice in her head, the one that sounded an awful lot like Cruz, wouldn't shut up. "I found your missing employment information when I was getting everyone else's together."

"Oh?"

"It was back in the folder this afternoon and filed under *C* rather than *M*." A feeling she could only define as reluctant grief washed over her. "Someone took your file then put it back, probably assuming I wouldn't notice it was gone. I don't misfile things, Cruz."

"No. I wouldn't think so." His statement was slow, thoughtful, and did little to ease her anxiety. "I don't suppose you lock your office?"

"I never have." There'd been no reason to. The idea

she'd have to start doing so triggered that dormant anger she'd pushed aside. "But that doesn't mean it's someone who works for me. I mean, someone could have come in as a patron and snuck up here."

"You really think a customer could come up here without being noticed by someone? Your wait staff? The people in the bar?" Cruz shook his head, dismissing the idea as quickly as she had. "Someone's trying to cover their tracks."

"It also means they're suspicious of you." She knew it was his job, but if these people were as dangerous as he claimed, she wasn't the only one in danger.

"Don't worry. I can take care of myself." He made an attempt at that cheeky, borderline-defiant smile of his but failed miserably. "I am sorry about earlier with Sam. And for messing up in the kitchen tonight. I've been distracted."

"So I noticed."

"This morning threw me off. After I dropped you off today." He lifted the file containing her employee records in a helpless gesture. "It's just been one crap day."

She took a deep breath and let it out slowly, along with her frustration. Darn it. How was she supposed to stay mad at him when he was admitting fault? But it wasn't just that, she thought as shadows crossed over his handsome, bearded face. There was something more going on.

Let it go, she told herself. Let him be and deal with whatever difficulties he was having on his own. But that wasn't who she was. Even with her own future at stake, as easy as it would be to walk away and let his investigation go wherever it needed to, it was clear that in this moment, the man standing in front of her was in pain.

"What happened?"

He shook his head. "It's not important."

Tatum gnashed her back teeth to the point her jaw ached. What was it with men and not talking about what was bothering them? Her cousins were the exact same way, especially Heath. It took a crowbar to get the man, the successful president of Colton Connections, to open up even to those he cared about the most. It seemed as if far more men were cut from that stubborn piece of cloth than she realized.

She dropped her bag and jacket on the table by the door and walked over to him. She sat beside him, close enough to feel the tension rolling off him in thick, heavy waves. "What happened?"

He stared straight ahead while she looked at him. His Adam's apple moved as if he were pushing down whatever he was feeling. The anger that had been her companion for the past few hours faded in the silence. Tatum reached out, slid her fingers through his and took hold of his hand, squeezing in what she hoped was comfort. She rested her head on his shoulder, settling in for him to finish fighting whatever battle raged within.

His hand tightened around hers, pulsed in what she suspected was the same rhythm as his heartbeat.

"My friend is dying." The quiet statement cracked her heart. "That's where I went this morning. To meet with his doctors. Whatever brain activity there was…" He shook his head as if he couldn't quite believe it. "He's dying and there's nothing I can do to stop it."

She closed her eyes, let the grief he felt wash over her. It had been easy to forget Cruz was more than a cop who had her business in his sights. Easy to forget that there was anything beyond her own situation and circumstance. There was more, so much more to the man with the dark-eyed gaze, gentle, firm touch, and generous, pulse-kicking smile. He had a life, one that was just as fraught and complicated as her own. She didn't have a monopoly on pain. How arrogant of her to think otherwise. "I'm sorry." The most useless words, she knew, but still she uttered them. They were all she had at the moment.

"Yeah, me, too." He pinched his thumb and index finger against the bridge of his nose, squeezed his eyes shut and released a sigh of complete defeat. "He had so much going on before this happened. He was looking at houses, was going to propose to his girlfriend. I even helped him pick out a ring." His suppressed laugh had her lips twitching. "Like I know anything about engagement rings." She reached up, locked her hand around his arm and squeezed. "He never had a chance to give it to her."

"Life turns in the blink of an eye." She'd learned that herself only last month when her father and uncle had been murdered. "And it's not particularly kind to those left in its wake."

"No, it's not, is it?" He looked at her and in that moment, the case, the threat he posed to her future, melted away. "I screwed up, Tatum. I should have had a plan to explain this." Cruz tilted her chin up, his gaze skimming over the still sore bruise on her forehead. "Especially knowing how bad a liar you are. I saw how hurt you were today, after my fight with Sam." He cupped her cheek in his hand, stroked his thumb over her skin. "The last thing I want is to hurt you."

She wanted, more than anything, to believe him, but no matter how many times he said it, she couldn't escape the truth. Cruz's very presence did just that. His investigation threatened her career, her reputation, her livelihood, and now it was threatening her employees' future. And yet. She lifted a hand to his face, stroked the backs of her fingers down the beard. The sensations exploding against her skin had her silently gasping. Maybe for tonight they could set everything else aside and just be…friends. "How about we end tonight on a good note." Her smile widened at the sudden spark of interest in his eyes. "Not that good a note, Valentino," she teased, happy to see him grin. She pulled free of his hold and got to her feet. "I've got a cure-all guaranteed to help you feel better. You game?"

"I've got these files to go through and reports to fill out, but…" He let out a soft laugh, amusement and maybe a bit of gratitude shining in his eyes. "Sure. Why not?"

"Great. I'll drive. And when we get there you can tell me all about…" She hesitated. "What's your friend's name?"

"Johnny," Cruz said. "Detective Johnny Benton."

Her heart twisted at the professional add-on. "Okay, then." She held out her hand. "Let's go. And you can tell me all about Johnny."

The time would come, Cruz thought a little later, when Tatum Colton would stop surprising him. He wasn't in any rush for that day. There was something to be said for the unpredictability and mood-lifting endorphins that came with the unexpected. But he had to admit, midnight hot dogs near the lake was something he wouldn't have expected at any time from a four-star, award-winning chef.

The air was warmer than a typical March night in Chicago, as if Mother Nature couldn't quite make up her mind which season they were in. He could still see their breath puffing into the night sky, along with the fragrant steam billowing out of the food truck cranking out after-movie snacks and late-night dinners. He inhaled the aroma of grilled onions, spicy peppers and oil-coated fries as he kicked one leg over the bench of the worn picnic table near the edge of the lake. He set the bottles of water down, along with a collection of napkins and utensils.

He'd barely glanced at the menu before Tatum was chatting with the cooks. Obviously they were old friends and he was unnecessary to the conversation. Leaving them to their discussion, he'd stepped back and instead embraced the silence of the night.

"You really don't strike me as the hot dog type of girl," he teased when Tatum joined him a few minutes later and lowered two stacked cardboard trays onto the table.

"Ricky's is one of the not-so-well-kept secrets in the neighborhood. Oh, shoot." She snapped her fingers. "Forgot the fries. Back in a sec." She hurried off, leaving Cruz on his own to enjoy the view. Not the lake. Not the surrounding area. But her. He wondered if she had any idea how stunning she was. How breathtaking. Not in how she looked, necessarily, but in how she presented herself, how she moved and acted. How she cared about people.

No wonder Sam had come to her defense. She inspired loyalty in people, even in people who had every reason not to trust. But they trusted her. Even tonight, when it had been clear she was angry with him, she'd pivoted and ended up giving Cruz comfort, despite his intention to bring her some peace of mind.

She was also, as evidenced by the loaded and unusual-looking hot dogs she'd ordered, a bottomless pit when it came to food.

"You can't have these dogs without their double-fried garlic taters with lemon aioli." The third box was just as large as the other two. "So." She sat down and cracked open her bottle of water. "We've got my favorite, the Asian-inspired teriyaki, mango and sriracha dog. This is the homemade lobster sausage, and then the beef and blue cheese. But this one…" She lifted an old-fashioned, did-his-heart-good, Chicago-style replete with the requisite neon green relish and chunky tomatoes. "This one was my Dad's go-to."

"Your dad ate here?" Yeah, Cruz ordered himself as she cut each hot dog in half, he really needed to stop being surprised by her.

"Mmm-hmm." She lifted half of the teriyaki and bit in, held up her hand until she swallowed. "First time he brought me here was my first trip home after starting culinary school. I'd been so excited about going. I was nineteen, on my own for the first time, and so sure I knew everything." She lifted a fry, seemed to admire it a moment before she popped it into her mouth. "I nearly burned down the school kitchen on my first day. And it got worse from there."

Following her lead, Cruz chose the teriyaki and bit in. He nearly swooned at that ear-pleasing snap of the casing and the explosions of flavors on his tongue. "Worse how?" She had to be exaggerating. He'd seen her in the kitchen. She moved like a fish in water, as if it was where she belonged. Nothing frustrated or frazzled her, not even tonight, when things were off from the start.

"Let's just say I set off enough fire alarms to make my teachers cringe when I walked in the door. For that semester anyway. I felt defeated when I came home for that first break. Like I couldn't do anything right. I was ready to quit. Cooking was all I'd thought about for years. There was nothing else I wanted except to own my own restaurant, and I felt it slipping away. I don't think I got out of bed that whole first day. My mother told me to stop wallowing, but my dad..." She slowed down, wiped her hands and looked out over the moonlight-kissed lake. "He knocked on my door that second night I was home, said he had somewhere he wanted to go and for me to get dressed and come with him. I was not happy at the prospect. I am a first-class sulker," she added.

"Noted." Cruz toasted her with his dog.

"He brought me here." Cruz could see the tears in her eyes, but they didn't fall. And her voice didn't break. It was as if she'd found a memory she could share without breaking her own heart. "Ricky Sr. owned it then. He and my dad were friends back in the day. We ordered four dogs, just like I did tonight, along with fries and sodas my mother never would have approved of," she added with a laugh. "We sat right here. At this table. And he told me to eat. I was still in my food snob phase, turning my nose up at what I of course saw as utter pedestrian fare. I had plans to be a Michelin-rated chef. Hot dogs? As if I'd deign to eat these." She took another bite. "But these were, are anything but pedestrian. They were flavor explosions, made with love and affection and attention to detail. Because the people who work in that truck over there, they're doing it because they want to. Because they have to. Feeding people fulfills them. That's what my dad wanted me to understand. That cooking was about more than degrees and plans and techniques and star ratings. It's about people, and feeding not only them, but their souls. Food creates memories and memories create lives. Full lives. From that night on, things smoothed out. I found my way." She plucked up another fry. "And whenever I came home, Dad and I would make it a point to come here and have midnight hot dogs together." One of the tears slipped out of her control and slid down her cheek. "I haven't been here since he died. But tonight it felt right. He'd approve, I think," she added and gently wiped the tear away. "So." She took another bite of hot dog. "You and Johnny were partners? For how long?"

"Three years," Cruz answered automatically, as if talking about Johnny didn't feel like a knife to the gut. "I'd just finished a case that showed me I wasn't cut out for undercover. Well," he added at her raised brow. "Not deep undercover. The kind that kept me cut off from my family for months at a time. Being your sous-chef is a little bit different than building up a reputation as a drug dealer's best friend. True is a much more hospitable environment than drug dens and flophouses."

"Good to know." Her mouth twisted as she pondered her choices, eating more fries as she debated her next hot dog. "What happened with Johnny?"

"One of those fluke things." Despite his stomach twisting in knots, he continued to eat. Partially to honor her tradition with her father. In part because it gave him something to do. "He made arrangements to meet with a CI, confidential informant. I was supposed to meet up with him later that night, compare notes. When I got there, he was already down, barely breathing." He winced. "The bullet caught him in the neck. I remember kneeling there, hearing that death rattle breath we're all taught about but never want to hear, knowing the man who had shot him was getting away. I couldn't stop the blood." Some nights he woke up expecting to find his hands covered in it.

"Cruz." Tatum reached across the table, took his hand. "I'm sure you did everything you could. Like you said, it was just one of those fluke things."

He set his food down, reached for his water. "Flukes like that shouldn't happen. If I'd just gotten there sooner, or if I'd just gone with him." How many times had he replayed that night in his head? IA had cleared him without much fanfare, despite the fact their original suspect had gotten away. "Jade, that's his girlfriend, and I both had hope he'd recover, but the doctors made it clear this morning it's time. We have to decide when we'll let him go." It was not a decision he ever thought he'd have to make. He didn't want to make it, but Jade couldn't do it alone. He owed her, he owed Johnny, at least that much.

"I can't imagine what it must be like, worrying about someone you love, being in a job like you have." Tatum's observation sounded almost wistful. "My sister January is dating a cop. Sean Stafford."

"I know Sean." Cruz found his appetite returning. Or maybe the hot dogs were just that good. "He works Homicide. My partner before Johnny was Harry Cartwright, who's worked with Sean recently."

"The Chicago Police Department is one big happy family, then?"

"Well, we're a family, I guess," Cruz agreed. "Not sure happy applies. Dating a cop isn't easy." It felt odd, making that statement sitting across from a woman he would definitely like to shift from the professional side of his life to personal. "I'm sure she worries about him a lot. Like Jade worried about Johnny."

"That must have been the call she was dreading," Tatum said.

"It's the call all family members of cops dread," Cruz said. "Just ask my mother," he added at her nod. "When I was done with deep cover work she made me promise never to do something like that again. She said it felt like she was dying a little each day, just waiting to hear I'd been hurt or worse. I guess now I understand a fraction of what she felt."

"Because your mother loves you." Tatum squeezed his wrist. "Just like you love Johnny. You'll do right by him, Cruz. From what I can see, you already have."

He nodded, finished off one of his dogs, but barely tasted it. "The kid who got away, whoever shot Johnny, they're connected to the investigation I'm running now." He watched as her eyes glazed over and she pulled away. "I can't walk away from the case that cost Johnny his life. I can't. I'm sorry, Tatum, but that's the truth. And I need to work it the way it needs to be worked."

She nodded but didn't make a sound.

"I need you to understand why this is so important to me. I don't want to destroy your business, Tatum. I don't want to hurt you or Sam or anyone working for you who's innocent, but shutting this down, exposing them once and for all gets me that much closer to finding whoever shot my partner. I can't let that go." No matter how much he might want to.

Watching the disappointment and hurt flash across her face had him wishing he could do just that. If it was anyone else, would he feel the same? Would he feel so torn and conflicted about doing his job? He didn't want to know the answer.

The answer couldn't matter.

"Just promise me you'll do your best to minimize the damage." Her tone sounded almost teasing, but she wasn't laughing. "And that you'll keep me informed. Promise me you'll let me protect True in every way I can."

"I promise to try." It was the best he could offer, and it seemed his best was enough. At least for tonight. "Now, tell me—" he cleared his throat and pointed to one of the uneaten hot dogs "—which was that one again?"

"You didn't have to walk me upstairs," Tatum told Cruz at two in the morning, as they climbed the last of the stairs. "I'm fine once I'm in the door."

"I needed the stairs to walk off those dogs. Honestly, woman, where do you put it?"

"Onto my treadmill," she laughed. "It's currently under a painting tarp, but it'll definitely get a workout in the morning." Nerves sparked through her blood. It had been a nice night, under the cold spring stars, sharing gourmet hot dogs by the lake. Heart-wrenching at times, for both of them, but lovely nonetheless. When they reached her door, she stuck her key in the lock and faced him. "I guess this is where I say see you at work tomorrow."

He nodded. "As much as I'd love to suggest otherwise, I don't think tonight's meant for anything else.

Besides, I think polishing off those garlic fries canceled out any amorous activity for tonight."

She smiled. "Actually." She moved closer to him. "Since we both ate them, the garlic cancels out. They teach you that in culinary school."

"Do they?" His hands snaked around her waist, his fingers brushing up and under the edge of her shirt. Temptation to slide his hands, his palms, over her smooth, warm skin had him pulling her closer and dipping his head. "I think that's a theory I'd like to test."

When his lips claimed hers, she was ready, oh, so ready for this and more. She heard her own moan in the back of her throat as she slipped her arms around his neck, her fingers diving into the soft, silky length of his hair. The more she kissed him, the more she found his beard achingly arousing as his lips and tongue invaded and challenged her to rise up and meet him.

There wasn't an inch of her that wasn't overheating like a blast furnace. Reason drained out of her head while desperate thoughts of dragging him inside and into her bedroom threatened to override sense.

How was it that the absolute wrong man at the wrong time could feel so right?

"I should go." His protest whispered against her mouth. Was it a question? she wondered. "We're on the precipice of breeching protocol. For both of us." His gaze bored so deeply into hers she felt as if he'd dragged her into a trance. His fingers stroked the side of her face now, as if memorizing what she looked like. "Tell me to go, Tatum." He kissed her again, a mere pressing of lips. "Tell me."

"Go." The word emerged on a whimper, a desperate, regretful whimper she wanted to pull back, but instead she moved out of his hold and reached for the handle of her door. "I'll see you at work tomorrow."

"All right. Lock up when you're inside." He reached out, touched her face again. "Tatum?"

"Yes?"

"When this is all over? When the case is closed? We're going to finish what we've started." She'd never believed anyone more in her life.

Every cell in her body gave a joyous cry of release. "In that case." She cleared her throat and attempted to sound stern. "Might I suggest you work a bit faster, Detective?"

Before he said anything more, she walked inside and closed the door.

Chapter 10

"What's going on with Tatum Colton?"

Cruz choked on his coffee as his lieutenant's question shot at him over the cubicle wall. He sputtered and got to his feet, reaching for a pile of old fast-food napkins shoved into the corner of his desk cubicle. "Going on?" he managed and gave himself points for not cowering beneath Lucille Graves's steely stare. "Ah…" Coherent words were nowhere to be found, even as he scanned his fellow detectives' empty desks. "Fine. Things are going fine, I guess."

"Uh-huh." Lieutenant Graves motioned for him to follow, which he did, and found himself in what he would now laughingly call the break room. As well-supplied, organized and decorated as True's break/locker room was, the precinct offerings left much to be desired. They might very well be cause to call in the biohazard disposal unit. Three other detectives sat around the room at mismatched tables and scarred, padded chairs, drinking their coffees and mulling over their phones or open files. The windowless room maintained the scent of scorched coffee, day-old pastry and stress. "Haven't heard much from you since you started working at True. Any progress?"

"Some," Cruz said and declined a refill on his coffee. He'd kept one eye watching his back as the job at True drove him into nightly exhaustion. He still needed to get to the restaurant by one, but he'd forgone his morning workout in favor of sleeping in before coming into the station to catch up on stuff. Even with the extra hours, he was dragging. How did Tatum do this night after night, week after week? But he was quickly falling into the routine of a powerhouse restaurant that met every expectation of perfection.

"I'm making my way through the employees." So far he'd kept the break-in and the theft of his employee file to himself. His lieutenant was already on shaky ground with the time this case was sucking up. He didn't want to give her any reason to shut him down. Besides, nothing beyond that had happened, so whatever they'd read in his file must have passed muster. Not surprising given Tatum's attention to detail. So far as he knew, his cover was still in place. "I have someone in my sights I hope to make progress with tonight." Ty Collins had yet again passed on the afterwork nightcaps with his fellow workers. While Cruz hadn't seen the ex-con hanging around True after-hours, near as Cruz could tell, he had no alibi for the night Tatum had been hurt.

The only difficulty he was having was finding time alone to get a deeper look at the restaurant itself. So far his plans were to continue observing the staff, tail a different employee home each night and look into their financial records. Of course he couldn't do the latter until his warrant was approved, and red tape being what it was, he was still waiting. That said, he'd pretty much cleared Colby, Chester and Bobby Quallis. Nothing they did raised any suspicions, and their loyalty to True and Tatum seemed genuine. She garnered loyalty, which meant either someone on the inside was an excellent liar, or he was off base with his suspicions.

"Hmm." Lucille Graves opened an overhead cabinet and, after digging into the back, came out with a tin of butter cookies. "Don't tell Sheryl about this," she said in much the same way she told her detectives to be careful on the streets. "My wife is trying to kick sugar before the baby gets here, so I've been relegated to work-hour binges only."

Cruz held up a hand and refused a cookie. Since having partaken in Tatum's homemade and back-of-house cooking, he found himself avoiding packaged and processed food. This morning he'd actually fixed himself an omelet instead of emptying out a box of cereal. All the while he could swear he heard Tatum laughing and urging him on.

"Is your gut still telling you True is at the heart of the distribution?"

"Yes." He was stubborn enough to cling to his belief, even though he didn't want to cost anyone at True anything, especially Tatum. But what choice did he have? He needed to see this through. He had a job to do. End of story. "Tatum's not a part of it."

"Because you've examined her financials?"

"I've gone through them right up to last year." He

planned to finish tomorrow, on his day off from True. "The fact she's turned everything over and given me access is legit."

"Well." Lieutenant Graves polished off a cookie and slapped her crumb-coated hands together. "Let's keep things moving along, shall we? You've got three days to make some progress, otherwise I'm shutting you down."

"You can't be serious." His disbelief sent the break room into an uneasy silence. "Ma'am," he added at his lieutenant's arched silver brow.

"You and Benton had six months, Cruz. That means we're going on eight with you solo. There's only so much circling you can do before you have to pounce. Unless there's a reason you're dragging your feet?"

"I'm not—" His temper caught, but before he tanked his career, he pulled back. "I'm not dragging my feet. And even if I was, like you said, I'm single-handed now, aren't I?"

"That's by choice." His LT looked far from entertained. "It's also something I can fix easily if that's the problem. You want another partner, I can make that happen by the end of the day."

He didn't want another partner. He didn't want another one ever again, but he was also a realist. He was on borrowed time as a solo detective. And he had to make use of every minute. That said, he also wasn't going to admit, out loud anyway, to being overly cautious in order to prevent Tatum from paying a life-altering price. "Give me a week, LT. Three days won't do it."

She picked up her coffee and walked out of the break room, leaving Cruz no choice but to follow. "All right. One week from today. You want to close down this drug

ring, you want to find whoever it was who put Benton
into that coma, I suggest you focus, Cruz. We've got
dozens of other cases that could use your attention.
While I appreciate your determination to finish what
you and Johnny started, you don't have an open cal-
endar. Bring me something substantial by then or I'm
pulling the plug."

"Yes, ma'am." He resisted the impulse to salute,
mainly because he didn't want to lose the week he'd
been given. Instead he glanced at his watch, cringed,
then cursed. Cruz hurried back to his desk and grabbed
his jacket. He was going to be late.

Again.

It was a line Tatum resented walking: lying to her
staff for the greater good while having to suspect one—
or maybe more of them—were involved with drug distribution. She found herself distracted and at the same
time hyperattentive to everyone around her as she
watched for hiccups, inconsistencies, little things that
would somehow prove Cruz right or wrong.

Midshift during one of True's busiest nights of the
week was not the time to have this epiphany, but nonetheless, there it was, staring her right in the face. Why
was she trusting Cruz, a man she'd never laid eyes on
before last week, more than the people who had helped
make her business the success it was?

It didn't help that her increasingly frequent calls to
her sister Simone were going unanswered. Simone was
her sounding board, her go-to when things got tough.
And these last weeks since losing their father, there
wasn't anything that had been easy. But Simone was
dealing with things in her own way, according to her

mother, who was growing increasingly worried for her firstborn. Psychologist Simone was determined to find an explanation behind the murders, something that would help them make sense.

But nothing ever would. Tatum had already suspected that before Cruz confirmed it. And if anyone should know about such things, it was a decorated detective.

She flipped the three filet mignons over in the stainless steel pan, spooned luscious, golden herb-kissed butter over the top to ensure that glistening crust. Behind her the line chefs had the plates ready for the table full of carnivores outside. Roasted baby carrots and radishes lay piled on one another and were treated to an extra sprinkling of flaked sea salt before Tatum pivoted and deposited the steaks between the fresh, farmers market vegetables she and Sam had picked up this morning. Her aim was always to present farm to table with as few stops on the way as possible, and the ever-expanding daily market was the perfect place to make that happen. Having Sam accompany her was unexpected, but Ty had called in sick for the second day in a row. The timing of that—coincidental though it might be, hopefully—had her stomach knotting every time she thought about it.

"Order up. Three filet specials." She pushed the plates across the table for pickup, glanced up when Richard waved to catch her eye. "What's up?"

"Got a minute?" Richard pointed toward his small office down the hall toward the loading bay.

Tatum glanced at the clock, then wiped her hands. "Sure. Sam? You and Colby have this?"

"On it," Sam said and moved effortlessly from the

pizza oven to the main burners. "Cruz, holler if you get behind."

Tatum watched Cruz slide the classic margherita pizza from peel into the oven with practiced ease. The way he moved in the kitchen shouldn't be possible, not with as little time as he'd spent there in the past. But inhabiting other people's lives was part of his job, wasn't it?

"Tatum?" Richard called again.

"Yeah." Tatum grabbed a bottle of water and followed him into his office, a bit guarded at the uncharacteristic glee spinning in her manager's eyes. "Slow night?"

"Full up," Richard said. "Susan's managing fine for right now. I finally heard back from Constance Swan. She's agreed to review True for her vlog."

The water halted halfway to Tatum's mouth. "You'd better not be kidding, because that would be the cruelest joke anyone has ever played on me."

"Not kidding." Richard's chest puffed out more than usual. "I wanted to get everything set before I told you. Next Friday. I could have made it sooner, but I figured you'd want more lead time with the menu."

"Oh, wow. Okay. Wow." Tatum's head spun. Less than a week. Not a lot of time, but she could do it. Constance Swan was to online food communities what Martha Stewart was to home perfection. She'd been the leading voice in the culinary world for almost a decade, and had a worldwide following of millions on every social media platform available. Tatum had been trying to snag a review ever since she'd first opened True. "How'd you do it? What magic wand did you use?"

"You can thank Nancy."

"Your wife?" Tatum chugged water, feeling exhilarated and anxious to get started on fresh and new menu offerings.

"Turns out they're in the same Pilates class." Richard sat on the edge of his desk and folded his arms over his chest, the barest hint of ego glowing on his fashion-doll handsome face. "Their last class got canceled, so they went out for coffee. Conversation ensued and Nancy turned on the charm, told her all about you and how amazing this place is."

Tatum actually squealed and grabbed his shoulders, kissed his cheek. "I am going to send your wife a case of her favorite wine first thing tomorrow." She needed to write that down. She needed to write a lot of things down. "Do you know what a positive review from her would mean? We wouldn't just be made here in Chicago, True could become a destination dining experience. Oh." She fanned her face. "Oh, man, I could even think about opening a second restaurant." A dream she'd only let herself have after the best of nights. "You are the best! I can't wait to start planning. Staff meeting first." She snapped her fingers, pushed him aside and grabbed a notepad off his desk. "Or maybe I'll tell everyone tomorrow before we open, after we're done eating. Yeah, that's what I'll do." She was babbling. She didn't care. Right now she felt as if she could walk on air. "Let's make sure we're booked for that night. I want every table filled. I bet I'm not going to sleep at all this week."

"It's all in your hands now," Richard said as she danced out the door and plowed straight into Cruz.

"Oh!" Cruz locked his hands around her upper arms before she bounced back against the wall. "Sorry."

"What's wrong?" She saw the cop light in his eye, brighter, steadier and more critical than she had seen in the man who had been cooking in her kitchen the past few days. "Something happen?"

"Something amazing!" Professionalism out the window, Tatum took his face between her palms and pressed her lips to his. The tingle of attraction that zoomed through her wasn't dulled by her happiness. "Constance Swan has agreed to review True."

"Congratulations?"

Tatum rolled her eyes at his confusion. "She's only the biggest and most influential food critic in the country right now. I so needed some good news. I'm not telling anyone else until tomorrow, so keep it to yourself. Hang on—" she frowned, craned her neck to try to see back into the kitchen "—what are you doing here? Who's manning the pizza oven?"

"I'm on a break and Chester is covering." He ran his hands down her arms. "Relax, Tatum."

"Easy for you to say." Right now she felt like she had a swarm of bees buzzing inside her. "We're already a man down tonight."

He drew her away from Richard's office, down the hall toward the exit into the storage area and loading bay. "I want you to leave with the rest of the crew tonight. Don't stick around after-hours."

"Why?" Just like that, the balloon of expanding excitement inside her popped.

"Because I have something I need to do, and I won't be here to escort you home."

She fluttered her lashes and pressed a hand to her chest. "But however will I take care of myself without a big strong man around to protect me?"

"Tatum."

She'd known him long enough to recognize that warning tone; not that it had any effect. "I don't need anyone looking after me, Cruz."

"Tell that to your head." He brushed gentle fingers against the bruise that was finally showing signs of fading. "If you aren't going to leave with the others, I'll just have to make sure one of them sticks around so you aren't alone."

"No." As much work as she had to do, she didn't want to put anyone else at risk. "I don't want you to do that. I don't want any of them knowing about this, remember?"

"Great. So you'll leave right after we close?"

"Where are you going?" Did he notice she didn't answer his question? "Is it to do with the case?"

"Everything has to do with the case."

Did the man have to be so infuriating? Nonanswer answers were not productive. "I need to know what's going on. If you're onto something, I need to know." She swallowed hard. "Even if I don't want to."

"All right, then." He lowered his voice. "I'm going to find out why Ty hasn't been coming in to work."

"Because he's sick." Even as she said it she could hear how naive she sounded. "You don't think he's sick at all." Her stomach rolled. Not Ty. Please, not Ty.

"I don't believe in coincidences. Someone breaks in and steals my employment file, and soon after, one of your employees stops showing up for work?"

Tatum pinched her lips tight. There had to be another explanation. Ty was her stalwart sentry; she'd been able to rely on him from day one. Never once had she got any inkling of an ulterior motive from him. She couldn't have been wrong. She wasn't wrong. Not about him. But darn it if Cruz's suspicion had doubt creeping in. And a tiny part of her resented Cruz for that.

As if reading her mind, his tone shifted to what she could only describe as total cop. "I still have a job to do, Tatum. But I can't focus on that if I'm worried about you. I need to know you're somewhere safe. And right now, if I can't be with you, that means you need to be at home."

Even with the obvious frustration in his voice, the sentiment warmed her heart. She moved a step closer, felt that tingle of attraction shoot straight up her spine when he dropped his hands to her waist. "You worry about me?"

"Constantly." There was that twinkle again. Just a flash, but enough to convince her he was right. Until they knew for certain, until he'd cleared everyone in her employ, she wasn't safe here alone.

"You know what?" She linked her arms around his neck and inclined her head. "I think I like the idea of you worrying about me."

"What happened to professionalism in the work-place?" he asked when she lifted a finger to his lips. He kissed her fingertip. She bit her lip and wondered how or even if either of them was going to be able to hold out until the case was closed. There wasn't much more she wanted right now than to get Cruz Medina into her bed.

"I told you. I'm very happy tonight." And she wasn't going to let anything, not even the so-called suspicions he had about True, ruin it. "And when I'm happy I—"

A box came skidding down the hall floor, stopped right at their feet. Tatum spun just as Quallis stepped into sight. "Might want to start putting up warning signs, boss," the big man said with a naughty glint in his eye. "Never know when someone might walk up on you two."

"Thanks for the warning." Cruz squeezed his hand on Tatum's hip to keep her quiet. "Not a lot of places for privacy around here."

"Then you aren't looking hard enough. Loading bay is full of them. Not that I'd know personally," he added at Tatum's sudden interest. "As you were." He moved past them and, pulling out a pack of cigarettes, headed out the loading bay door.

"I thought you quit smoking!" Tatum yelled after him, but Quallis only shrugged and flicked open his lighter. "Going to have to come up with an incentive for him," Tatum muttered.

"I've still got a few minutes left on my break," Cruz said when she faced him again. "It would probably be best if I didn't take them with my boss."

"I suppose not. Rain check?"

He hauled her to him and kissed her quick and hard. "Count on it."

She slipped away, fingertips to her mouth and smiling to herself.

It wasn't until Tatum was out of sight that Cruz realized she hadn't promised not to stay late at the restaurant. She'd distracted him. Effectively. When was the last time a woman occupied his thoughts and overwhelmed his senses so completely he forgot to do his job?

"Never," he muttered as he followed Quallis's path into the loading bay. Being distracted was not going to help him close this case. Or get him through the maze of shelving and storage. "Guess there really is a first time for everything." His break time could no longer be used to recuperate from the hours he spent on his feet and in front of a hell-fire-degree pizza oven. He had a week to make significant progress on the case or else he'd lose it forever. No way was he going to let Johnny die for nothing. If his partner was leaving this world, the least Cruz could do was to lock up whoever was responsible for killing him. That meant refocusing. Besides, the sooner he solved this case the sooner he and Tatum could work out whatever it was raging through both their systems.

Nice to know the sexual frustration went both ways, sure, but man. He pushed through the slatted plastic curtain into the dim warehouse-type setting. His empty-bedded nights were becoming excruciating.

Why True? What did someone see here that made this place useful to them?

Stacks of boxes and aisles of the same metal racks that filled the walk-in refrigerator stood in a type of labyrinth, leading this way and that. The lack of temperature control meant the air was chilly and would no doubt be roasting in the summer humidity. Keeping one eye on Quallis, who he could see was standing by the open landing bay door, Cruz set his phone timer, clicked on the flashlight app and took a look around.

Multiple skylights provided light during the day, and as far as he could tell, sporadic fluorescent bars illuminated the space when needed. The overstock of towels, aprons, tablecloths, napkins, plates and all the table fixings were neatly arranged. A clipboard hung off the side of each rack, a continuing inventory for catering and supplies for the restaurant. The number of glasses alone had him gaining even more appreciation for Bernadette and Pike, who made them all sparkle and shine.

Most everything else seemed to be transportation items, like insulated food carriers, multiple sizes of wheeled ice chests. Everything around the catering van was neatly arranged. He moved around the truck, smoothed a hand over the gold-and-black lettering of the True logo.

"You looking for something in particular?" Quallis's voice carried in along with the cold night air. "Or are you naturally nosy?"

Cruz shook his head. "Just getting a feel for the place. You know." He shrugged off his having been caught and continued his inspection in clear sight this time. "I like to know everything about a place I work in."

Quallis crushed out a cigarette under his foot, checked his watch, then lit another. "The other night we had a bit of a joke about you and Tatum."

"So I recall." Cruz trailed his fingers along the hood of the van. Ice-cold. Hadn't been driven in a while, or today at least.

"I didn't think it much of a joke, to be honest." Quallis waited until Cruz faced him. "Tatum's had a rough few months. You know about her father and uncle?"

Cruz nodded. "I do. We've talked about it."

Quallis's bushy eyebrows went up. "I guess that's good news, then. Now's not a good time to be messing with her, is all. I'd appreciate it if you kept that in mind going forward."

"I don't plan on hurting her." It was true. Didn't mean it wasn't a possibility. "Is someone going to warn me off every night like a ritual or something? You all taking turns?"

Quallis shook his head. "Sam had his say. Colby and the others, they think it's built-in job entertainment. Me?" His eyes narrowed. "There's something I can't quite figure out about you. I'll work it out at some point, though. I always do."

"Translation, you'll be watching me."

"You catch on quick." He tossed his cigarette down, crushed it out and slapped that now familiar hand on Cruz's back. "Good not to have to spell things out. See you back in there." He headed back inside, leaving Cruz out in the alley, the faint and familiar sounds of night traffic and meandering crowds echoing against his ears. There was something oddly comforting in being warned by Quallis. Comforting and affirming.

If the big guy was part of the drug running, Cruz doubted he'd have been so light-handed in his advice. More likely he'd have used his girth and strength to try to intimidate Cruz out of a job. Instead he'd come across as a big brother, something Cruz appreciated and, in a strange way, welcomed.

Alone now, Cruz finished his search of the warehouse-like area, finding nothing that raised his suspicion. If he hadn't witnessed the break-in the other night, he'd be seriously reevaluating his suspicions about True. He needed to find something, and fast.

Otherwise the case was going to be closed. And Johnny would have given his life for nothing.

Tatum rarely appreciated being told what to do. Especially in that assumptive, borderline-condescending tone Cruz tended to use. Was she special? Did he use that particular intonation just for her? Part of her hoped so. The other part wanted to stuff those words down his throat and make him swallow them.

She'd do as he suggested and leave with the rest of the employees, but beyond that...

"Early night tonight?" Colby swung her bag over her shoulder as she joined Tatum in the bar. The place had been cleaned and ready for tomorrow's shift; the bar was sparkling against the dim glow of the after-hours lights. The ever so faint echoes of conversation and banter made their way through the depths of the almost empty restaurant.

"Shaking things up," Tatum confirmed and earned a smile from Colby. "You doing okay?" The revelation that one or more of her employees might be using her business as a front for crime had Tatum realizing she hadn't taken as much personal interest in their lives as she probably should have. She considered them all her friends, but were they? Friendship worked both ways, didn't it?

"Yeah, I'm good." Colby's raised brows confirmed Tatum's suspicion. "You want to join us for drinks over at O'Shannahan's?"

"I'd love to," Tatum started. "But I've got plans for tonight. But I will soon. And I'll buy the first round." Right now she couldn't wait to get started on planning the perfect meal to offer Constance Swan.

"Wicked good." Colby nodded in approval. "So you and Cruz have plans tonight?"

"Remains to be seen." Tatum was really getting tired of Cruz being right, but letting those at True believe she and Cruz were involved really did make sense. That said, he was also right that Tatum was a terrible liar.

"If not, I'll just have a quiet early night. Work on some new recipes. Maybe drink some wine." A lot of wine.

"He seems nice." Colby tugged on her jacket. "Wouldn't have thought he was your type, but what can you do." She shrugged. "The heart wants what the heart wants."

Tatum's lips twitched. Funny how she'd been thinking that herself these past few days. "What about you? Are you seeing anyone special?"

Colby's cheeks went almost as pink as her hair. "Maybe. It's too early to talk about yet." She looked away when the kitchen doors swung open and the rest of the crew appeared. Considering the group consisted of everyone from Jeremy Pike to Quallis, there was no telling who Colby's paramour might be. But he was here. That much was evident. "Hopefully soon, though."

"Boss is cutting out early, huh?" Sam elbowed Chester in the ribs and earned some hearty chuckles from Quallis, Pike, Bernadette, and even Cruz. "Check the news reports, because hell might have frozen over."

"Ha ha." Tatum pushed open the door and waved them all out, then locked up behind them. Colby, Sam and Chester broke off and headed across the street to O'Shannahan's while Bernadette, Pike and Quallis made their way to the parking lot on the far side of the building.

Tatum walked right past her own car and followed Cruz to his. "So where are we going?"

"You're going home." Cruz walked around and pried her fingers off the passenger door. "Remember?"

"I remember you telling me what to do. I don't recall agreeing."

He sighed, dropped his head back as if asking a

higher power for patience. Why did she find it entertaining to irritate him? After a moment, he planted his
hands on the car on either side of her, blocking her escape, and leaned in close. His breath was warm against
her face, making her shiver in the cool, early spring
air. "I cannot keep having this same argument with
you, Tatum."

"Stop arguing and we don't have to." She patted
the oversize bag on her hip. "I made stakeout snacks.
There's enough for two."

"You made…" The fact he struggled not to laugh
boosted her mood. And her optimism. "Okay, here's
how it's going to be. You're going to go home and stay
there until you leave for work tomorrow, or I'm going
to get on the phone and tell your mother exactly who
I am and what I'm doing working at your restaurant."

The warmth drained from her face, probably, Tatum
assumed, with all her color. "You wouldn't."

"Try me." He slid his hands down her arms, slipped
one hand around hers and gave her a gentle tug. Seconds later he waited while she climbed into her car. "Go
home, Tatum. If I find something out you need to know,
I will tell you. *That* was part of the deal."

She sat there, hands on the steering wheel, engine
rumbling, and glared at him. "You're no fun."

"Glad to hear it. I'll see you tomorrow." He closed
her door and backed away.

"Wait!" She scrambled for her bag, dug through it to
find the pair of containers she'd packed from leftovers
at the restaurant. Powering down the window, she held
them out. "In case you get hungry."

He strode back, accepted the offering, then bent

down, caught the back of her head in his hand and kissed her.

The time for lazy, curious, testing exploration was over. His mouth was hot, insistent, demanding, and tasted like heaven. She found herself whimpering and grabbing for him when he stepped away. "Go home."

"Right." She nodded, her head a bit fuzzy as she slid the car into gear. Being kissed by Detective Cruz Medina definitely had lasting effects. She bit her lip, caught between sighing and smiling. She could almost, almost forget her life's work was balancing on a very, very thin edge.

Cruz found Ty Collins's house as easily as expected. He'd already searched it out on GPS, knew it was in a neighborhood not altogether different from the one Cruz had grown up in. He parked amid the cars across the street, near a park and out from the glare of streetlamps.

Ty's saltbox-style house, even close to midnight, was ablaze with lights. The yards on the street were neatly tended for the most part. Bikes and toys littered lawns and swing sets sat behind weathered wooden fences. Dogs barked. Windows flickered with the glow of televisions, and behind him thrummed the incessant beat of music turned up too high.

Cruz brought out the employee files Tatum had given him, and on the tablet he pulled out of his center console, he logged into the department database and pulled up Ty's arrest record. It wasn't long, but it was varied, starting back more than thirty years to the man's first arrest and adult charge for breaking and entering. The rest of his criminal résumé had everything from forging checks to criminal trespass, nothing particularly violent. The single assault charge, given Cruz's own experience with the man, seemed out of character, but this wouldn't be the first time a felon had surprised or disappointed him. Nowhere did he see any connection to narcotics. Not before or after he served his time. Logic and Ty's sudden disappearance told him he needed to look deeper; someone inside True was involved. But Cruz's gut told him this was the wrong direction.

Cruz glanced up as a car approached from behind and turned onto Ty's street. The aged, rusted sedan wheezed and knocked as the driver parked in front of Ty's house. Instincts spinning, Cruz tapped open his camera app, angled the phone and snapped a shot of the plate. Typing it into the police database, he pulled up the information on one Eddie Russo.

White. Thirty-one. Felon. Connections to various white power gangs operating within the prison system. Convictions included… Cruz's stomach took a bit of a dip as he scanned his screen. "Possession of narcotics with intent to sell." Was that the connection he'd been looking for? But as he read further, doubt crept in. Domestic assault. Possession of an unlicensed weapon. Those charges explained the restraining order currently out against him. As did his pleading guilty to endangering the welfare of a minor…

Cruz glanced up as the man exited the car and the front door to Ty's house opened. Dim light streamed out as Ty stepped outside, his girth and stance unmistakable. The curtain overlooking the front porch shifted. Cruz sat up straighter at the sight of a smaller person darting out of sight. Smaller person? That was a child.

Instinct and experience had the pieces dropping into place. He swore, and leaned over to retrieve his badge and weapon out of the glove box. He ejected the magazine, checked it, slammed it home and chambered a round.

Setting the gun on the center console and shoving his badge into his back pocket, he powered down the window and strained to hear, hand poised on the door. He didn't want to interfere; he wasn't looking to blow his cover where Ty was concerned, but he'd be damned if he'd let Ty get hurt because Cruz was too busy protecting his case.

The voices rose; rage and frustration wafted off the visitor in thick, pulse-kicking waves. Ty took a step down off his porch when Eddie kicked his way through the yard gate. The shouting split through the night.

Unlit porch lights suddenly blazed on. Doors were opened, heads poked out, curiosity getting the better of them until they assessed the situation and ducked back inside.

Cruz wasn't going to assume any of them were calling the police. He picked up his cell and dialed. "Yeah, Dispatch, Detective Medina. Badge seven-oh-seven-two-two. I need two squad cars rolling to…" he rattled off Ty's address. "Possible felonious assault in progress. Be advised undercover on scene. Situation is escalating. I need backup."

Assured someone was on the way, Cruz clicked off, shoved his phone into his back pocket and, grabbing his gun, pushed open his door.

Ty took a step toward Eddie. Eddie didn't budge, but his hand did move toward his back. In the dark, Cruz couldn't be certain the man had a weapon, but he wasn't going to take the chance. Ty had a good four inches, twenty years and at least a fifty-pound advantage, but that didn't seem to matter. The closer Cruz crept, the better picture he got of Eddie Russo. Shaggy hair, unshaven face, ragged, filthy, too-big clothes meant he was in a bad way, and probably, given his record, hyped up on something.

Eddie seemed to spring like a cat, but Ty's hands shot out and slammed solidly into Eddie's chest, knocking Eddie back a few steps. Cruz was closer now, close enough to see the sweat beading on Ty's forehead. Close enough to see, even at a glance, the face of the young boy standing at the window, eyes wide in terror and glistening with tears.

"You're trespassing." Ty's words echoed through the street and brought Cruz back to attention. "I'm not going to tell you again, Eddie. Get gone."

"You can't keep me from what's mine!" The younger man twisted and groaned, pulled something out of the back of his belt.

Gun raised, finger poised beside the trigger, Cruz stepped out of the shadows and into Ty's line of sight. "Don't do it, Eddie."

Eddie Russo seemed to trip over his own feet as he spun, the gun in his hand nearly slipping free of his grasp as he struggled to catch his balance.

"You're in violation of your parole, Eddie." Cruz kept his voice calm and even. The trembling hands, the wide, spinning eyes. He was strung out, panicked, and hopeless. The trifecta of horrible combinations.

Sirens sounded faint in the distance, not loud enough to convince Cruz his backup was close. He was going to have to handle this himself. He moved in, slowly, keeping his weapon aimed center mass, just as he'd been taught in the academy. He'd do everything he could to avoid shooting him, but he was ready to do what was necessary to keep Ty and whoever else was in that house safe.

"I just want what's mine, man." Eddie's pathetic whine might have had some effect had Cruz not seen the abject terror on what had to be Eddie's son inside Ty's house. "She's keeping me from my kids. They're my kids. Mine!"

He sounded like a spoiled toddler who hadn't gotten his nap. But he looked like a crazed, pushed-to-the-edge addict who might be willing to do the absolute worst before this was over.

"You aren't going to see your kids, Eddie." Cruz stepped in through the gate, flicked his gaze to Ty, who looked at him with both confusion and relief. "You think about that. You think about where you are at this minute. You hear that?" He inclined his head as the sirens approached. "I've already called for backup. You're going in, Eddie. Like Ty said, you're trespassing and you've violated a restraining order." He'd skimmed the document; he knew the threat he posed. "You've got maybe seconds to decide how this goes down. You put that gun down and surrender, and there's still a chance you'll see your kids someday. You don't?" Cruz shifted, made certain Eddie saw he had control of the situation. "This only ends one way."

Two squad cars screeched around the corner, came to a halt outside Ty's house.

Eddie's hand continued to shake. The barrel of the gun shifted from Ty to Cruz, who, in that moment, saw an image of Tatum flash in his mind. Of all people, at all times, he could see her. Hear her. Feel her.

"Eddie, you need to put the gun down." Cruz took

one more step forward, shifted the gun to his right hand, held out his left to keep the patrol officers back. "Detective Cruz Medina," he yelled without pulling his gaze from Eddie. "I've got this, Officers."

One more step. He could see the rim of the barrel wavering, the terror take hold behind Eddie's frantic gaze.

"Cruz?" Ty's voice held its own ring of fear, fear he recognized as concern for the welfare of the children in his house.

"I've got this. We've got this, don't we, Eddie?" Cruz trusted his gut, listened to his instinct, and as he took one final step toward Eddie, he lowered his own weapon as he reached out to grab hold of Eddie's.

The gun fell free of his grasp and Cruz held it out for one of the officers to take as the uniformed officers flooded in through the gate. He set the safety on his gun and shoved it into the back of his waistband. "Okay, Eddie?" He lowered a hand onto the shaking man's shoulder. "You did real good. It's going to be rough for a while, and it'll take work, but you did the right thing. It's a good first step."

"I want to see my boy. And Katie. My little girl." Eddie's eyes filled with tears that took even Cruz's jaded heart by surprise. "I want to see my kids."

Cruz held off the officers for another moment. "You don't want them seeing you like this, Eddie. You aren't good for them this way. You aren't good for yourself."

For a moment, Cruz saw clarity in the older man's eyes.

"You do your time, Eddie." Cruz turned him away from Ty, reached out and wiggled his fingers at one of the officers, who handed over his cuffs. Cruz snapped them around Eddie's wrists. "You do your time, you get clean and sober, then maybe you'll stand a chance of being part of their lives. You keep going like you're going and you'll die. One way or the other." He passed him off to the officers. "You have a decision to make, Eddie. If you can't make the right one for yourself, you make it for your kids." Eddie was escorted to one of the patrol cars.

"Detective Cruz Medina working his usual junkie magic."

Relief surged through Cruz as he recognized the senior patrolman on scene. "Manny." He actually laughed, a release of adrenaline, he was sure. "Hey, man. How's it going?"

"Same old, same old." Manny Santiago, senior patrol officer with more than twenty years' experience and the gray hair to prove it, gave him a smack on the arm. "Cruz, what are you doing around here? I thought you were Narcotics these days. Now you're adding neighborhood watch to your résumé?"

"I was visiting a friend." The lie came easily. "Got here just as this guy turned up with that." He pointed to the gun one of the officers had now. "I'd charge him with trespassing and attempted aggravated assault." Personally he'd go with attempted murder, but Eddie hadn't gotten a shot off. "You need a witness, you've got one." Or maybe two. He glanced at Ty, who hadn't moved from his last position.

"Dude's seriously strung out," one of the patrolmen said. "We might want to run him by the ER on our way to booking."

"Never pass up a trip to the ER." Manny's smile actually widened. Cruz patted the older man on the back. Manny's wife of eighteen years was an ER nurse and frequently worked the night shift. "Get your statement tomorrow?"

"You got it. Thanks, Manny." Grateful the arriving officer had been a friend, Cruz stood on one side of Ty's fence while Eddie was hauled away, along with his shotgun.

He and Ty stood there in Ty's front yard as the neighbors got their curiosity quotient filled for the night.

"So." Ty cleared his throat, shoved his hands in his front pockets and rocked back on his heels. "You're not a chef."

Cruz shook his head. "No."

"If Tatum put you in her kitchen, she must have a good reason." He hesitated, leery eyes considering. "She in trouble?"

"Yeah." Cruz wasn't going to sugarcoat it. And he wasn't going to lie to Ty. Not now. And not about this. "Yeah, she is."

"Well, I owe you for the assist, so you may as well come inside and fill me in. I'll get the coffee going." He turned as the door opened and the young boy Cruz saw in the window peeked out. "Julian, I told you to stay in the house." Ty moved lightning-fast to scoop up the little boy and tuck him securely in his arms.

"Is the bad man gone, Grandpa?" Cruz judged the boy to be about six, but he was burrowed into his grandfather so deep he couldn't really see him. Other than the construction vehicle pajamas he wore that were sagging around the butt.

"He's gone. And he's not coming back." Ty rubbed the boy's back. "Where's your sister?"

"Hiding in the bathtub." Something in the way he said it told Cruz that Julian had been there not too long ago, as well. "It's where Mama always tells us to go when there's trouble."

"Well, let's go get Katie and put you both back in bed, all right? Cruz?" He headed inside. "If you want to get the coffee going while I—"

"Take your time," Cruz assured him and felt his heart pinch at the relief on the older man's face. "I've got all night."

There were few truths in life, but for Tatum the very idea of a nationally renowned food critic coming to True was enough to give her a second wind. She practically floated into her condo and straight into the shower. Donning sweatpants and an old T-shirt from a rock concert she and Simone had gone to well before their youngest sister, January, was allowed, put her in the perfect creative mood. The ratty, faded fabric always brought a smile to her face, and that was definitely needed for creating a stellar menu selection for Constance Swan.

The wine she'd assured Colby she'd drink hit her glass in a healthy splash. The kitchen, her world, beckoned.

It wasn't enough to yank out every cookbook on her shelves, or to spread printouts from True's menus from the past three months. She did a quick survey of her pantry and refrigerator contents and found both sorely lacking. Obviously, she was in a severe creative slump. More than an hour passed with her scouring her favorite foodie websites for inspiration, the notes scribbled beside her almost unreadable thanks to her abundance of excitement.

"This isn't cutting it." She glanced at the clock. Just

after 1:00 a.m. Tatum bit her lip, the idea forming before she could stop it. Five minutes later, she'd stuffed
her feet into sneakers, grabbed her bag, notebook, jacket
and cell phone, and headed back out to the twenty-four-
hour gourmet market located a few blocks from her
house. Not wanting to deal with the gate and parking,
she walked. Being out in the cool air, with the streets
and sidewalks pretty much empty, let her mind continue to flow through and over the ideas she couldn't
get control of.

It had been over a month since she'd felt this level
of anticipation and excitement. She'd begun to wonder if her father's and uncle's deaths had robbed her of
the ability to do anything but maintain the status quo
at True, but tonight was proving to be the beginning
of—what would she call it?—a reckoning? A reawak-
ening, maybe.

She needed to get all her ideas out and organized as
soon as possible so she could start testing and tasting.
And maybe, if he was very, very lucky, Cruz would
benefit from both. The idea of cooking for Cruz, using
him as her guinea pig, sent an unexpected and unfamiliar thrill of exhilaration through her. The good detective was featuring more and more in her thoughts,
and she wondered where they'd end up, when all of
this was over.

"Other than bed, you mean." Yeah, Tatum grinned
as she stepped through the automatic sliding doors of
Barley & Bakes Market. They'd definitely end up there.
Instantly she was welcomed, both by the night staff as
well as the comforting aroma of briny olives, fresh fish
and meat, and the promise of oven-baked bread awaiting the first bake of the day.

Cart obtained, Tatum put all plans and preconceived ideas out of her head and began meandering up and down the aisles, beginning in the gourmet imported-food section where she filled her cart with jams, chutneys and a selection of cheeses that would be lucky to make it home. She was already veering away from the typical fare she'd been serving of late. There was only so much pasta she could make, only so many ways to cook chicken and steak. She wanted new. Different. "Unexpected." She needed to think beyond her normal borders, challenge herself. She found herself examining the fresh olive bar and the imported saffron that was on sale. Spanish. She'd read most everything Constance Swan had ever written, and Swan had mentioned Spain multiple times.

Images of freshly roasted seafood, tender chicken and spice-kissed saffron rice had her thinking paella and tapas. Something caught in her mind and began to spin. How could she make those dishes her own?

Her cell phone went off, filling the empty aisles with the melodic tunes of Julia Child's theme music. Who would be calling her at this time? She dug inside her purse, pulled it out and didn't recognize the number on the screen. "Probably a midnight owl telemarketer." She still answered. "Hello?"

"Is this Tatum Colton?"

The officious-sounding voice had her thinking instantly of Cruz. "Yes. Who is this?"

"Officer Pearson, ma'am. Your sister January asked me to call. I'm afraid there's been an accident."

"Jany?" Shopping spree forgotten, Tatum yanked her bag out of the cart and raced to the door. "Where is she?

Is she all right? What happened?" She looked up and down the street, judging the quickest route to her condo.

"Car accident, I'm afraid. She's being taken to the hospital. She'd like you to meet her there. Mercy General."

"Yes, of course." Heart racing, she was mentally calculating how long it would take her to run home for her car. "I'm on my way now. Please tell her I'm on my way." Cell still clutched in her hand, she stepped out into the parking lot.

The sound of squealing tires didn't register until she caught the flash of headlights out of the corner of her eye. She froze, almost an instant too long, as the car barreled right at her. In the dim light, she saw a flash of gold inside the car. A thick-banded ring. She leaped to the side and bounced off the trunk of a parked car. As she rolled off, the tail end of the speeding vehicle clipped her at the last second and sent her plummeting face-first to the ground. Her purse soared out of her grasp, but her fingers tightened around her phone as she rolled, feeling every inch of asphalt along her side. The air was driven out of her. Her head spun and she looked up, blinking her vision clear as the car continued its race away. She angled her phone, managed to tap her camera open and click as the car skidded and turned out of sight.

Footsteps sounded all around her, voices shouting, uttering commands. Gentle hands touched her arms, her torso, but nothing computed. Nothing made sense. She couldn't answer the questions she was asked, and didn't want to move. There was only one thing she could think to do. Hands shaking, she lifted her phone and called Cruz.

Chapter 11

"So you're a cop." Ty finally joined Cruz in the minuscule kitchen of his house, poured himself a cup of the coffee Cruz had taken the liberty of brewing. One a.m. didn't seem a great time for caffeine, but it didn't look as if he was going to be getting any sleep tonight anyway.

"I am." Cruz, seated at the small circular table by a window overlooking a backyard containing an old swing set and a collection of baseball equipment, toasted him with his half-full mug. "How are they?"

"Asleep. I think." Ty retrieved a container of leftover Chinese, held it up in question. "You hungry?"

"No, thanks." Thinking of the snacks Tatum had made for him, he found himself looking forward to eating them once he was on his way home. "So you're a grandpa."

Whatever suspicions Ty had of Cruz vanished beneath the flash of pride. "Two times over. My daughter, Deena, she works nights as a bookkeeper for a chain grocery store. Up until a few weeks ago she had a sitter come stay with them, but since Eddie got out—" he slipped two cartons into the microwave and set the timer "—she was afraid something like this might happen." In that moment, Ty looked exhausted. "I was never much of a father to her. Was in and out of prison for most of her life. Last time I got out I promised that was it, that I'd be here for her no matter what. When she asked for my help watching the kids at night—"

"You couldn't say no." Cruz nodded. "You don't have to explain taking care of your family, Ty. It's nice to know where you've been, though." It felt good to have his first impression about Ty confirmed. The man had turned his life around. He'd put family first.

"That sounds like relief to me."

"It is." He'd never been so grateful to be wrong.

"You going to tell me why you're working at True or do I have to guess?" The microwave beeped. After Ty dumped what looked like sweet and sour chicken and fried rice into a bowl, he sat across from Cruz and dug in. "Is Tatum being stalked?"

"Stalked? No. Why would you think that?"

Ty shrugged. "You seem to always be around when she needs you. And you certainly watch her every minute you're in the same room together. I thought maybe you started out protecting her and it's changed to something…else."

Cruz squirmed. Put that way, a lot of what Ty surmised seemed right. "I don't watch her that closely. Do

I?" He'd never been that careless before and he didn't like the idea that he'd been so now.

Ty grinned and some of the tension melted away. "So whatever's going on between you two doesn't have anything to do with why you're working there. Tatum's pretty picky about who she lets work in her place. Richard's suggestions are always a hard sell. She likes giving people a chance, but sometimes they just don't work out. You, uh, haven't worked in a kitchen before, have you?"

"Does my mother's count?"

Ty shoveled in more chicken. "Not really. You're good at it, but it's not where your heart is. Knowing you're a cop?" He took an extra beat, seemed to be peering into Cruz's very soul. "That definitely makes more sense. You don't have to worry about me blowing your cover. Provided you're there to help Tatum and not hurt her."

Was that warning the True company motto or something? "I'm investigating the new influx of drugs to the area. Heroin in particular. You know anything about it?"

"Heroin?" Ty shook his head, but there was no deception in his expression that Cruz could find. "Only thing I know is that overdoses are up, and whatever people are using is as pure as you can get. That's one side of things I never got into. You need an example of why, you just have to look at Deena's ex. Kid was as straitlaced as they came in high school, then he went away to college and got hooked. Doesn't stop her from loving him. Thankfully, it does stop her from being with him. What does a drugs case have to do with Tatum?"

"My case puts True right in the middle of the distribution area."

"True?" Ty sat back in his chair, wiped his mouth.

"Nah, man. You have that wrong. No way Tatum has anything to do with drugs."

"I didn't say she did. But someone who works there does." He was taking a chance, a big one, by coming clean with Ty, but there wasn't much more he could do on his own. He needed some extra cover, cover he didn't want Tatum to have to provide. "That knock on Tatum's head? She got that when someone broke in the other night. They shoved her in the freezer. Knocked her silly."

Realization dawned in Ty's eyes. "Well, that explains that. Never did buy she tripped. Woman's more graceful in the kitchen than Misty Copeland is on the dance floor. My granddaughter, Katie," he added at Cruz's blank stare, "she's taking ballet lessons. Misty's her idol."

"Right." Cruz's lips twitched. "Near as we can tell, nothing other than my employment file was taken. And then it was returned the next day."

Ty swore. "Meaning someone working at True, or at least with a working knowledge of True, was responsible. All right." He took a deep breath, resumed eating. "So what's the game plan? You getting a look at everything you need?"

"I'm examining the financials, but nothing's popping. Is there anything I should know, maybe something Tatum doesn't know, that you can share?"

Ty didn't answer for the longest time, and when he did, there was an odd determination—or was it resignation—in his voice. "I've never been one to snitch on anyone," he said finally. "If I thought it would help Tatum, I would. Keeping that in mind, I think you're wrong about this, Cruz. I've been around criminals most of my life. I am one. It'll be in my obit when I leave this earth. I know that world and it's not at True. Not that I've seen. Not that I've felt. You're wrong, Cruz. You're just wrong."

It wasn't something he wanted to hear; admitting that meant he'd taken a wrong turn somewhere, wasted time and energy and promises to find the person who had shot Johnny. In a way it would be easier to admit defeat and walk away, go back and see where he'd gone wrong, but…there was something there, in the back of his mind, that wouldn't allow him to let go.

"I've got over a decade as a detective telling me otherwise." He didn't know how else to explain it. "But if you honestly believe there's nothing there…" Cruz's cell phone vibrated in his pocket. Used to late-night calls from the station, he pulled it out, glanced at the screen. Seeing Tatum's name pop up had him both smiling and wincing at Ty's snort of instant comprehension. "Stop it," he warned the older man, who held up his hands in surrender. He clicked to answer. "Tatum, you'd better be calling me from—"

"Car. Parking lot. Took picture."

"Tatum?" Cruz shot to his feet, held up a finger when Ty followed him. "Tatum, what's wrong? Where are you?"

"Car. Plate. Picture. On my phone."

He strained to hear, but all he could pick up were voices shouting and the sound of a siren. "Tatum?" He was yelling now and heading toward the door. "Tatum? Answer me."

"Hello?" Someone else's voice came on the line. "Um, I don't know who this is but the lady's passed out. She got clipped. Not sure how bad. We called an ambulance. I can hear it now."

"Tell me where you are," Cruz demanded.

"Parking lot of Barley and Bakes Market. It's on—"

"I know where it is. I'm on my way." Cruz disconnected, faced a worried-looking Ty. "Tatum's been hurt. I need to go."

"Yeah, go, go. Call me when you know something."

Cruz barely heard him as he was already running.

"For the tenth time, I don't want to go to the hospital. I want to call my sister!" Tatum didn't know how many more times she could repeat herself. "Please." She looked to the female EMT currently taking her blood pressure. Again. "Please just get me my phone."

"Ma'am—" The woman's partner had his hands locked around Tatum's ankles, attempting to keep her still on the stretcher. "You need to let us do our job." The stern tone of his voice reminded her of Cruz. Instead of the notion calming her, it only irritated her. The crowd that had formed in the parking lot wasn't huge; it wouldn't be this time of night. But there were enough people for her situation to be embarrassing. The manager from the market had come out with a bottle of water for her while they'd waited for an ambulance. Once she'd regained consciousness. She didn't remember passing out. She wasn't entirely sure she had. But she did have one whopper of a headache. Worse than the one after her freezer encounter.

"I'll make you a deal." Tatum stopped trying to kick her way off the stretcher at least. "You get me my phone and I'll let you haul me wherever you want."

The male EMT looked to his partner, who simply

shrugged and moved the stethoscope from the crook of Tatum's arm to her chest. "Her vitals are okay. Not great," she added at Tatum's snort. "From what we've been told you bounced off a car and landed pretty hard." She set the stethoscope aside and reached for a penlight, flashed it into her eyes. "We're going to take you in for a CT scan if nothing else. What's this?" The woman pressed her finger lightly against the bruise along her scalp.

"I bashed my head at work a few days ago."

That seemed to settle things. "Yeah," the woman said. "You're going in to check for a concussion. Ms. Colton… Tatum," she said when Tatum started getting restless again. "You need to be checked out, and fighting us isn't going to make this any easier."

"I need. To call. My sister." Humiliated tears formed in her eyes. She couldn't think beyond the idea that January was hurt in a hospital somewhere and she was here, being poked and prodded in a parking lot. "Please find my phone."

"I've got it." The male EMT returned, held up her phone.

Tires screeching into the lot had a scream forming in Tatum's throat. That sound. She'd never forget that sound for the rest of her life. The next thing she knew, Cruz's SUV pulled to a stop and he jumped out, heading straight for her.

"Cruz." She couldn't help it. She reached for him, and when she grabbed hold she instantly felt calmer. "I need to call January. She's been in an accident. I need to know if she's all right."

"Okay, we'll do that." Had he just patted her hand? "Just give me a minute."

"No, now!" Tatum blinked the tears free. "Cruz, please. If something's happened to her—" She couldn't finish the sentence. If January was hurt or worse… Tatum could barely breathe around the terror threatening to strangle her. She couldn't lose anyone else she loved.

"Tatum." Cruz's voice gentled and intensified. He caught her face in his hands and forced her to look at him. "I'm going to check on your sister. I promise. But right now I need to know what happened and how you are." He looked to the female EMT. "Detective Cruz Medina. Tell me what you know."

Tatum could only imagine what the EMT thought about her, but she didn't care. She sat there, shaking, worrying, as the EMTs listed a litany of possible injuries and why she needed to be taken to the ER.

"You were hit by a car." Cruz's deadpan statement had her wincing. "For the love of… Tatum, why are you arguing with them?"

"I got a call from an Officer Pearson." She was so tired of explaining. "He said January was in a car accident and I should get to the hospital." She ground out each word as if it were glass under her frustrated foot. "Now let me call my sister!"

"Do you have her phone?" he asked the EMT, who handed it over. "Tatum, I'm going to check on January for you, okay?" He pocketed her phone, caught her face once more. "I want you to go to the ER in the ambulance. I'm going to follow you there and I'll let you know about your sister when I get there. All right?"

"You promise?" She hated that her chin wobbled. Hated that she sounded so…pathetic. "You said you wouldn't lie to me, so if you promise, I'll believe you."

"I promise." He bent down, pressed his lips to her forehead. "I'm glad you're all right." She reached up, wrapped her hand around his wrist and felt the unsteady, frenetic pounding of his pulse.

"You were worried about me." The joke had him smiling. A little. "I'll see you at the hospital."

She swore she heard the male EMT mutter "finally," but she chose to ignore it as they belted her in and lifted her into the back of the ambulance.

"My purse!" she yelled at Cruz, who nodded and retrieved it from an onlooker. The last thing she saw as the ambulance siren sounded and the vehicle pulled away was Cruz dialing his phone.

"Yeah, Ty, she's okay. As far as I know." Cruz started the call before pulling his SUV into the emergency lot of the hospital. He felt like he'd been on a roller coaster of emotions ever since Tatum called. The abject fear pulsing through him on the unending drive to the market was not something he was used to. Adrenaline, yes. Anticipation? Of course. But not knowing what he'd find when he got there, the idea she'd been seriously hurt or worse… He swallowed and forced himself back into cop mode. His feelings were going to have to wait. "They're going to run some tests, I'm sure. She knocked her head again and had some bruises and scrapes, but I think she was lucky."

"Was she?" Ty's question wasn't anything Cruz hadn't already thought himself. He'd been so focused on everything around Tatum he hadn't considered she was deeper in this than either of them realized. This was twice someone had tried to hurt her, twice someone in the shadows had struck out, the fear of whatever threat she posed more powerful than their desire to stay hidden. He'd missed that and it had put her in danger. What else had he missed? "After what you told me about what you suspect, Cruz, this can't be an accident."

"No," Cruz said as he found a parking space. "It wasn't." She was supposed to be home, safe and sound. What had she been doing at the grocery store? He scanned the lot for the familiar face he'd called less than an hour ago, saw a pair of headlights turning in. He climbed out of the car, grabbed Tatum's purse. "Let me get a handle on this before we call anyone else from the restaurant. You're the only one I can count on right now, Ty. You up for it?"

"If it'll help you find whoever hurt Tatum, you bet. The restaurant's closed today. My daughter's going to pick up the kids around ten. With Eddie in custody, I shouldn't have them at night anymore. You tell me what you and Tatum need and I'll be there."

"We'll make it work. I need to go. I'll call when I know more."

"Okay. Thanks."

"Sean." Cruz hung up and approached the couple heading toward the emergency room doors. They looked as shaken as he felt. "Cruz Medina."

"Yeah, sure. Cruz." Detective Sean Stafford slipped an arm around the woman at his side. She was shorter than Tatum, a bit curvier, and looked significantly younger than her age, but her eyes were all Colton. "This is January Colton."

"Nice to meet you." Cruz gave a short nod. He almost said he was glad to see she was all right, but that would only raise more questions than Tatum's sister no doubt already had. "She'll be glad to see you."

"Thank you for calling." January's soft voice was controlled, but he could hear the worry nonetheless. He took the lead, holding open the door and then finding out what cubicle Tatum was in. When he drew back the curtain, the relief at seeing Tatum not only awake but very clearly irritated nearly drove him to his knees. It took him a moment to catch his breath and he stepped back as January raced around him to her sister's side.

"Jany?" In that one word, in that one moment, Tatum broke down. "Oh, thank God you're all right." She wrapped her cord-encased arms around her sister and nearly dragged her down onto the bed with her. "I was so scared…"

"Shhhh. It's okay, Tate. I'm here. I'm fine." January glanced back at Sean, a confused furrow on her brow. "Everything's fine now."

Clearly, Cruz thought as Sean led him away, January hadn't been told everything. "You didn't tell her."

"That someone told Tatum she'd been hurt? No. I wanted her to see Tatum was all right first." Sean didn't look one bit remorseful. "She'd only have worried and that wouldn't do anyone any good. She's where she needs to be. So." He straightened, shifted from concerned boyfriend to detective in the blink of an eye. Only an inch separated them in height, but Stafford's build dwarfed Cruz in a way. Sean's reputation as a stand-up, no-nonsense cop preceded him, and bolstered Cruz's opinion he'd made the right call. "Tell me what this is about."

It didn't take long to fill Sean in. The department gossip mill ran smoothly enough and fairly accurately that he could speak in common cop code. Hearing his girlfriend's sister's restaurant was under suspicion for drug trafficking didn't, however, apparently sit well with his fellow detective.

"You should have come to me," Sean said, an icy glint in his eyes that matched his tone. "I'd have told you you were off the mark on this one. No way is Tatum—"

"I know that," Cruz cut him off, probably more sharply than he should have, but darn it, why did everyone assume he thought Tatum herself was involved? Anyone who met her would know she wasn't capable of deception, let alone long-seated criminal activity. As it was, his cover at True wasn't going to hold much longer now that Tatum, Ty and Sean Stafford knew what he was really doing there. "And for the record, she was supposed to go home tonight. And stay there. What kind of person goes to the grocery store at one in the morning?" He glanced at the clock above the nurses' station. It was going on three, and Cruz was beginning to wonder if he'd ever calm down long enough to sleep again.

"A chef," Sean said simply. "January says she cooks at all hours, whenever inspiration hits. Shopping, cooking, eating. It isn't just what she does. It's who she is."

"Right." He needed to accept that. She wasn't a nine-to-five kind of woman. She didn't fit into any stereotype, let alone any box he might tag her with. And he wouldn't have her any other way. Not that he had her at all. But maybe… "Right. Okay, so." He pinched the bridge of his nose. "Since January is just fine and there wasn't any accident—"

"There's no Officer Pearson in the department."

Cruz stared at him.

"Not in patrol, not in any investigative unit. I figured you had enough on your mind," Sean offered, an almost friendly smile breaking across his face. "I made some calls while January got dressed. And before you ask, I had them check citywide. Whoever called Tatum wasn't a cop."

Cruz swore. Someone had purposely lured her out of the store. Right into the path of that car. So much for them being in the clear. His suspicions were proving correct. But beyond the drugs, someone wanted Tatum out of the way and that someone knew her routine and her habits. Given work was her life, that person had to be connected to True.

"Sean? Cruz?" January poked her head out. Her smile didn't quite reach her eyes, which flashed dangerously at Sean, as if warning him there would be a long discussion later. "Tatum wants to talk to you."

"Right. Good, thanks." Cruz returned to the cubicle and this time he was the one standing at Tatum's side. "You doing okay?"

"Mmm. Good now." She smiled and her head lolled to the side. "Nurse gave me a shot."

"Just to relax her," January clarified. "They want her conscious for the tests, just not so tense."

"Nice big shot." She made an injection motion with her fingers before she tapped them against Cruz's chest. "You're pretty."

Sean snorted. January smacked him. Cruz's face went hot. Even as he took hold of her hand and kissed the back of her fingers. "I don't suppose you saw the car that hit you?"

"Yep. Big. Big car. So big." She started to hum. "Got a picture. After it hit me. I clicked it with my phone." She seemed to focus for a moment, just long enough for the fear she must have been feeling at the time to flash in her eyes. In that instant, Cruz felt such overwhelming rage he had to take a deep breath as he held on to her. "Do you still have my phone?"

"I do. I need your face."

Tatum laughed. "He needs my face," she said to her sister, who was clinging to Sean and clearly torn between laughing and lecturing. "Here you go. Cheese!" She grinned and tried to keep her eyes open as Cruz held her phone up to unlock it. Once he did, he quickly disabled that feature so he could access her call log and photos. "Okay, yeah, got it here. It's blurry." He winced. "But I'll get it to our techs. I can just make out a few of the..." He trailed off, the buzz of realization clouding his mind. Son of a— He recognized that car. It was the same SUV that had been parked outside the loading bay the night she'd been shoved in the freezer.

"They've got her scheduled for a CT scan," January said. "But it's going to be a while. If it comes back clear they'll send her home."

"No other injuries?" Cruz asked as Tatum continued to hum and wave her hand in the air as if she was conducting an orchestra. He pressed a hand against her shoulder, needing, wanting to feel the warmth of her body.

"She's a bit battered and will be sore for a few days. She'll need help at the restaurant."

"Can't keep her from going back, I suppose," Sean said.

Both Cruz and January snorted, and in that moment, seemed to bond. "She's got a bigwig food critic coming in on Friday night," Cruz said. "We'll be lucky if she isn't at True twenty-four seven until then. That said, I've got help on standby. True will be fine if she needs a couple of days off. Since she's going to be out—" he glanced down and saw Tatum playing Itsy Bitsy Spider with her fingers "—I'd like to run this car's info down."

"Why don't you two go and do what you do? I'll stay here," January said. "I'm going to wait until morning to call Mom and Simone. Neither will be happy about me waiting, but the ER wouldn't appreciate being taken over by Coltons. Go on." She patted Sean's shoulder. "We'll talk later."

"Okay." Sean tipped up her face and kissed her. "I'll be back soon and I'll bring coffee."

"And a bagel? I'd love a blueberry bagel."

"You got it. Cruz?"

"No bagel needed," Cruz joked as the two of them left. "But I'll take an assist with the lab."

Chapter 12

"Cruz is going to kill you when he finds out you helped me escape."

"Yeah, well, he's got work to do." January finished tucking Tatum into the corner of her sofa not at her condo, but at her ranch house in Livingston. "You know we should call Mom, right?"

"And tell her what exactly?" Tatum had been waiting for this ever since the ER doctor came in to tell her the CT scan was clear, but that she was to take it easy for the next twenty-four hours at least and not overdo it when she did go back to work. "It was an accident and I'm fine. Let her and Aunt Fallon keep decorating. I can't deal with either of them hovering right now."

"You're mostly fine and it wasn't an accident," January retorted from the kitchen behind Tatum. "Stop pretending like it was."

She wasn't pretending exactly. She just wasn't in the right frame of mind to deal with the fact someone had tried to kill her. Tatum didn't respond to January's comment. Her sister was puttering in the kitchen. Her kitchen. She gnashed her teeth. She didn't like anyone in her space.

Space was one thing in abundance in this place. As cozy and practical as the condo near True was, the ranch house was her refuge, where she went to rejuvenate and relax and tune the rest of the world out. Her family knew this, which was probably why when she'd been discharged from the hospital, January had driven her here.

She loved the open floor plan of the old house. She'd had it completely remodeled before she'd moved in, eliminating the walls between the living room, kitchen and dining area, and replacing walled-in windows with big plate glass ones. The front third of the house was now one big open space outlined with glass and overlooking the drought-resistant and low-maintenance landscaping. She didn't get here as often as she liked, but when she did come out, she didn't want to spend what time she had puttering in the yard.

Besides, other than herbs, she wasn't the greatest gardener.

"Maybe we should compromise and call Simone," January said right before a clatter of pots and pans had Tatum's nerves fraying. "Oops. Sorry. I'll just…" Crash. Bang. Cursing followed by a triumphant "aha!" had Tatum shaking her still sore head. Maybe she should have accepted that prescription for painkillers after all. "I got it."

"Got what?"

"Never mind. You just stay there and relax."

Having someone in her kitchen was not relaxing. In any way.

"Did you let Sean know where we'd be?"

"Considering I absconded with his car, I didn't have a choice. Not that he deserves me telling him anything right now. Oh, good. You have milk. And bread! Score."

"I haven't been here in over a week, so if you're looking for produce—"

"Being run down in a parking lot does not call for salad. And you changed the subject."

"Yes, I did." It was bad enough January had been brought into the situation; she didn't want her sister or mother anywhere near what was happening with True. She'd tell them. Once she was on the other side of things. When January started humming, a signal to Tatum that she was done talking for the moment, Tatum snuggled down in the corner, tucked her feet in and gazed into the dormant fireplace.

Strange. An odd pang struck, and she realized, as his face flashed in her mind, that she missed Cruz. Seeing him in the parking lot had erased a lot of the rising fear, and when he'd finally arrived at the hospital, the anxiety and worry had faded, as well. She'd seen the concern in his beautiful eyes, felt the worry in him when she'd clung to him. There was a gentleness she didn't particularly accept, and seeing it on full display had broken away whatever pockets of resistance still dwelled inside of her. In the space of a few days he'd managed to slip into her world, into her life, into her thoughts, and—she dared to think—into her heart.

She jerked herself awake, unaware she'd dozed off. The very idea she may very well be falling in love—

with a cop, no less—might just keep her awake for months.

"Spooked?" January was standing over her, a steaming mug in one hand and a plate of bread in the other. "What's wrong?"

"What's that?" Tatum sat up and accepted the mug, sniffed at the contents. The familiar combination of chocolate, cinnamon and cardamom soothed her senses and her thoughts. "You remembered."

"Your cure-all? Of course. Both Simone and I are experts at it now." January sat on the other end of the sofa and set the plate down between them. "How many broken hearts, broken dates, failed exams and late-night gossip sessions have we had over your hot chocolate and Simone's cinnamon toast?"

"Too many to count." Tatum sipped, swallowed and sighed. The warmth slid down her throat and spread through her body. "Thank you."

"Yeah, well, after this your cupboards are bare." January drank her own cocoa and took a piece of toast. She grinned and laughed. "I used way too much butter." She licked her fingers.

"Nothing wrong with that." The sound of crunching bread and the aroma of hot, spicy sugar had Tatum claiming her own piece. Definitely too much butter. And it was delicious.

"So." January rested her arm along the back of the sofa. "You and Cruz. What's going on there?"

"He's working a case. He needed my help."

"Uh-huh. Not what I meant. I mean you *and* Cruz. Am I right in thinking the Colton sisters might have a type?"

Tatum continued eating her toast, crust first, saving

the buttery, sugary goodness for last. "I like him. A lot. I also like to think the attraction is mutual."

January kicked her with her foot. "You don't have to think. I saw it. He cares about you. I'm not sure he's happy about it, but he cares."

Tatum shrugged. "He's got a lot riding on this case." She had to remind herself of that. The case was important to him. His partner's life—and impending death—was important to him. She could only hope he understood how important True was to her. She'd certainly told him enough times. "We'll see what happens once it's over."

January frowned. "You mean you two haven't—"

"No, we haven't." Now it was Tatum's turn to kick, and when she did, she felt a twinge of pain in her leg and hip. "It's complicated."

"You do know complicated sex is the best kind of sex, right?"

"I've been hit by a car, Jany. I don't need a sex talk from my baby sister."

"Obviously you do. You want to know what I've learned being with Sean?"

"In the entire month you've been with him?" Tatum fluttered her lashes. "Oh, do tell."

Her teasing didn't elicit a smile, not much of one anyway.

"There's no guarantee of tomorrow." January's eyes shifted and it seemed as if a curtain she'd been keeping in place dropped away. "Being a cop…it's scary for the people who love them. The people they love. I never know if when my phone rings it'll be his CO telling me he's been hurt." She swallowed hard. "Or worse. And I get that there are plenty of people in the world who feel that way about their loved ones, for various reasons. Nobody ever knows, but I don't take one minute I have with him for granted, Tate." She held up her hand and with her thumb, spun the ring Tatum hadn't noticed until now on her finger. "That's why I'm going to marry him."

"Seriously?" Thoughts of hot chocolate and toast abandoned, she grabbed her sister's hand with both of hers to get a closer look. "Oh, January. It's beautiful." Tears misted her eyes as she looked at the delicate collection of smaller diamonds circling a solitare. Unpretentious, simple and perfectly suited.

"He found it in an estate sale. The woman who had it before was married to her first love for over sixty years." January sighed. "Beneath that cop heart lies a romantic." Tatum's brow lifted and her sister laughed. "Maybe deep down. But my reasoning stands. I'm not going to waste one single second and I plan to take advantage of him being crazy about me every chance I can."

"Translation, you jump him when he walks in the door." Despite her sister's obvious joy, there was still a trace of concern. It wouldn't be evident to everyone, just to those who knew January Colton best. Wanting to ease her sister's worry, she reached out her hand. "Sean's a good guy, Jany."

"He really is. And from what I can see, Cruz is, as well. You could have died, you know."

Tatum drew in a deep breath. "Jany—"

"You're sitting here worrying if his job might be too dangerous for you to deal with when he was the one who got the call last night you'd been hurt. None of us gets a pass on the future. We've learned that the hard way. If we can lose Dad in the blink of an eye, anything can happen. If you want to be with Cruz, if you want to take that chance, that swing at happiness, take it."

"You think?"

"I really do." January drank more cocoa. "You know what else I think? Pretty soon the Chicago PD is going to be overrun by Colton women."

Tatum laughed and finished her toast. There were definitely worse things to have happen.

"Thanks for doing this, Ty."

Cruz stepped through the doors to an eerily silent True. The older man had met him across the street at O'Shannahan's, where they'd waited for the last of the cleaning crew to leave the restaurant. Now, at nearly noon, Cruz was finally able to put some of his frustration to work. The fact his frustration stemmed from not being where he really wanted to be—with Tatum—was something he was trying not to think about.

"What is it you're hoping to find?" Ty followed him up to Tatum's office where Cruz took a seat, and after a few keystrokes and work-arounds, found himself in the business's system.

"Remind me to educate Tatum on the importance of passwords and a firewall. After I'm done," he added at Ty's chuckle.

"What do you think is on here that—"

"It's not just Tatum's computer on this network. Don't worry." He flashed Ty a grin. "It's all covered by a warrant."

"It's not legalities I'm worried about," Ty said. "It's Tatum. When she finds out what you're—"

"If it saves her business she won't care how I did it. That's at the top of my list."

"What else is on that list?"

"Taking a better look at the storage area and loading bay. The intruder the other night went in and out like he knew the place. That tells me they're familiar not only with True but also with that section of the building. The way it's set up, you have to know where you're going, to get to the kitchen."

"But why use True in the first place?" Ty's annoyance mirrored Cruz's. "What possible good could a restaurant be for moving drugs? Especially one that's been in the spotlight like True?"

Cruz had his suspicions, but nothing concrete enough to share. Yet. "Pretty much everything I've learned about how this place works is that privacy is pretty much impossible. There's always someone around." One of the reasons he'd had a difficult time getting away to search various spaces of True. "It's been more of an elimination of ideas rather than proving myself right." Anger popped like tiny bubbles of fire in his blood. He may have been convinced he was wrong if Tatum hadn't been nearly killed. "Why go after her now?"

"She must have set them off. Did something, said something."

"Inadvertently, yeah." He scanned through files and folders, clicking open anything that didn't look like it fit or made sense. "She's made someone nervous, if not before, then by hiring me."

"What put you onto True in the first place?" Ty asked and took a seat across the desk from him.

"GPS. We've been looking at GPS and phone locations for drug arrests in the past year. There's a lot of overlapping area they cover, but there are two sections in the city they have in common. The warehouse district a mile and a half south and the four-block radius around True. You and Sam have worked here the longest, right?" Click and copy. His flash drive hummed.

"Yeah." Ty's brow furrowed. "Quallis came on board a few months later. She's had wait and bar staff come and go, and there's high turnover for the dish room, no surprise. But no one who stands out as a criminal mastermind."

"And you can't think of anything that happened in say the last year that seems strange in hindsight?"

"Other than Daria quitting out of the blue, no."

"Daria." Cruz stopped, mentally flipping through the employment records Tatum had given him. "She was the manager before Richard, wasn't she?"

"Yeah. Daria Naughton. She helped Tatum open this place. Of course, back then Tatum was still a control freak. She didn't really let Daria do much more than manage the front of the house and consult on staff. Some of us wondered if that's why she quit. Tatum wouldn't let her do a lot of what she could or should be doing. She resigned and that weekend she and her husband were killed in a car accident."

Definitely horrible. And another coincidence Cruz didn't buy into. "When did this all happen?"

"Seven, eight months ago?"

Around the same time the drug distribution kicked into high gear.

"Tatum didn't give us any details," Ty went on. "She just said Daria resigned unexpectedly and that she was going to be hiring a new manager. A couple days later we heard about the accident. Tatum was devastated. I think she thought Daria was upset with her about something and they could never clear the air. Probably why she's let Richard take over so much of what she used to do. She didn't want to make the same mistake."

"Do me a favor." Cruz gestured to the filing cabinet. "Go through those and see if Daria's file is still in there?" He remembered coming across the name, but because her employment period hadn't seemed connected, he'd moved on.

"It's locked."

Cruz reached to the narrow table behind him and flipped the photo of Tatum and her sisters around. The key was wedged into the back. "Here."

Ty's brow went up. "I guess Tatum really does trust you."

While Ty rummaged for the file, Cruz quickly accessed the network settings, clicked on remote-connected computers and…yeah. He clicked to upload files from the other laptop on the system. The light on the flash drive started blinking like crazy as it downloaded.

"Here it is." Ty handed over Daria Naughton's file, flipped it open as Cruz took it. "She was a sweetheart. Enthusiastic. Excited about being in on a restaurant from the ground up. Smartest woman I've ever known. Tatum included."

Cruz glanced down at the photo. The woman was older than he expected. Forty-four at the time she'd started at True. Degrees in business and hospitality services. Married. No kids. Chicago… "Daria Naughton." There was something familiar about her. Something he couldn't quite… He checked the file again for her husband's name. "I remember this." He plucked out the resignation letter dated seven months earlier, then pulled out his phone and called Sean. "Hey, can you look up a name in our database? Daria and Nathan Naughton?"

"Sure thing. When you're ready, can you give me a lift to Tatum's? January took her home in my car and I'm stuck at the station."

"She's out of the hospital?" Why wasn't he surprised?

"You've met Tatum, right?" Sean asked slyly over the sound of clicking keys. "The CT scan came back clean. Doctors cleared her to be released. January took her to the ranch house. Figured she'd take it easier there. Also Tatum didn't want to take the chance of running into her mother. Also I should have the info on the SUV by the time you get here."

"Okay." Cruz shook his head. "I'll pick you up as soon as I'm done here. You find anything?"

"Yeah. Daria and Nathan Naughton. Killed in a one-car collision seven months ago. It was ruled accidental death, mechanical issues with the car. I remember this one. They hit a power junction. Knocked power out to a couple thousand homes and businesses for half a day."

"What's the date of the accident?"

"September 17. Why? You find something?"

"Yeah. I think I did." He handed the letter to a curious Ty. "I'll see you in a bit."

"What?" Ty asked when Cruz hung up. "I don't see it."

"The date." Cruz pulled out the flash drive and pocketed it, then turned off and disconnected Tatum's laptop to bring with him. "How many people do you know quit their job after they're dead?"

"Why am I not surprised to find you in the kitchen?"

Cruz spoke in what Tatum now called his "I surrender" voice.

"Because I'm going stir-crazy in my own house and

this is the only thing that helps. Here." She waited for him to set the grocery bags on the counter and held up a sauce-covered spoon. "What do you think?"

"And by what do you think, she means tell me you love it," January instructed as she started unloading.

"No lie, it's delicious." Cruz grabbed hold of the spoon and brought it back to take another taste. "Spicy."

Tatum grinned. "That's the sriracha powder. You hungry?"

"Starved." Sean clapped his hands together. "When do we eat?"

"When we get home." January abandoned her task and quickly retrieved her purse and jacket. "I'll call you tomorrow, Tate. Sean, we're leaving."

"But I just got here." Tatum laughed at Sean's little-boy whine. "And I'm sorry, babe, but your sister is a much better cook than you are."

"You aren't in enough trouble?" January asked and dragged him by the arm. "Save us some leftovers!" The door slammed behind them.

"How are you feeling?" Cruz set a gentle hand on her shoulder and squeezed. The sensations rocketing through her, the emotions swirling as if they couldn't grab hold, nearly overwhelmed her.

"Better than I should." She got a new spoon and stirred the sauce. The pasta dough was resting in the fridge and the breadsticks were doing a final proof before baking. Imperishable staples had saved her sanity this afternoon as she waited for word—any word—from Cruz. Reducing the heat, she took over her sister's unloading. "I see you got my list."

"Might have been easier to tell me what not to get."

They reached for the fresh basil at the same time, his hand covering hers.

She glanced up, heart pounding, as he tugged her close and slipped his arms around her. "I'm glad you're all right." He brushed his lips over her forehead, across her mouth. "All I wanted was to be with you today."

"That's all I wanted, too." Emotion clogged her throat. "I'm feeling a bit unsteady, Cruz. I don't know what's going on."

"I know." He smoothed her hair away from her face, his palm caressing her cheek. "I'm working on it and I think I'm making progress. But before we get into that, there's something you should know."

"Okay." She swallowed hard, braced herself.

He kissed her. Slow, deep, a kiss filled with such promise she cried out when he lifted his head. "Until this is all over I'm moving in." He inclined his head toward the oversize duffel by the front door.

"Oh." She blinked, tried but for the life of her couldn't come up with an argument. "All right. Just one problem." She lifted a hand, tapped a finger against his lips. "I never got around to furnishing the guest room, so you'll have to share my bed." Her smile was slow, deliberate, and filled with as much promise as she'd felt in his kiss. "That work okay for you?"

"That works just fine."

"Good. Now here's a beer." She stepped out of his arms, pulled a bottle out of one of the bags and handed it to him. "Go sit down and relax while I finish dinner."

It was, Tatum thought as he wandered off with his beer into her living room, a routine she could most definitely get used to.

* * *

There was little that made Tatum happier than a full fridge, a warm sauce simmering on the stove and a pile of fresh pasta awaiting its baptism by boiling water. The aroma of fresh-baked garlic breadsticks wafted through the air, along with the sounds of classic Hollywood soundtracks drifting from her television. Cruz was stretched out on her sofa, arms crossed over his chest, beer by his side, sound asleep.

Suddenly the full fridge, et cetera, didn't hold the appeal it had moments before. She lowered herself to the sofa, careful not to touch him for fear of waking him. Given what had happened last night, she couldn't fathom when he would have slept, and while she had certain plans for the evening, she couldn't bring herself to wake him.

Dinner would wait. Her plans would wait. Wanting nothing more than to wash the day away, she headed into her bedroom suite to shower and change.

By the time she emerged, damp hair clipped to the top of her head, towel wrapped around her wet body and knotted between her breasts, the sun had dropped low enough to cast the garden outside her window into the prettiest of shadows. She'd seen the bruises forming along her side, on her hip and torso, felt the aches fade beneath the pulsating hot water. She was lucky, she told herself. Things could have been, could be, so much worse.

"And here I was thinking you should have woken me up."

Tatum smiled, keeping her back to him. "You needed to sleep."

"I'm not complaining." He stepped into her room,

moved in behind her, rested his hands on her bare, damp shoulders. "I'm glad I didn't miss this." His lips brushed away the droplets of water on her skin and made her shiver. "I missed you today."

She lifted a hand to cover one of his. "I missed you, too." She turned, tilted her chin up to meet his eyes. "Are you hungry?"

"More than I have been in a long time." His thumbs caressed her shoulders before his fingers trailed down her arms. With one hand he pulled the clip in her hair free. The damp tangles dropped over the backs of his fingers.

"I meant for dinner."

"Did you?" He dipped his head, placed a whisper of a kiss on her mouth. "I've never been less interested in food. How about you?"

"I—"

His smile told her he was teasing. "Why don't you get dressed and we'll—"

"How about I don't?" She reached down and released the knot and let the towel drop to the floor. She was already reaching for the hem of his T-shirt when he stepped back to admire his view. "You're severely over-dressed for what I have in mind, Detective Medina."

"Tatum, I—" The words seemed to catch in his throat. He caught her hands as they slipped beneath the fabric of his shirt. "You were nearly run over by a car just hours ago."

"Nearly." She'd expected the protest, the concern. But as much as it touched her, she wasn't in any mood to add another frustration to her life. She could deal with the bruises and aches. She couldn't deal with waiting any longer to be with him.

She tightened her hold on his hands, made certain he was looking at her when she spoke. "The gift almost being killed gives you is you realize how much you want to live." She slid one hand up his chest, her fingers tingling at the feel of his taut form. She curved it around his neck, drew his face down and to her. "I know what I want, Cruz. I want you."

When she kissed him, it was with all the passion and attraction she'd felt since he'd first stepped into her restaurant. She'd thought of, dreamed of this moment to the point of distraction. There had never been another man who had stoked desire to the levels he did simply by walking into the room. His beard scratched gently at her skin, heightening her senses as her mind fought to keep up with her body.

If he had any reservations, they seemed to evaporate the moment his lips captured hers. She couldn't get enough of him. While her lips pressed and pushed, her tongue seeking and tempting, her hands shifted and moved down his back and under the edge of the fabric so she could flatten her palms against his back. Her bare breasts tightened against the roughness, and when he lifted his mouth for the mere moment it took to pull his shirt over his head, she cried out.

A fraction of a second was too long to wait. For him, too, and he locked his hands around her waist, turning her toward the bed as he lifted her against him. The moment her breasts met his bare skin she gasped, tore her mouth free and dropped her head back to expose her throat.

"This isn't going to be slow." She heard more determination than seduction in his voice. Even if she'd had the compulsion to slow things down she couldn't have.

Her mind could no longer function beneath the intensity of sensation sparking through her. Everywhere their skin touched, every step he took closer to her bed left rational thoughts spinning into oblivion.

She felt the mattress brush against the back of her legs before he lowered her to the bed. They stood there, in the barely-there light, the only sound in the room their ragged breathing. "You're still overdressed." She brushed the backs of her fingers against his cheek, drew her fingers down the tight brown skin of his throat, his shoulders, around to his chest.

He was hers. She saw it in the dazed passion of his dark gaze, felt it in the restless, exploring touch of his hands. Felt it beat against her palms as she pressed her hands flat against where his heart resided.

She slid her hands down, lower, to the waistband of his jeans, made quick, determined work of the zipper and button that kept them separated. His breath hot against her face, she lifted her chin, found his mouth waiting and dived in. Tatum felt the hard length of him straining, throbbing behind the jeans she couldn't help him discard fast enough. "Cruz." She murmured his name and the answering moan she received as she wrapped her hand around him had whatever reason she had left shattering.

His hips moved, pushing him more firmly into her hold. His breathing came in short, determined gasps as she adjusted her hold, moved up and down his hot arousal.

"Enough," he growled and reached down to catch her hand. "You keep touching me like that and I won't be able to wait."

"Maybe I don't want you to wait." She pressed her

lips against his throat, gently nipped with her teeth. "Maybe I want to see exactly what I do to you."

"Tatum." He released her hand, caught her face between his palms and, after kissing her so deeply she lost her breath, pressed his forehead to hers. "I left the condoms in my bag."

She smiled, slid her hands down his sides and pushed his jeans down over his muscular thighs. He kicked them free and sucked in a breath that echoed through the room as she grasped him once more and brought him to her mouth.

It only took one open-mouthed kiss on the most sensitive part of him to have him reaching down and hauling her to her feet. "When I come, I want it to be inside you. Not before." His mouth took hers again, his tongue doing now what she had only dreamed of. "Let me go get—"

"Nightstand drawer." She locked her hands around his wrists when he started to set her away. "You aren't the only one who planned ahead."

He stood there, his hands deep in her hair, looking down at her in a way that made her heart skip a beat. "I love you, Tatum."

"Because I bought condoms?" she teased.

"No." Another kiss, one that all but melted her bones. "Because you're you."

"I also opened the box," she prodded. "I didn't want to waste time..." She'd barely uttered the words before he had the drawer open, the foil packet ripped and the condom in hand. She couldn't tear her eyes away as he covered himself, yet another form of protection that had love swelling inside of her.

She sat on the edge of the mattress, moved back as he

moved over her. Tatum lay back, reached up her arms to encircle his neck as he stretched out above her. She opened for him, her legs falling apart and he settled as if he'd been made for her. "Now," she whispered and arched her back. She could feel him, hard, covered and ready, against the part of her that was waiting and wanting. "Cruz, please."

She slipped her foot up the back of his leg, wrapped herself around him as he pressed into her, full, throbbing and thick. She moaned, absorbing both him and the sensations rippling through her as he joined their bodies. Her hips moved in time with his thrusts, slow at first, giving her time to adjust to him, adjust to them.

"Look at me, Tatum." His rough order had her blinking through the stars in her eyes, and when she gazed into his eyes she knew that this was where she belonged. In this moment. With this man. "Tatum?"

She lifted her hand, touched his cheek. He was hers. All hers. "Take us over." Her other leg came up, her thighs locked around him, pulling him in deeper as his breath moved out in a rush. "Take us over together."

She wanted to keep them here, in this moment, but she could feel the pressure and passion building, her body igniting under his touch and invasion. She met him, move for move, thrust for thrust, and when he fused his mouth to hers and erupted inside of her, she crested that final edge and soared with him.

The orgasm tore through her, locking her around him as she hovered in that perfect moment of ecstasy. Her cries caught in his mouth as he held her and she rode it out. When she came down from the high, when he lay in her arms pressing light butterfly kisses along her jaw, she smiled. He was hers. This man was, and always would be hers.

"Cruz." She murmured his name, drew her fingers through his hair. "I love you, too."

"Yeah?" He shifted, keeping them linked as he drew the sheets over them.

"Yeah." She snuggled into him, feeling herself begin to drift. "Most definitely yeah."

Extricating himself from Tatum's arms, Cruz reached over and lifted his vibrating and buzzing cell off her nightstand, careful not to wake her. The message from his LT acknowledging that he had enough to keep him moving forward with the case should have eased his mind.

Instead, he turned his phone over and lay there, in the dark silence, unable to sleep.

Tatum let out a sigh and shifted, her still damp hair spilling over her shoulders and across his chest. He dropped a hand down, took a moment to appreciate the feel of it sliding through his fingers.

This wasn't supposed to happen.

Moonlight streamed through the skylight above, casting its gentle shadows at the sliding doors into the garden beyond her house that, growing up, was a dwelling he could barely have imagined.

He'd found paradise, a sanctuary he hadn't known existed within the confines of the city he called home. He'd liked her condo, the practical, convenient space, but this place removed from their real lives felt almost like a mirage in the middle of a crazy, whirlwind desert. He'd known, well, he'd hoped they'd end up right where they were, wrapped up with and in each other to the point of distraction.

But falling in love?

That wasn't supposed to happen.

He trailed his fingers up and down her arm and a surge of masculine pride shot through him when she moaned in her sleep and snuggled closer. He turned his head, closed his eyes and inhaled the floral fragrance of the shampoo she'd used only moments before he'd seen her standing at that window, glistening, beautiful and perfect. It was in that moment, before he'd touched her, before he'd made love to her, that he realized it fully.

He was in love with Tatum Colton.

Not only in love, but in serious like. She made him laugh. At life, at himself. She made him think. She drove him nuts. And she made him worry. He'd never been as afraid as he'd been last night when he'd gotten that call. He understood now why some people believed love made you weak. How could he function, how could he do his job knowing one wrong decision, one wrong step, could take him away from her? And he was bound to, wasn't he? Something was bound to come between them, no matter how hard he worked to stop it.

Was it selfish to want this to last? To want to stay here, in this place, hidden from everything out there, where the two of them could live off her cooking and each other? Of course it was. But he could still dream it.

This moment couldn't last. Not with what he had to do. But he'd draw it out as long as he could. He'd do whatever it took to keep her safe, sacrifice whatever he needed to. He had hours, maybe days before he confirmed who was behind True's involvement with the drug cartel that had its hooks in the city. Until that time, until he had to do what needed doing, he'd take what he had now and embrace it. Enjoy it.

He'd love her.

And hope, when all this was over, that she'd forgive him.

Chapter 13

Tatum couldn't remember the last time she slept so late. Or so well. When she opened her eyes and looked at the bedside clock, she had to take an extra beat to compute what she was seeing. And…she sniffed the air. Ahhh, coffee and…

She rolled over, stretched and let out a very satisfied sigh before she sat up. The bedroom doorway suddenly filled with a very sexy, very shirtless, and barefoot detective. No one man should ever look that good in a pair of unbuttoned jeans. Even as her cheeks warmed and she tugged the sheet up to cover herself, she smiled. "Good morning. What's this?" She scooted back against the brass headboard as he approached with a tray. When she looked down, tears misted her eyes. "You made me waffles." She inclined her head. "In the shape of a heart."

"I did." He sat on the other side of the tray, scooted it closer so she could get a look at the berry-laden syrup spilling over the crisp, golden cakes. "I heard somewhere they're your comfort food. Which explains your fetish for waffle irons."

She picked up a knife and fork, cut, and took a bite, her starved palate singing in response. "Oh, wow." She took another bite, swallowed and sighed. "These are amazing. What's this?" She scraped her fork over the white melted into the grooves. She tasted, frowned.

"The Medina special ingredient." He leaned forward and kissed a drop of syrup off the corner of her mouth. "Marshmallow fluff."

Tatum gaped. "I, um. Okay." The laughter bubbled up from her toes. "I guess I've neglected to test that particular ingredient's superpower. Consider me a convert." The light, sweet, ultra-crispy texture definitely deserved closer inspection. "I need to eat quick and get going. I'm already late."

"If you mean for the fish and farmers market, it's already taken care of." He nudged her coffee forward. "Ty and Sam have already headed over. You're taking the day off."

"I most certainly am not." That she could declare that even as her body throbbed like one large bruise was a minor miracle. "Do you know what this week is?"

"I know about Friday and I know how important it is." He sat back as if he'd mentally rehearsed this conversation. "I also know you were nearly killed the night before last and are lucky to be alive. I think you can take one day off to recover."

She shook her head, unable to stop shoveling waffles

into her face. "Can't. I don't even know what I'm going to serve Friday night yet. I need time—"

"You need time to focus and create and make this the best dinner service True has ever offered. This seems the perfect place to do so."

"I need my people around me. I need to tell them what's going on."

"You can do that on a video call later this afternoon, once everyone's in. This isn't a discussion, Tatum. You aren't leaving here today. Tomorrow is another story, but for today, I need you safe and protected. And by protected, I've got two officers outside keeping an eye on things while I go to work."

"You really think someone's going to try to get at me again? Cruz, if I don't turn up—"

"They'll think they succeeded in putting you out of commission, which is precisely what they hoped to do. Just be grateful it wasn't permanent. You've got the best people working for you, Tatum. If you can't trust them for one day…"

That he trailed off and seemed to be waiting for her to finish the thought had her grumbling around her breakfast. Previous conversations pushed back on her, and as she swallowed, her mind cleared. "You've put your faith in Ty. That must mean you don't think he's a suspect anymore."

"No, I don't." He quickly filled her in on Ty's situation with his daughter and grandchildren.

"I knew he had a daughter, but he never talks about her. Or them." Tatum sat back, coffee clasped in her palms. "I supposed I should have." Maybe if she'd been paying attention to other people's lives as much as she did her own, she would know a lot of things. "Are they okay?"

"Yeah, they're fine. And Ty's going to be our go-to until the case works itself out. I told him everything I could. And he won't say anything until we're on the other side of this. And we will be soon, Tatum." He lifted a hand to her face and she leaned in to his touch. "I promise."

"You're making progress, then." She turned and pressed her lips into his palm. "Tell me. Please."

"The license plate you caught belongs to the same car I saw that night at the restaurant. We've traced it to a company here in town. A company we suspect is a shell company for the drug cartel. We have an all-points out for it, but I'm betting it's been ditched."

"Ditched?"

"I'd be surprised if we don't find a burned-out shell in the next couple of days. They want you out of the way for some reason. We won't get lucky a third time."

"All right." As much as she hated to surrender, the idea of spending the day alone in her kitchen, with her cookbooks, sounded more appealing by the minute. "Will you still be working at the restaurant?"

"I will. I'm going in around one. Ty's going to have you call in on video chat around three. He'll have told them you're taking an inspiration day. His suggestion. He said they'd understand that once you let them know about Constance Swan's reservation."

"You two just thought of everything, didn't you? Oh! We have a catering job tomorrow." She snapped her fingers. "Sam and Quallis—"

"Sam's on top of it."

"He'll need to get the final details from Richard—"

"Yep. He knows. They all know. You've trained them well, Tatum. Now let them do their jobs."

Tatum flinched, his words hitting too close to a target she'd closed off months before. "I'm a control freak, I know." She pulled her knees in as Cruz moved the tray, wrapped her arms tight and locked herself in. "Since you've been going through the files, you probably know about Daria." Even now, all these months later, the thought of her friend could still make her heart weep. "She quit because I didn't let up. It was a hard lesson to learn, losing her that way."

"Then don't learn it again." He leaned forward and kissed her. "I need to go into the station, catch up on a few things before I head to True."

"Okay." She grabbed hold of him and hung on, deepening the kiss. "Did you already shower?"

"I did." His mouth lingered, lightly trailed down the side of her throat. "But I can always scrub your back?"

"Now that—" she kissed him again "—sounds like the perfect start to the morning."

It had taken him a while to form his plan of attack when it came to convincing Tatum to stay home for the day, but the time had been worth it. She was safely ensconced in her house, a pair of patrol officers securely in place and on watch, and a grocery delivery system on call should his shopping run last night not have provided her the appropriate supplies. He had a good four hours before he needed to get over to True and back up Ty during their video conference call between Tatum and the rest of the staff.

He'd barely taken a seat at his desk when his LT appeared. "Progress report?" She stirred a steaming cup of what could loosely be called coffee and blinked as if trying to stay awake.

"Ah, right. Here?"

"In my office." Luce headed down the hall before Cruz could reply. He found his commanding officer slouched in her chair looking completely exhausted. "Took Sheryl to the hospital last night." She smothered a yawn. "Braxton-Hicks contractions."

"False labor?"

"Four hours' worth. When your time comes, save up your vacation time because you're going to need it."

"Do you know something I don't?"

Luce looked at him, gaze narrowed. "It looks like maybe I do. You and Tatum Colton seem to have set off some sparks from what I've heard. That going to be a problem?"

"No, ma'am."

"Cut the ma'am crap, Cruz, and sit down. Don't be snippy. If your relationship with Colton is going to complicate the case—"

"It won't," he repeated. "Did the warrant for Richard Kirkman's financials come in?"

"Pending. Should be late tomorrow, Thursday morning at the latest."

Cruz cursed. He needed that information now. "Why the delay?"

"The bank is playing hardball. Sicced their lawyers on the assistant DA assigned to the case. The woman's already juggling four big cases, so her attention's a bit divided. We'll get it, don't worry."

"There's a catering job being run tomorrow. I'm hoping that'll give us the last of the evidence we're looking for."

"Pretty sneaky, using the catering service."

"But it makes sense. Talking to Ty and Tatum, I found it was Kirkman who brought up the idea after Tatum had True cater her father's funeral reception. The timing lines up. Distribution in the neighborhoods around True increased in the weeks following. They only have one continuous customer, so I'm going to check that out on my way in today. I was able to access the delivery schedule. They have a big one coming in right before this job. That has to be it."

"Move carefully," Luce advised. "I know you're anxious to get this case behind you, but we need it closed clean with as many big fish in the net as we can catch."

"That's the plan." He already had Ty working on a way to conceal his presence in the loading bay so he could observe the delivery. "Kirkman's the inside guy. He's been the point person from the jump. Whether he had Daria Naughton killed or not, he was certainly there to help pick up the pieces. Not that any of that will matter if we don't get into his financials."

"Agreed." His LT nodded. "And what about Tatum Colton? How much have you told her?"

"About Kirkman? Nothing. She still thinks I'm looking." He hated, no, he loathed lying to her, but he didn't have a choice. "Whatever buttons we've pushed, they see Tatum as the threat, not me." That was the only thing that still nudged at him. "I'll know more tomorrow. Then once we have what we need to use against Kirkman, we can bring him in, flip him on the cartel and finally shut them down." *And Johnny will be able to rest in peace.*

"Draw up the arrest warrant so it's ready to go the second you need it," Lieutenant Graves said. "I'll get you a backup team for when you need, and yes, before you ask, I put out the alert on his name. He tries to make a break for it, we'll be ready. Surveillance on his residence will be in place by tonight. He makes some weird move at True, you phone it in, understood?"

"Yeah." He let out a long breath. "The fallout from this, it's going to be bad." He hadn't meant to voice it. Didn't want to. "Even if everything goes right."

"You knew that going in," Luce reminded him. "It's your call how much you think Ms. Colton needs to know. You sure you don't want to fill her in?"

"I'm sure. She's a terrible liar." He managed a quick smile as if he'd made a joke. He'd do what he had to in order to protect her. As for protecting her business? He couldn't let himself dwell on that. "I need to catch up on some stuff before I head in to the restaurant. Hope Sheryl has that baby pretty soon, LT. You look beat."

"Spoken like a true man," Luce said with a strained smile. "Just for that I'm putting you on the babysitting list. Go on. Get going." She waved him out. "And Cruz?"

"Yeah?" He glanced over his shoulder.

"Be careful."

He supposed she meant with the case, with his safety. But as he returned to his desk and dug into the mounting evidence against Richard Kirkman, he had to wonder if maybe she was referring to his heart.

Kirkman's use of True's catering service as a decoy was the inspiration for Cruz's surreptitious visit to Belma Trade, located, according to their website, on the sixth floor of a high-rise half a mile from True. The small business district housed multiple financial investment and law firms, as well as one well-known hole-in-the-wall pizzeria.

Cruz called in and paid for an order for three large and loaded pies, gave Belma Trade as the delivery address, then parked across the street from the building and waited.

Less than a half hour later, he spotted the delivery person, familiar blue visor on his curl-encased head, heading toward the office building. When he ducked inside, Cruz waited a good few minutes, then got out, tugged his shirtsleeves down and straightened the tie he'd donned. The next second, the delivery guy emerged, a confused, anxious look on his face. He turned, looked to the number on the building and rechecked his phone.

Cruz jogged over. "Hey! Are those for Belma Trade?"

The kid practically sagged with relief. "Yeah, that you?" He pointed to the spinning glass door. "You know your offices are empty, right?"

"No one up there?" Cruz pulled out his wallet.

"Place is a ghost town. Name's on the directory, but it's all dead space. They move without telling you?" The kid laughed but didn't seem convinced it was funny.

"Not exactly." Cruz held a fifty up between two fingers. "Anyone asks, the delivery went fine. No surprises. You get me?"

"I got you, yeah. You want these?"

"Absolutely." Cruz hefted the pies out of the kid's hand, and the kid took the money and walked away.

He had the pieces. All the pieces, as well as the framework, and finally, he could see the complete picture. A picture he was almost reticent to finish. Whatever happened now, he'd done what he'd set out to do:

he'd have a major supplier of narcotics off the streets and soon he'd have leverage to find out exactly who pulled the trigger and shot Johnny. Nothing else, nothing else, he told himself firmly, mattered.

He didn't believe that for one flat second.

When he walked back into the station, he dropped off one of the pizzas to the front desk, carried the other two up to Narcotics, where the best group of detectives had helped him get to this point. Those detectives gave him a bit of a cheer when he left the pies in the break room, but he didn't stop until he reached his LT's office. He wasn't hungry. He wasn't sure he'd ever be hungry again. He rapped his knuckles on the doorframe, ducked his head inside. "Hey, LT?"

"Yeah?" She glanced up from her computer. "Well?"

"We got them."

The combination of adrenaline, anticipation and potential triumph made for one powerful fuel that catapulted Tatum through the week. Armed with a plethora of new menu ideas and riding high on the positive benefits of excellent and mind-numbing sex with one seriously hot cop, she had True and its employees buzzing like serious worker bees determined to please their Queen.

Word that Constance Swan would be dining with them on Friday had been the injection they'd all needed and everyone was on board to present the best food, the best experience of their careers.

Friday morning, do-or-die day, she was up and moving well before the sun, unable to sleep. But Cruz was out, sprawled on his stomach in her bed, black hair a stark contrast against her daisy yellow sheets. The sheet currently riding low across his narrow and quite agile hips. As the barely-there rays of the morning sun peeked through the skylight, she sat for a moment, tempted to trail her fingers down and along the toned, taut, tempting sight of him. It wouldn't take much. This she'd learned fairly quickly. But he'd been wiped out last night, and not, funnily enough, because of her.

She curled her hand into a fist, resisting the urge, and grabbed her yellow robe before padding into the kitchen, where she put on the coffee and set to work.

A little over an hour later, coffee in hand and the homemade cinnamon buns she'd made last night after getting home from work securely in the oven, she sat at the table with her computer and notebook, and got to work.

When she sniffed the air a while later, she set a mental clock, and sure enough, not ten minutes after, Cruz wandered in, nose first. "Woman, you are magic to wake up to, you know that?" He stopped long enough to capture her mouth with his, his hand massaging the back of her neck as she leaned into his kiss. "That said, if you don't stop baking I'm going to have to get my butt back to the gym." Cruz grabbed what was now his coffee mug off the counter and filled it.

"I think we're managing just fine with our own workout routine, don't you?"

"We're getting by. So." He took a seat. "You ready for tonight?"

"As ready as I can be." Nerves were taking hold; she could feel their tiny catlike talons creeping around inside her, leaving marks in their track. "I keep telling myself it's all going to be fine. Even if she hates us, there's no such thing as bad publicity, right?" He didn't laugh with her. He barely smiled as he sipped his coffee. "Hey." She reached out, closed her hand over his. "Everything okay?"

"Yeah, of course." His lips quirked up. "I just feel like we haven't stopped for a while."

"That's because we haven't. Last night you said you had something you wanted to talk to me about. I assume it's the case?"

"Yeah." He nodded, caught her hand when she pulled away. "Yeah, it's about the case. You have some time now?"

"Sure. Oh, wait a second. Hold that thought." She practically bounced out of her chair when the oven timer went off. She nearly swooned when she pulled the pan of fluffy, springy, fragrant rolls out. "Are you a gloopy icing kinda guy?" She set the pan on the counter and retrieved the batch of cream cheese icing off the back counter.

"Isn't everyone, with cinnamon rolls?" He stood, walked over and, coffee in hand, watched her slather the still steaming buns. When she started to lick her finger, he reached out, took hold and brought her fingers to his mouth, kissing and licking the icing clean.

"These are just as good warm as they are hot," she murmured, shifting and moving closer to him.

"I have no doubt." He brushed his sugarcoated lips across hers and she wondered if she'd ever tasted anything so completely wonderful. "But about that conversation."

"Right. The case." Because she knew it had to happen sometime, she put some distance between them and slid a knife around the edge of the pan. "I've been assuming no news is good news."

"We found the car that ran you down in the parking lot. It hadn't been burned out, but it was stripped. Registration information shows it was reported stolen three weeks ago. The plates were from another car altogether, so I'm afraid that's a dead end."

"Meaning?"

"Meaning whoever this is, they still have you in their sights."

"And you're here." She focused on the buns because there wasn't anything she could do about the other. "I've been back at the restaurant for days. Nothing's happened. Everyone's been great and as normal as usual."

"Yeah. That's what's worrying me."

"Well, I can't let it worry me." She took a deep, controlled breath. "Today is literally the biggest day, the biggest opportunity of my career. It can and I'm hoping will set up everything that comes next. So unless you're going to tell me to cancel dinner reservations tonight—"

"I'm not."

"But you did consider that, didn't you?" She may have only been sleeping with him for a few days, but there wasn't any doubt in her mind he was hedging that answer.

"I did. Things are…moving fast. Faster at this point than I think I can stop."

Her throat tightened, frustrated and disappointed tears pressing for release. "If that's your way of telling me you were right and I was wrong, congratulations." She locked her jaw, refused to look at him, and the iced buns wavered before her eyes.

"Tatum—"

"You're choosing to tell me this now, today of all

days." She finally found the courage to look him in the eyes.

"I…" He seemed to be struggling.

"Give me today." She could feel herself begin to shake. "Tomorrow we can sit down and hash it all out, but please, Cruz." She lifted a hand to his face. "Please just give me today."

He turned his head, kissed the inside of her palm, in the same way she'd done to him days before. "This isn't going to go away, Tatum. No matter how much you want it to."

"I know that." Did she? Everything about the last few weeks had been almost surreal, from being suspected of being a drug trafficker to having an undercover cop in her kitchen who then ended up in her bed. There wasn't anything about the days since she'd met Cruz Medina that weren't completely out of the ordinary for her, so why wouldn't she be able to keep pretending everything was fine? "Tell me one thing." She tried to keep her voice steady. "Did you mean it the other night when you said you loved me?"

"I did. I do. I wouldn't have said it if I didn't believe it."

"Then that's enough for today. You won't hurt me, Cruz. I believe that as much as I believe I've never loved anyone the way I love you. This matters." She caught his hand and clasped it between hers. "We matter. If we both acknowledge that, if we both accept it, we can tackle whatever happens. Together, right?"

His free hand came up and brushed her cheek, tucked a loose tendril of hair behind her ear. He smiled, a sad, resigned smile that didn't exactly make her heart leap. But at least it kept beating. "Together. Now." His gaze flicked to the counter. "Are you going to keep torturing me or am I finally going to get one of those cinnamon rolls?"

"This is a sign." Tatum was talking to herself again. Talking and pacing and examining each and every nook and cranny of True hours before they were scheduled to open. "This new seafood vendor is already exceeding my expectations." She lifted a fresh head-on prawn to inspect it. "Sorry little fella, but you are getting star billing tonight." She set it back on the ice on the plastic-wrap-covered tray and waved Colby to the refrigerator.

"How's she doing?" Ty's question had Cruz glancing over his shoulder. "She's been like a spinning top for the past two days. I don't think she's stopped to breathe."

"She has. It's called crashing," Cruz said, then offered a sheepish grin. "Sorry. That was a bit crass, I suppose."

"Only a bit. What's going on with Kirkman? You get what you need yesterday when you followed him on the catering job?"

"I think so." Cruz angled his head and urged Ty to follow him into the break room. Never in his wildest dreams would he have considered Ty his partner in all this, but the man had proven a worthy one, working with him to gather information and keep an eye on people Cruz couldn't. A quick check of the locker rooms confirmed they were alone. "Kirkman accepted a delivery yesterday afternoon. Had them load it right into the catering van. I couldn't get anywhere near it."

"So you don't know what was in it?"

"I only know Sam and Pike helped load up the van

with the food orders and Richard headed out. When he came back, the van was empty."

What he had managed to do earlier in the week was put a tracking device on the van. His people knew everywhere that van had gone in the past three days and it hadn't gone near any of the addresses listed on the delivery invoices.

"Bastard really is using Tatum's place to distribute drugs. There won't be a hole deep enough for him," Ty said. He started to say something else, but Cruz held up a hand, motioned to Ty to look busy.

Ty shifted to the coffee machine and pushed Brew.

"You two going to join us or not?" Sam sounded more stressed than Cruz had ever seen him. "No main entrée pizzas tonight, Cruz. Tatum wants you working prep with Chester."

"Understood." Cruz nodded and straightened his jacket.

"Ty, you've got pastries. Remember not to overdo it on the saffron."

"Right." Ty nodded. "It's going to be fine, Sam. We all know what we have to do."

"Good, good." Sam let out an uneasy laugh. "Sorry. I guess I'm wound tight. Tatum called me into her office earlier. After this weekend she's going to put me in charge of the catering side of things. Including the menu." He straightened and beamed with pride. "She says she trusts me with it. Best news I've had in a long time. One step closer to my own place. Catering for True. Can you believe it?"

"You're going to do great," Cruz assured him. "And yes, I can. Once we get through this weekend, we'll celebrate. Maybe even get Tatum to join us."

"Yeah, well, we all know who has an inside track on that happening. You guys get to work, okay? We've got food to prepare."

"What's going to happen?" Ty asked when they were alone again. "After?"

"I don't know. But I plan to do everything I can to minimize the fallout." He offered a tight smile and together they returned to the kitchen to help make Tatum's dreams come true.

Chapter 14

"T-minus thirty minutes to open!" Colby yelled out as she rinsed a huge colander of mussels under running water. "Let's get it done, people!"

"Look at her, all cheerleader." Susan, tablet in hand, paced in front of the serving area where Chester and Pike were busy loading dishes onto the shelves. "Front of house looks good. Everyone's pressed and polished. Don't worry." She held up her hand when Tatum started to comment. "They don't look like they're trying too hard. Everything is just tip-top. Promise."

"Good, okay." Tatum glanced at the clock, which at times seemed to jump into warp speed. "We've got two and a half hours before Constance is due to arrive. Just do what we've been doing and everything will be fine."

"I've got you coming out to greet her shortly after eight thirty. That still work?"

"Yep." Tatum tightened her apron band. "But feel free to remind me. Where's Richard?"

"He had to take a call. He should be…yeah, here he is. You ready?"

"Absolutely." Richard smoothed a hand down the front of his suit jacket.

"Everything okay?" Tatum recognized one of his nervous twitches.

"Yeah, fine. Just had a call from Nancy. Nothing to worry about." He slapped his hands together. "Tonight is going to be one for the books, I don't have any doubt. I'm going to head out, do one last check. Good luck, Tatum."

"You, too." Relieved to know the space beyond the kitchen was in good hands with both Richard and Susan, she felt a little bubble of apprehension burst. They'd spent the last two days rearranging some of the kitchen equipment to make room for the large paella pans she'd purchased, enough for one per table. She'd gone back and forth between single-serving plates, single-serving pans and family-style. Given the inspiration for tonight's menu had been Cruz and his Spanish heritage, she'd taken the chance and gone with family. The rest of the meal, appetizers, salads, and desserts, would be served in their normal way, but the paella, when ordered, would steal the show.

Which meant it was time to start. Paella done the right way took dedicated time, and that was where Tatum was putting her energy. Everything was at her fingertips, from pans to rice, seasonings and seafood. Spicy chorizo they'd made fresh in-house was ready to be cooked, organic chicken was cut up and undergoing its precook treatment of salt and pepper and a hint of smoky paprika. She could already smell and taste the herbs and spices permeating the steamy air of the kitchen.

She took a deep breath, let it out and found her gaze shifting to Cruz. He was watching her, those dark eyes of his so penetrating, so piercing. So perfect. He gave her that smile she'd come to love, the one that said so much without a word, that she touched a hand to her heart, absorbing the support, confidence and approval.

Embracing all the encouragement he sent her, she turned to her stove and got to work.

Wrist-deep in chopped onions and peppers, Cruz felt his phone vibrate against his hip. He glanced up at the clock. The doors had been open for over an hour. Orders were brisk and constant. Constance Swan was set to arrive any second.

He swore. No cell phones were allowed in the kitchen, but he didn't have a choice. Not with the case about to burst wide open. Stepping to the side, he turned his back on Chester and the prep area and pulled out his cell. Seeing his LT's number did not make him feel better.

"You got this for a few, Ches?" Cruz asked his fellow prep chef. "I have to take this."

"Tatum sees a phone in here she'll skin you like a chicken." But Chester nodded. "Be quick."

"Right." Nothing like having a twentysomething kid tell you what to do. He ducked into the hall and hurried into the storage room. Ignoring the voice mail she'd left, he quickly called Luce back. "What's going on, LT? I'm up to my neck—"

"Kirkman's booked a one a.m. flight for two to Mexico. Saw his name pop on the alert we set up. He's running, Cruz. He's running tonight. And he's running scared, because he didn't even try to hide this."

"Why now?" It didn't make sense. Or did it? The chaos of the night, the frenetic energy spinning in and around True. What better time to disappear when people would be too busy to notice. "Only reason to do that would be if he was running scared, but I don't think he is. I watched him on those deliveries yesterday, LT." He'd barely seen a hint of nerves on the man as he conducted a drug handoff as easily as one might cash a check.

"We can ask him why in questioning. We're out of time, Cruz. You need to make a decision."

"What decision? We pick him up when he gets home."

"We just took his wife into custody. She was on her way to the airport, two suitcases and passports with her. She had instructions to meet him at the gate. If we want him, we'll have to grab him at the restaurant."

No. Cruz felt the blood drain from his face. No, not here. Not tonight. He glanced over his shoulder. "LT, I can't do it to her. Tonight means—"

"We have one shot at this, Cruz."

"Then grab him at the airport!" Anywhere but here.

"There's a workers' strike, remember? The logistics would be a nightmare and we risk the chance of losing him. We have a clear shot at him right where he is. I warned you this could happen. You want to close your case or protect your girlfriend?"

Cruz's mind raced. *Girlfriend* seemed such an inadequate descriptor for what he considered Tatum to be. She was...well, she was just it for him, wasn't she?

It hadn't taken long for him to understand he didn't see—didn't want—a future that didn't include her in it and yet…

And yet Johnny was lying there hooked up to machines thanks to someone lurking in the shadows of this case. Tatum could be everything to him but Johnny would never have that chance. And Cruz couldn't let the people responsible get away.

"Ticktock, Medina." Luce's voice snapped him back. "What's it going to be?"

"Do it." As he said the words he could all but feel the connection between him and Tatum snap. "But I'll take lead. Have the team meet me around the corner."

"It doesn't have to be you, Cruz."

Yes, it does. "It's my case." He wasn't going to shirk the responsibility just because of his feelings for Tatum. Once he started down that slope, it wouldn't stop. "We go in fifteen."

When Cruz hung up and turned around, he found Ty standing in the doorway. Arms crossed over his chest, eyes cool as a freshly honed blade. "What are you doing, Cruz?"

"What I have to." He tried to move past, but Ty stopped him with a solid hand on his chest. "Let me by. I need to talk to Tatum."

"It's too late. She's out on the floor."

Cruz steeled his jaw, clenched his fists. "Richard's skipping town. There's nothing I can do about this, Ty."

"Sure there is." Ty's voice turned cold. "You just don't want to. No." He pushed Cruz back, took a step toward him. "If you're going to walk out on her you go out the back." He pointed out the loading bay door. Unwilling to take on another fight for the evening, Cruz acquiesced and walked away. "You disappoint me, Cruz." Cruz froze at Ty's statement. "I thought you understood what was really important. I guess I was wrong."

Nausea rolled thick and slippery through him. He did understand. He understood more than Ty could imagine. But he'd made a promise, and Cruz was nothing without his word. Tatum of all people would understand. Cruz reached up and unbuttoned his chef's jacket as he walked. He turned down the alley, tugged it off, wadded it up, and as he passed, tossed it into the dumpster. "Someday she'll understand."

Tatum made it a point to greet a number of other guests before making her way to Constance Swan's table. Everyone in True was always given the same service, the same quality food and the same attention. As anxious as she was to connect, she slowed down, took her time. *Make it count.*

"Ms. Swan, it's lovely to meet you." Tatum shook the offered hand of the woman who could put True on the culinary map. Petite and far more slender than any food critic had a right to be, Constance Swan introduced her fellow dining companions. "Welcome, all of you." Tatum looked to each of them, Constance's publicist, her web designer, and her daughter Margaret, who looked to be about Tatum's age but had far more polish and presence than Tatum could ever hope to have. "I hope you're enjoying your evening at True so far."

"It's been sublime, and it's Constance, please."

Tatum gave Susan a glance that had her hostess moving away. "We were thrilled to hear you were interested in dining with us," Tatum continued. "I admit to taking advantage of the privilege and using the opportunity to stretch my cooking wings a bit." She motioned to the paella.

"It was a nice surprise," Constance told her. "I went to Spain on my honeymoon and had the best paella. I've talked about that trip and that meal often over the years."

"Spain was my father's favorite vacation spot," Margaret clarified.

"What you've given us here is as close to that experience as I could ever hope to recreate," Constance said. "Especially now that he's passed."

"My condolences," Tatum offered. "But I'm glad I could bring back some good memories. That's what food should be about, isn't it? Connecting with our emotions, our pasts. Our experiences. That's what I strive for every day I'm in the kitchen. Connections."

"Well, from where we are sitting you're accomplishing that perfectly."

Not wanting their food to get cold while they chatted, Tatum stepped back. "I'll leave you to your meal, then. Please, if you have any concerns or questions, I hope you won't hesitate to let Susan know. We'll do our best to accommodate you."

"I wonder." Constance caught her hand when she began to walk away. "If a tour of your kitchen would be possible? I would love to meet the staff who helped prepare such a wonderful meal."

"Absolutely. Only—" Tatum hesitated, glancing around the filled dining room "—would you be willing to wait until closer to the end of service? I'd be happy to send over another bottle of wine, on the house of course. Once we've caught up with orders I'd be pleased to give you a tour."

"That would be fine." Constance nodded. Tatum stole a look at the others seated at the table. Given their approving expressions, Tatum wondered if she'd just passed some kind of test.

"I'll have Susan bring you back as soon as…" Tatum trailed off at the unexpected flash of movement at the entrance by the bar. Uniformed officers flanked the glass doors outside. And three men with polished badges hanging around their necks stepped in.

Two of the men were utterly unfamiliar, but the third? That glossy hair, the neatly trimmed, thin mustache and beard. The determined spark in dark eyes that didn't miss a single thing. "Cruz." She hadn't realized she'd spoken out loud until she noticed Margaret turn her chin up.

No, this wasn't possible. She tried to swallow but couldn't. He wouldn't… He was supposed to be in the kitchen, working prep with Chester. It wasn't possible he'd…and yet it clearly was.

Tatum's breath caught in her chest. She reached out and grabbed the back of Constance's chair to stop her legs from folding. Cruz spoke to Susan, who, from behind her podium, turned her head and locked wide, disbelieving eyes on Tatum. Her gaze instantly shifted behind Tatum, to where Tatum had seen Richard moments before.

Richard.

A million questions flew through her mind in an instant, spinning around each other, too fast for her to even attempt to find an answer.

Of course. It was the only answer that made sense, wasn't it? Richard, who had access to her books, who had the run of the place whether she was here or not.

Richard, who had been so solicitous and caring when her father had been killed. It had all been a ruse so he could get his claws deeper into the restaurant that may as well be her beating heart.

Cruz had told her this morning, warned her that he'd found the connection, but she hadn't wanted to listen. She hadn't wanted anything marring her perfect day, but she never, not in a thousand years, would have believed Cruz would use it against her. Not tonight.

"He wouldn't." Recalling that first night he'd come here, with that self-assured I'm-not-wrong attitude that had somehow slipped through whatever sense she might have had, she thought he would. *When someone first shows you who they are, believe it.* Her father's voice echoed in her mind.

But as he walked toward her, she looked at his face and knew. He pointed to the kitchen doors, and the two men with him took up position there, turning and holding up their hands when Ty, Quallis and Sam pushed their way out. Pike and Colby emerged as well, but were held back by Ty. Pike quickly ducked inside, and seconds later Chester and Bernadette joined their fellow employees; all shared the same dumbstruck, confused expression Tatum could only dream of wearing.

Her world moved into slow motion. Nothing made sense. And she could hear the ever so faint sound of her future beginning to crumble. She was peripherally aware of people grabbing their cell phones, recording every torturous moment, cementing True's reputation in online scandal even before she could remember how to breathe.

Cruz made his way through the tables as effortlessly

as he'd slid into her heart. Conversation stilled as he came closer, as if muting customers as he passed.

"What's going on?" Richard's tight-throated question had Tatum's hand clenching around the back of Constance's chair. "Tatum, what's your sous-chef doing?"

Tatum couldn't stop herself. She stepped between them, planted a hand on Cruz's chest, her fingers brushing against the badge he wore, and lifted pleading eyes to his. "Don't do this now, Cruz. Please. Not tonight. Not here." Didn't he see? Couldn't he feel anything other than blind obligation and duty?

"I'm sorry, Tatum. I don't have a choice." While he kept his voice low, in the graveyard silence of True, everyone would hear. "There's nowhere for you to go, Richard. We have your wife in custody along with your passport. You need to come with me."

"You're a cop?" Richard's relief might have been comical if the entire situation wasn't so…Shakespearean. "You're a damned cop? Tatum, what the…you let an undercover cop into your kitchen?"

"Please," Cruz tried again. "Don't make this worse for Tatum."

Tatum went cold inside. There wasn't an ounce of warmth, not in her blood. Not in her body. Not in her heart. This was the man from the bar, the man she'd refused to believe. Not the man she'd fallen into bed with. And certainly not the man she'd fallen in love with.

"Worse than you're making it?" Richard scoffed. "Like that's possible."

"Are we really going to do this this way?" Cruz challenged Richard.

"Richard, please, just go with him," Tatum urged. "If it's a mistake—"

"Of course this is a mistake! What are the charges? I demand to know what I'm being charged with." Richard turned gleaming, if not defiant, eyes on Tatum. "Tell me why you're arresting me. I want witnesses." In that moment she knew exactly what he was doing. And she wasn't going to let him get away with it. "I want everyone to know."

"He's arresting you because you're a drug dealer," Tatum said before Cruz could find the words. He reached out for her, but she stepped away. The last thing, the very last thing she could deal with right now was Detective Cruz Medina touching her. "You've been using my business to distribute drugs in the city, Richard. You've been using me. Using all of us. Was it you who tried to run me down the other night? Did you try to kill me?"

"No." Richard blinked as if coming out of a trance. "No, Tatum, I swear, that wasn't me. That was—"

"Doesn't sound like a denial on the rest of it." Cruz spun Richard around and slapped handcuffs on him. That clicking sound as they tightened would haunt her for the rest of her life. "Since you wanted witnesses, how about they hear me read you your rights. Richard Kirkman, I'm arresting you on charges of…"

Tatum didn't hear the rest. Would that she could have melted into the floor and disappeared, but that wouldn't happen. She walked behind them, more than aware of every single eye on her. She stopped at the podium when Cruz stopped at the door.

"Tatum," Susan whispered and then stopped, as a middle-aged woman stepped forward, her cool, controlled cop expression aimed at Tatum.

"Ms. Colton. Lieutenant Luce Graves. I'm sorry, but

I'm afraid I need to ask you to close your restaurant immediately."

"Why?" Susan demanded, but Tatum shook her head and looked to Cruz.

There it was. The final nail in the coffin.

"Because it's a crime scene," Tatum said softly. When she continued, she did so with her gaze firmly on Cruz. And she waited until he met her eyes. "I'll take care of it, Lieutenant. On one condition. You make certain I never see *him* again."

Cruz winced.

"Ms. Colton—"

"That's the condition." She didn't want the sympathy she heard in his boss's voice; she didn't want platitudes or explanations. He'd lied to her. Over and over. From the moment he'd sat down at the bar all the way up to when he'd said he loved her. He didn't. It wasn't possible he did, when he'd just blown up her entire world. "Do we have a deal?"

"Yes." Lieutenant Graves nodded and motioned for her cops, including Cruz, to leave. "I'll be sending in a team—"

"Can this wait a few minutes?" Tatum cut her off. She'd never felt so in control and yet so detached in her life. "Susan, show the lieutenant to the bar and help her with anything she needs." She didn't wait for agreement or understanding before she faced her customers. "Ladies and gentlemen, I apologize for…" She cleared her throat. "It's with my deepest regret that I ask you all to leave. There will be no charge for your meals. I can't offer any explanation at this time. I hope to in the near future. Please." She stepped up onto the bar stair, stood with her hands clasped behind her back and willed them all away. Slowly, silently, people gathered their belongings and did as she asked.

She stood there, chin up, eyes dry, heart pounding a staccato in her chest, as they filed by, one by one. The tears would come later, much later, when she was alone and could scream them free. She nearly lost control when Constance Swan stopped and reached out her hand. Tatum clasped it and found only warmth.

"I'll take a rain check on that kitchen tour," the older woman said.

It was no doubt an offer made out of pity, but Tatum managed a small smile and nod. When the last customer stepped out and the door closed behind them, Tatum walked slowly through her empty restaurant. She heard Ty's and Sam's outraged voices echoing against the glass, but she couldn't talk to them. Not now. Not yet.

She made her way around the scattered tables and chairs, casting tear-filled eyes upon the partially eaten meals and half-filled wine glasses. Tatum climbed the stairs, one by one, slowly, deliberately, until she reached her office.

And closed the door behind her.

Chapter 15

"It's all over the internet." The declaration shot at Cruz from across the squad room like a bullet, hitting him square in the heart. A heart he couldn't afford to listen to at the moment if he was going to do his job.

And he would do it. Not following through would mean he'd betrayed the woman he loved for nothing. He would never, for the rest of his life, be able to erase the image of Tatum standing there, in the middle of her beautiful restaurant, looking utterly and completely defeated. And yet...

And yet she'd stood. She'd done what she had to do, because she was Tatum Colton and anything less would be utterly unacceptable.

As much as she loathed him now, he'd never loved her more.

To top it all off, he was an internet star, which meant his days as an undercover anything were officially over.

"Medina, you ready? They've got him in interview three."

He didn't answer. Instead he pushed to his feet and went to the break room to distract himself with some coffee.

"Cruz." Luce leaned in the doorway and crossed her arms. "You did what you had to do. You did the job. I know it wasn't easy—"

"No," he said, not wanting to discuss it with anyone, but especially his boss. "It wasn't. But it's over and done." He dumped a crap ton of sugar into his coffee, prayed the combination of sugar and caffeine would get him through the next few hours. "I'm letting him stew. A couple of hours should do it."

"Hours? You sure?"

He looked at her. "Has he asked for a lawyer? Even once? Asked to see his wife? Asked for anything?"

"No." Luce inclined her head.

"It won't take much of a push to get him to talk. He's already scared, and the longer he's in here, the more worried his partners will be. I want him shaking when I go in there." He took a sip of coffee, winced, and accepted it as appropriate punishment. "Maybe then I won't choke the life out of him."

"Cruz, it'll blow over. You'll talk to her. You'll work it out."

"Is that what you'd do if you destroyed Sheryl's career? Any hope she has of advancement? How do you think she'd react if you made her a social media sensation for employing a drug dealer?"

Luce didn't answer. She didn't have to, because they both already knew the truth.

"Sometimes what we have to do seriously sucks,

Cruz. I'm going to head back, see how the team's coming along with their search. Anything you want me to tell her?"

Tell her I'm sorry. Tell her he wished there was another way. Tell her if he could, he'd turn back the clock and tell her everything that morning when she'd waved him off. "No." There were no words that would fix or change what had happened. The only thing he could do now was close the case and lock Richard Kirkman and his partners up for the rest of their lives. "Just watch out for her for me, will you?"

Beyond that, there was nothing else he could do.

Who knew a police search could take so long? She should have asked Ty or Quallis or Sam about that, but she waited it all out, opening her door only once when Lieutenant Graves came up to give her an update.

"The restaurant will have to remain closed for at least the next few weeks."

"You can't be more specific than that?" Tatum asked, wondering if this situation could possibly get any worse.

"I'm afraid not."

"Don't plan things out very far, do you?" She had yet to remove her chef's jacket; it felt like the ultimate surrender, but the fabric was beginning to feel more like a straitjacket than her uniform of choice.

"I'd say I'm sorry," the lieutenant said. "But I have the feeling you wouldn't appreciate it."

"You're right. If you and your team are finished, I'd like to lock up and go home." She gathered her purse and jacket and led the older woman downstairs. She waited until the lab techs and officers walked out her front doors, then turned out the lights and locked up.

She dug into her purse for her set of spare keys and handed them over. "In case anyone needs access and I'm not here."

Lucille Graves looked down at the collection of keys. "About Cruz—"

"I'm sorry." Tatum held up a hand. "When I said I didn't want to see him again, that included I don't want to talk about him."

"He cares about you, Ms. Colton."

"All evidence to the contrary. I'd say thank you, but I wouldn't really mean it. Good night, Lieutenant."

"Good night."

Tatum couldn't stop swallowing on her way to the parking lot. Her car felt a million miles away, but the tears were just beneath the surface, waiting for one tiny crack in her control to flow free. She lifted her face into the cold wind, let the chill take care of them. She stopped when she saw her car was surrounded by her employees. By her friends.

Sam and Quallis and Colby and Chester. Bernadette and Susan clung to each other. Every server, every bartender, every bus-person and Ty. All of them stood there in the cold March air waiting for her.

When Ty stepped forward, she couldn't stop herself. The tears spilled and she held up her hand, shook her head. "Don't," she whispered. "Please." But he did. He moved in and wrapped his arms around her, drew her in to an embrace that reminded her so much of the ones her father had always provided that her knees buckled.

The sobs nearly choked her as she clung to him, the cold fading as the others encircled her, rested their hands on her shoulder, on her back.

"I'm sorry," she managed between sobbing breaths.

"I'm so sorry. This is all my fault. I never should have let—"

"You have nothing to apologize for," Ty assured her. "If you want to blame someone, blame me. I helped him. I trusted him. Should have known better than to trust a cop. Especially a cop who lies for a living."

"We're going to fix this," Susan insisted. "Somehow, someway, we are going to get True back on track."

"You can't really think there's any hope of that." But it meant the world to her that they at least pretended. She'd seen the videos online. They were trending on Twitter and had been splattered all over Facebook. The food world would be next, especially once Constance Swan added her two cents. "We're closed. Indefinitely. I'll pay you all through the end of the month at least. After that, I don't know when or if…" There was every real possibility she might never open those doors again.

"Come on, boss," Sam urged when she stepped back and got herself under control. "Let's go get a drink across the street."

She wanted to. Tonight of all nights, but she couldn't. She was exhausted and the last thing she wanted to do was rehash it over and over. "Another night. I'm going home. I'll call you when I know something," she insisted and made her way to her car.

Tatum didn't look at them as she drove away. She couldn't bear to. She drove by rote, heading for the ranch house only to pull over to the side of the road halfway there. Her home, in the last week, had somehow become theirs. Everywhere she looked she'd see him, hear him. Smell him on her sheets. Imagine him lounging on her sofa while she cooked or acting as taster as she experimented. There wasn't a part of that place that wouldn't haunt her tonight.

She turned the car around, headed for the condo. She barely remembered getting there, parking, taking the elevator up. All she wanted was a shower and her bed and to sleep until she could forget.

But when she stepped inside, all those wants vanished. Her mother, her aunt and January all got to their feet. The space looked new, with its pale Wedgwood blue walls and elegant, gold-accented brocade draperies. Her furniture was rearranged into a more practical pattern, but most of all, they'd left her kitchen alone. It was beautiful. It was, she thought, perfect.

"Guess you finished just in time for me to move out."

When she buckled this time, her other family was there to catch her.

"How do you function on so little sleep?"

January stumbled out of the bedroom and somehow managed to perch on the barstool without tumbling to the floor. Her sister had never done particularly well with all-nighters, whereas Tatum thrived on them. Her mother and Aunt Fallon had finally headed home sometime after one, having given Tatum just enough time to wallow and wail before the anger set in.

Now, five hours, three loaves of bread and a vat of beef stew later, that anger was on a full-blast-boil.

"Coffee," January groaned. "For the love of all that is holy, coffee."

Tatum smirked and abandoned her puff pastry to do her sister's bidding. She waited to speak until her sister had had her first sip, then dived in.

"Somewhere between the sourdough and *fougasse*, I made a decision."

"Hmm." January looked doubtful. "Usually your best decisions are made over waffles. I say hopefully," she added, eyeing the waffle iron cabinet.

"Not today." That she now resented waffles only added to her mood. "Today, I take a stand. I'm not giving up."

"Well, duh." January rolled her eyes. "You're a Colton. It's literally a gene defect. We fight to the death. But, for clarification, are we talking about Cruz or True?"

"What do you think?" She had Cruz Medina solidly in her rearview mirror. Mostly.

"Ummm." January pressed her lips into a thin line. "Maybe we need Simone for the rest of this conversation."

"Mom said she didn't answer her phone last night when you all called her, but she did text."

"Whoopee!" January waved a finger in the air. "Such support she's showing you."

Because of her own issues with compartmentalizing, Tatum wasn't going to blame Simone for not being there with the rest. The longer the investigation went into their father and uncle's killer, the more determined Simone became. "She's having trouble dealing with Dad's death. You know this. Let her be."

"I'll remind you you said that at a later date. So, what's this plan of action you've come up with?"

"First—" Tatum brushed off her hands "—I'm going to call one of the local news stations and offer to give an interview, clear the air, so to speak."

"Can you do that?" January frowned. "I mean, will the police let you?"

"Let me?" Had she heard that correctly?

"Legalities and all. Due process and blah-blah-blah. Just…" January crinkled her nose. "And don't take this the wrong way, but you didn't like it when Cruz interfered with your career. Blindsiding him might not be the best idea. He has arrest powers."

Oh, he had a lot of powers. "The irony was not lost on me." Tatum folded her pastry, turned it and wrapped it in plastic wrap to set in the freezer for a half hour. "And don't worry. I'll clear any statement I make with Lieutenant Graves. I'm also thinking of writing something up for social media."

"Nah." January shook her head. "Let this ride out. Things like this burn out in days, replaced by some other attention suck that make people feel superior. The more you contribute to it, the longer the fire will burn. Trust me on this, Tate. Just focus on getting True's doors back open." She sat up, frowned. "I think that's my cell."

"Probably Sean again. He's been texting you all night. Don't worry," Tatum assured her when she got the glare. "I only answered once to let him know I was okay and that you were asleep. Call him back and tell him you're on your way home."

"Am I?" She looked down at the borrowed set of pink bunny shorts and matching tank. "I don't look like it. I don't like the idea of you being alone today."

"I won't be." She was already heading into her bedroom to get dressed. "I'm never alone at True."

Cruz managed to wait until dawn before interviewing Richard Kirkman. He wouldn't have made it that long if he hadn't taken a call from Jade and had a long, decision-making discussion with her about Johnny. It was time, she'd told him, only a short time to go. Cruz glanced at his watch, at the date below the time. Today was Johnny's thirtieth birthday. It was fitting, Jade insisted. To let him go on the day he'd been given to the world.

He'd sat there at his desk, multiple coffee cups lined up on the table. In hours he'd say a final goodbye. All that was left was to close this case and tell Johnny, before he was gone, that he'd kept his promise. Except...

He hadn't. Not yet. But he had managed to destroy the one good thing to come into his life. Tatum Colton had, in a very short amount of time, carved a permanent place inside of him. He'd never understood the idea of finding the person who fit, something Johnny had lamented for him on more than one occasion.

"Once you find her, man, you will never, ever want to let her go." Johnny's bright blue eyes and Hollywood-blond hair all but shone whenever he spoke about Jade. "It'll happen. One day. And I'll be there laughing my butt off even as I plan your stag party."

But there wouldn't be a stag do. For either of them. And that, Cruz thought as he scrubbed a hand down his face, was perhaps the greatest tragedy of all of this. Both their futures had disappeared in the blink of an eye, or, in Johnny's case, the flash of a muzzle.

The clock tick-tick-ticked its way to eight o'clock.

By this afternoon when he walked into that rehab facility, he'd have Richard Kirkman locked down as a witness against one of the biggest drug cartels in the state. And that would be his parting gift to his partner.

He stood up, stretched, and, catching his LT's eye, headed down the hall to interrogation. Cruz popped his head into the observation room, glanced toward the two-way mirror as Luce came in behind him. "He ready, you think?"

"Oh, yeah." The plainclothes detective sitting at a computer monitor, ready to record whatever happened, nodded. "He's about worn a trench in the linoleum. And he definitely should have to pee by now."

"Seems a good place to start. I'm going in."

"Cruz." Lieutenant Graves held out her hand. "Forgetting something?"

"Not really, no." But he handed over his sidearm anyway. When he stepped into the interview room, he knew instantly his instinct to let Kirkman stew had been right on target. The room smelled like sour sweat, guilt and desperation. His favorite combination. He motioned for the monitor officer to leave, murmured his thanks and closed the door.

Kirkman stopped his pacing and all but launched himself at Cruz. "Kept me waiting long enough. Where's Nancy? Where's my wife?"

"She's safe." Cruz held up his hands, pointed to the mirror. "You put hands on me we're going to have to add to your list of charges, Richard. I don't think you can afford any more."

Richard backed off, resumed pacing. "You don't know what you've done, Mendoz..." He stopped, whirled around, eyes narrowed. "That's not your real name."

"Close. Detective Cruz Medina. Mendoza was Tatum's idea. Keeping things as close to the truth as possible."

"Your admiration won't get you far anymore." Richard had the gall to smirk. "She won't have anything to do with the man who ruined her business."

"Then I guess we have something in common. Sit."

Richard ignored him. "You got this all wrong, Cruz. I've been protecting Tatum. For months! I'm the only reason she's still alive. Hell, I'm still protecting her!"

"Really?" Cruz pulled a chair closer, spun it around and sat. "Do tell."

"First you tell me where Nancy is. What are you charging her with?"

"Nothing. For now. She's being held for questioning. If she doesn't know anything—"

Richard scrubbed his hands down his face. "She only knows I screwed up. Cruz, she's innocent. You have to give her protection. You have to give it to both of us."

"Convince me. Tell me about Tatum and this fantasy you have about having saved her. You were a plant at the restaurant. You work for the Nacio drug cartel."

Richard sat, dropped his head into his hands. "I grew up with Javier Nacio. He was my best friend all the way through college. His father…his father considered me a second son. I didn't know what the family was about until it was too late. He paid for my college, bought my mother a house, made sure she moved into a safe neighborhood. And then I was in deep. So I went where they told me."

"Try again." Cruz shook his head. "No way Nacio Sr. would have had True on his radar." Cruz wagged a finger at Richard. "You should take credit for your ideas, Richard. That was all you."

"Okay, yeah, it was. I might have mentioned using a high-end restaurant like True would be a good cover for distribution, but I didn't know, I had no idea they were going to kill Daria Naughton to get me in the door."

That was one. Cruz made a mental note. "But once you were, you started pushing the catering idea."

"Yeah. It didn't get me very far until Tatum's dad was killed. That reception was the opening I needed. From there it was just a matter of creating the right client with the right system in place. In one month I managed to triple their supply."

"By accepting deliveries of drugs at True and transporting them in catering orders to Belma Trade."

"Yeah. Yeah, and it was all going okay until she hired you. I had someone all picked out. One of Nacio's lieutenants was ready for the sous-chef job and then there you were."

"And since Tatum hired me herself, you needed to get a hold of my employment file."

"I was ordered to. Nacio wanted to know who you were. He doesn't like coincidences."

Great. He had something in common with a drug lord.

"You didn't have to lock her in the freezer. You could have just gotten it during the dinner rush."

"Her office is all windows. She'd have seen me and I didn't have time to think about it. He had Nancy under surveillance. He probably did last night when you picked her up."

Cruz hoped his boss picked up on that. If Nancy

Kirkman was being watched by the cartel, then they knew she was in custody. Not being able to reach Kirkman himself was probably adding to their concern. "We'll take care of Nancy, Richard. I promise. What did they do when you gave them the file?"

"They told me you couldn't be trusted and that meant Tatum couldn't be, either. She needed to be taken care of, but I said I could do something without hurting her. That's when I had Nancy approach Constance Swan. Nothing distracts Tatum like potential to grow True. I just needed her to focus on something that didn't involve you and whatever you were looking for."

"And when it didn't work, you tried to run her down with your car."

"Not me, man. That was Nacio's deal. He put one of his best men on it. Cruz, you have to listen to me. This isn't over. Getting me, that's nothing. You want me to flip, great. Fine, yeah, you put me and Nancy somewhere where they won't find me, WITSEC, whatever, I'll take whatever deal you guys offer. But you have to get to Tatum and keep her away from True."

"But you're here. What threat—"

"You really think I'm the only one Nacio had working at True? It takes two people to drive those catering deliveries, Cruz. Man. Oh, man, this has all gone wrong. I told him this wasn't going to work. They always find out." He sagged forward, burying his face in his arms. "This has all gone wrong."

"What has gone wrong? Your last delivery—"

"The last drop-off didn't make it to the suppliers. He

took it, Cruz. He's stashed it to sell on the side. My cut was supposed to be enough to get me out of the country, but I felt things going wrong and planned to get out."

"Stop whining and tell me who else Nacio had working at the restaurant." His mind was already flipping through the employees. Susan, Sam, Chester, Colby... half a dozen servers, just as many bartenders. Ty, Bernadette and... "Pike. Was Pike driving that car that went after Tatum?"

Richard's head snapped up. "Yeah. He said she wasn't distracted enough. She needed to be taken out. He was furious when she walked back into True."

"Son of a... Pike is behind all this. Lieutenant!" He was on his feet and out the door. She popped out into the hall at the same time, held out his weapon. "Richard's low man on the ladder."

"But Pike's record came up clean."

"I'm betting that's not his name. Run a deeper background check. Talk to him." He pointed into the interview room. "I need to find Tatum."

"Wait, Cruz!" Richard tried to step clear, only to be stopped by the officer standing outside the room. "Pike's not giving up that stash. He's been ripping them off for months. He needs a scapegoat, someone to blame, someone to give Nacio as a trade-off."

"Tatum." Cruz felt the blood drain from his face. "He's going to turn Tatum over to Nacio. Luce?" He didn't even try to quell the panic spinning inside him.

"Go!" his boss yelled. "Take backup with you to the restaurant. I'll send a car to her house."

"And the condo." He yelled out the address as he ran through the squad room.

Please, please, he prayed as he raced to his car. *Don't let me be too late again.*

Chapter 16

It took all Tatum's focus not to do the math as she emptied True's refrigeration units of the leftover and unused food from last night. On the bright side, things had blown up on a Friday night, so she hadn't purchased food for next week yet.

She'd been able to cancel her standing order, and, having spent the past two hours on the phone with various vendors, assure them that payment was on the way and that there would be no outstanding invoices by next week. Only when she was caught up could she take a serious look at the accounting to see what other damage Richard had wrought on her restaurant.

"Not only Richard," she muttered and tossed multiple heads of lettuce into a plastic bin. She was just as responsible. She'd been mired in grief and all too happy to let someone else take control of what she should have been paying close attention to. She'd find a way, some way, to drag True back; she hadn't worked this long and hard to give up. She certainly wasn't going to give Cruz Medina the power to destroy her life.

True would be the phoenix of restaurants and rise from the ashes of scandal better and bigger than before.

As for the food she was left with, she would be spending her day making donations and deliveries to various food banks and homeless shelters. No way was she going to let any of this go to waste.

"Figured I'd find you here."

Tatum yelped, jumped back and pressed a hand to her racing heart. "Sam!" She all but shrieked at him. "What are you doing here?"

"Well, I was going to do what you've already started." He set his phone on the stainless steel counter beside hers. "Need some help?"

"I would love some."

Her phone buzzed for what must have been the tenth time in the past hour and she could tell by Sam's expression who it was. "Cruz?" she asked.

"Guy's got a set, I'll give him that. Man." He shook his head and joined her at the refrigerator. "A cop. Ty was right. I so should have seen that."

"If it matters, he never suspected you," Tatum said.

Sam hefted a box of produce, arched a brow at her.

"Okay, maybe before he met you, but not after." At least she didn't think Cruz did. Honesty wasn't exactly at the top of his list of positive qualities. The loading bay door rumbled. They stopped, looked at each other. "Someone come with you? Ty?"

"Nah. He has his grandkids today. Did you know he has grandkids?"

"I found out this week," Tatum said. "I've had a lot of information to process. Maybe it's Quallis."

"We need some more crates anyway. I'll go check." Sam set the box on the counter and headed for the loading bay.

Smiling for the first time in a while, Tatum resumed unloading the perishables from the walk-in. She heard voices, Sam and at least one other, muted. There was no way of telling who it was from here.

Curious, she closed the fridge and headed off to join them, clicking on the light in the storeroom.

"Sam?" she yelled. "Did you find who—"

Bang! Bang bang!

"Sam?" Tatum ran toward the sudden crash, skidding to a halt as she saw Sam lying on the ground, a thick pool of blood spreading under him. "Sam!" She raced forward, dropped to her knees and pressed her hand against his side, the only place she could see a wound. "Sam, what happened? Who did this?"

He blinked, his dark eyes wide with shock. "Tatum." Blood trickled out the side of his mouth. "Tatum, run."

"Run? No, you need help." She looked behind her but didn't see anyone around. The loading bay door was open, as was the van's back double doors. "I have to call an ambulance." She patted her bloodied hands against her shirt, over her pockets. "I left my cell. I need to go get it. I'll get help, okay?" She grabbed his face. "You stay with me, you hear me? I can't do this without you!"

"Go." He tried to sit up, but his face went ashen and he gasped, coughed up blood.

"Stay still. Sam, please, just don't move. I'm going to—" She turned to race back to the kitchen and slammed right into a solid form. She screamed, jumped back, and barely had a blink of a second to register what was happening.

He dived for her, grabbed her around the waist and threw her into the van. The doors slammed before she could scramble to her knees. She clawed for the handle, screaming for help. Two hands locked around her ankles and pulled her back. She slammed face-first onto the floor of the van. Dazed, she rolled onto her back, tasted blood in her mouth.

She pushed over onto her side as the engine roared to life and the van began to move.

"Tatum?" Cruz figured yelling his presence was enough of a warning as he pulled open the unlocked door of True. Irritation flickered. What was she thinking not locking the door behind her? If she wanted to strike out at him, fine, but he wasn't going to let her ignore him. "Tatum, I know you're here. I know you don't want me here but..." He slammed through the kitchen's swinging double doors.

Empty.

Crates and boxes of food were stacked around the kitchen, on the counters. The walk-in fridge was closed. Cruz pulled out his phone, dialed her cell again.

The buzzing from the counter had him walking forward. "Tatum!"

He picked up her phone, glanced at the second one lying beside it. He tapped the screen, saw an image of a laughing Sam with his mom appear. Of course Sam was here. Relief she wasn't alone surged through him, only to be stifled at the continuing silence. "Tatum? Sam?"

A crash exploded in the storage room.

Cruz raced down the hall, spotted the pile of boxes.

The catering van was gone. Something moved beneath the boxes. Moved and groaned. He threw them to the side, uncovered a trembling, bleeding Sam. He swore, ripped off his jacket and wadded it up to push against the younger man's chest. "Sam, what happened? Where's Tatum?"

Sam blinked hard to stay awake. "Pike." Blood continued to trickle out the side of his mouth. "Couldn't stop him. Took her. Get her back." He grabbed hold of Cruz's shirt, hauled himself up. "Go get her back."

"I will." Panic and terror battled for control, but Cruz eased Sam back, kept pressure on the wound and pulled out his cell. "Detective Medina, Narcotics. I need an ambulance in the back alley behind True. I've got a single gunshot—what?" he asked when Sam shook his head, held up three fingers.

Cruz swore again, yanked up Sam's shirt, then hauled him onto his side. "Be advised victim has three gunshots to the torso. Two appear to be through and through."

Sam coughed. His eyes rolled back in his head. Cruz pressed two fingers against the side of his neck. The pulse was there—faint, but still there. "You hang on, kid, you hear me? I expect you to kick my butt for what I did to Tatum."

He could have sworn he heard Sam try to laugh.

Footsteps pounded behind him. Cruz looked up and found two uniformed officers headed his way. "Over here!" he yelled. "Ambulance is on its way. I want you to keep pressure on this wound here." He dragged the young woman down into his position. "You, call in an all-points for one Jeremy Pike. He's driving a white van, with True Catering on the outside."

"On it," the officer said.

Cruz raced back through the restaurant and out to his car. He was pulling away as he hit Dial on his car's dashboard phone. Waited for his LT to pick up.

"Report, Medina."

"I was too late. Tatum's gone. Witness said Pike took her. I need you to access the GPS tracker I put on the True catering van." Thank God he hadn't had the chance to remove it yet. "I've got it bookmarked on my laptop."

"Give me a few."

Cruz drove mindlessly, uncertain where to head.

"Okay, Cruz, looks like he's headed to the warehouse area. I can get you a precise location in a bit."

"On my way."

"Backup's rolling. Ten minutes out."

Cruz hung up. Ten minutes. He had less than that before sirens rolled and all hell broke loose. Ten minutes to save the woman he loved.

"Pike." Tatum's vision finally cleared enough for her to make out the driver's profile. Even if she hadn't seen his face, that tattoo was unmistakable. "Pike, what are you doing? What's going on?"

She pushed to her knees and dragged herself forward. Another headache pounded its way through her skull.

"Just stay back and shut up." Pike's order shot out like bullets. "We're almost there."

"Almost where?"

"You're the only one who can get me out of this."

"Get you out of what? Shooting Sam?"

"Stupid of him to get in the way. Stupid, stupid!" He slammed his hand against the steering wheel.

"Jeremy, tell me what's happening. Please." It couldn't hurt to be patient, but something told her it would hurt a lot more to panic.

"They want their drugs." He looked at Tatum. "They think you have them. They want to talk to you."

Reality struck hard. He was taking her to the dealers working with Richard. No. The dealers working with him. "You're working with Richard."

"Richard was working for us! It should have been easy, should have been so easy, but then you had to bring in that cop. I knew, I knew I'd seen him before." He gripped the wheel, jaw pulsing. "Took me a while to remember, but when I did I knew, I knew he was a cop!"

"Where did you see Cruz?"

Pike laughed. "Like I'm going to confess everything to you. What do you think this is? A TV show?"

"I think I trusted you enough to hire you and I deserve an explanation." She looked at his hands, the way his knuckles went white as they tensed. The oversize gold ring on one finger. The same ring she'd seen flash in the glow of the grocery store parking lot. "It was you." She hadn't meant to say it out loud, but once she did, there was no taking it back. "You tried to run me down."

"You were supposed to be cooking! Supposed to be focused on the critic. But you couldn't be distracted. Not with that cop with you twenty-four seven."

That cop. Cruz. Hope sprung to life inside of her. He had Richard in custody. He'd probably questioned him. Was it possible...was there even a chance Cruz would know she was in trouble? She needed to stall, needed to give Cruz time to catch up with them.

"Pike, if you take me to these men, they'll kill me."

"Better you than me."

"You aren't going to get away. Not from Cruz."

"Cruz." Pike snorted. "Should have killed him that night I killed his partner. Then none of this would have happened."

She tasted bile in her mouth as nausea surged inside her. She pressed a hand to her stomach, willed the panic to subside. "His partner isn't dead."

Pike whirled in his seat, accusing eyes on her before he refocused on the nearly empty road.

"He's in a recovery unit," Tatum lied. "You haven't killed anyone yet, Pike. Please. There's still time to make something good come out of this. Don't do this. Don't take me to…" He turned into a fenced area of warehouses. All these buildings, all this space. There was no way Cruz would find her here. "Pike, please. I don't want to die."

"Too late." Pike hunched over the steering wheel. "We're already here. There." He pointed to the collection of cars just inside a wide-open door. "Don't worry. I've seen them do this before. It'll be quick. You won't know it's happening."

"Yes, I will." She spoke softly as her mind raced. Above the sound of the engine, she thought she heard sirens, but she had to be imagining it. Manifesting it. She needed to believe, even as she accepted the odds were against her.

These were the men, Pike and these cartel members, responsible for so much pain, so much suffering. So many deaths. The drugs they sold and dealt were only to line their own pockets, and their greed knew no end. This was what Cruz had spent his life trying to stop. He'd taken an oath, promised his partner, dedicated his life to protecting people and stopping the same kind of criminals who in a matter of minutes would kill her. Forgiveness, she realized, wasn't so hard to manage, after all.

If she was going to die, she wasn't going to die a victim. She'd go out fighting.

It was what Cruz would do.

Tatum threw herself forward, grabbed hold of the steering wheel and slammed her foot hard over Pike's. The van lurched forward, speeding up to the point the entire vehicle began to shake.

Pike tried to get his arms free, but she pushed all her weight into him, elbowed him in the face when he nearly knocked her aside. She lifted her foot, slammed it down again and wrenched the wheel to the side.

The momentum tossed her into the passenger seat. Her shoulder cracked hard against the door as the van spun, lost traction and, for an instant, seemed to be flying. She grabbed hold of the seat belt strap and yanked it down as the tires caught and flipped, once, twice, too many times to count.

She squeezed her eyes shut against the sound of crushing metal and a scream that went suddenly silent. When the van skidded to a stop, the sirens blared louder. Shouts and cries were followed by gunshots. Tatum lay there, bathed and covered in shattered glass. Tiny pinpricks of pain dotted her face and arms. She sat wedged between the dash and seat, tried to catch her breath and assess if she could move.

More shouting. Pounding footsteps. Two more shots. Tatum opened her eyes and found Pike's dead-eyed stare. Blood covered most of his face as he hung suspended by his seat belt, his arms dangling toward her.

Tatum whimpered, kicked out, desperate to get free. She could climb out if she could just—

"Tatum!" Cruz's voice blasted through the ringing in her ears. "Tatum!"

"Cruz." She had to clear her throat. "Cruz, I'm here! In here!" She pulled with her arms, hoisted herself up only an inch before Cruz appeared on top of the van. He lay there, half in the shattered windshield. She smiled up at him, half laughing, half sobbing. "Would now be a good time to tell you you're forgiven?"

"I don't think there's a better one." He reached out his arm. "Take hold, babe."

She released the belt and reached up. The instant her hand locked around his she knew, without hesitation, without reservation, that this was where she belonged. With him.

Minutes later he was pulling her off the van and hauling her into his arms, holding on so tight she couldn't breathe. And she'd never been happier.

"I was afraid I was too late." He led her away from the van, toward one of the waiting ambulances. "I was so sure I'd lost you."

"No way that's happening now." As she clung to him she looked around at the chaos she'd wrought. "Did I do that?"

"A woman of many talents. Thanks to your stunt driving we've got the entire cartel. Including Javier Nacio Sr."

"Pike's dead."

"Yeah, I saw."

"He shot Johnny." She felt him tense, then his hold tightened. "He could have shot you, too, but he chose not to. I'm so glad he did. It was maybe the only good thing he's done."

Cruz set her back, caught her face in his hands. "You aren't going to fight me on going to the hospital are you?"

"The hospital." She gasped and felt the first twinge of pain. "Sam! He shot Sam! Oh, Cruz…"

"He's alive," Cruz said with a nod. "Last I heard he was still alive."

"I need to be there."

"Yeah." Cruz pulled her back into his arms. "So do I."

"I am so done with hospitals," Tatum groaned as she uncurled from the torture device of a chair in the waiting room. She accepted the mediocre coffee Cruz handed her. She'd been checked out and discharged, but only because Cruz had promised to monitor her injuries. She had bruised ribs, multiple lacerations and another crack on the head. She'd be out of commission for at least a week, the same amount of time True would be closed.

The Chicago Police Department had also released a public statement thanking Tatum and the employees of True for helping to bring down a significant narcotics ring in the city. With Richard Kirkman cutting a deal with the feds, True and Tatum were in the clear to re-open with the restaurant's saved and praised reputation.

Or so Cruz's lieutenant had told her when she'd arrived at the hospital to touch base with Cruz. She sat with them and Sam's mother, who had been brought to the hospital by Ty. The rest of True's employees filed in to wait for word on their friend.

Hours ticked by. Tatum dozed, her head tucked into

Cruz's shoulder, the sound of his deep voice lulling her into a fitful sleep. By the time he shook her awake it seemed as if forgiveness, while not completely earned yet, was soon to come from the staff. Sitting among her friends, her family, peace settled over her corner of the world.

"Doctor's here," Cruz murmured as she sat up.

"Right, okay." She steeled herself. "Dr. DeSantis, how is he?"

"Very lucky." The female surgeon removed her surgical cap and gave an encouraging smile. "We removed his spleen and repaired some internal damage. He must have turned at just the right time. The other two bullets missed any vital organs. It'll be a while before he's on his feet again, but I expect he'll make a full recovery."

Sam's mother let out a relieved sob that brought tears to Tatum's eyes. "Thank you so much."

Dr. DeSantis left them alone.

Cruz swore when his cell rang.

"What?" Tatum wasn't sure she could take any more unsettling news today.

"It's Jade." He flinched, glanced at his watch. "I need to take this." He held up a hand at Tatum's curious expression. "Jade. Don't worry. I haven't forgotten. I can be there in—what?"

"What?" Tatum couldn't remember ever seeing him so shocked. "What's happened?" He reached for her hand, squeezed so hard she had to move in to ease the pressure.

"Okay, yeah. I'll be there as soon as I can. Tell him…" Cruz's eyes misted. "Tell him I'm bringing someone with me." He cupped Tatum's cheek. "Someone special. Yeah. I'll see you soon." He hung up. "It's

Johnny." He backed up, looked between his LT and Tatum. "He's awake."

"But…" Tatum couldn't process. "Is that even possible? I thought you said—"

"I told you what the doctors told me. They don't have a prognosis yet and he's definitely got a long road, but he's alive. And he's awake. He's talking."

"Well, don't sit around here," Sam's mother insisted. "Get going already. My boy's in good hands."

Tatum hugged her. "I don't want you to worry about hospital bills," she whispered to the older woman. "I take care of my family. That includes you and Sam."

"Your parents did a right good job with you, young lady." Sam's mother kissed both her cheeks. "My boy's blessed to have found you."

A few minutes later, Cruz and Tatum walked to his car. "It's been quite a day," Tatum sighed. "One I won't soon forget." Not that she wanted to. Well, maybe some of it. "What?" She asked when Cruz didn't respond.

"What are you doing Monday evening?"

"Considering my restaurant won't be open for business for a bit yet, I think my schedule's pretty clear. Why? You have something in mind?"

"Yeah, actually." He pulled open the passenger door, and as she sat, he said, "I'd like you to come to dinner with me at my parents'. It won't be anything fancy, but my mom's a pretty darn good cook. I want you to meet them. So you know what you're getting into."

She caught his face between her hands, pressed her mouth to his. "I would love to go."

Tatum laughed when his cell went off again. "What now?"

"Better get used to it," he teased. "Such is the life

of a cop." He glanced at the text. "Well, what do you know." The smile that broke across his mouth sent a zing of pleasure rippling through her. "Looks like the Narcotics division is getting a new member of the family. The LT's wife just went into labor."

"So we'll come back once you see Johnny," Tatum said even as she smothered a yawn. "You do know how to show a girl a good time, Detective Medina."

"And I plan to keep doing that." He bent down and pressed his lips to hers again. "For as long as you'll let me."

* * * * *

*Don't miss the next exciting story from
the Colton 911: Chicago miniseries:
Colton 911: Soldier's Return
by Karen Whiddon*

SPECIAL EXCERPT FROM

HARLEQUIN
ROMANTIC SUSPENSE

*Connie Shaw, VP of a security firm, is the only person
able to identify a murderer. Luckily, she has access to
protection in the form of her former one-night stand—
now coworker—Trace Halstead. As the lines of their
relationship blur, danger circles closer. Will Trace
be able to keep Connie safe while they explore the
connection between them?*

*Read on for a sneak preview of
Sharon C. Cooper's debut Harlequin Romantic Suspense,*
His to Protect.

"I'm glad you're okay."

"I'm fine. I just don't know if I'll ever get that man's gray eyes out of my mind."

Trace turned to her. "Exactly what were you able to ID?"

"I saw his eyes and part of a tattoo on his neck."

"Did he see you?"

Connie swallowed hard and bit down on her bottom lip, something she did whenever she was uncomfortable. "We made eye contact, but only for a second or maybe two. Then just as quick, one of the other men pulled him out the door."

"Damn, Connie. That means he might be able to identify you, too."

"No." She shook her head vehemently. "I don't think so. It was just a split second. Trace, everything happened so fast. There's no way he could've gotten a good look at me. Besides, he doesn't know who I am," she said in a rush, sounding as if she was trying to convince herself. "He knows nothing about me, and the FBI agent assured me that what I shared with them and my identity will be kept confidential."

Worry wound through Trace as he watched her carefully, noticing how agitated she was getting. He reached over and massaged the back of her neck.

"If you believe that, then why are you trembling?"

"Maybe because you have the air conditioner on full blast," Connie said, trying to lighten the moment. Trace wasn't laughing, though.

"It's like you're trying to freeze me to death," she persisted, trying again to ease the tension in the car. "Of course, I'm—"

"Sweetheart, quit deflecting and talk to me."

Don't miss
His to Protect *by Sharon C. Cooper,*
available April 2021 wherever
Harlequin Romantic Suspense
books and ebooks are sold.

Harlequin.com